MW01064325

The Kidding Pen

By

Dr. Hillrey A Dufner

Illustrations by
Esther Esquivel

ISBN: 1512131237

ISBN 13: 9781512131239

Forward

As is true of fiction I write, most incidents in this book are actual events, but not in this setting nor to people of the names used. Names used in this book are fictional. My involvement in public education for over forty years exposed me to many incidents of abuse perpetrated on children by parents, relatives, and people with opportunity because of positions of power or authority. Many of the perpetrators have not had to face their abuse and cruelty to those who could not defend themselves. When they are forced to face what they have done, it is my prayer that they change.

This book highlights abuses that have actually happened and are like those that continue to happen to defenseless children. This story, that weaves a few of these abuses into the fabric of a tale, is fiction.

One afternoon at the end of a difficult year as an elementary assistant principal, I was using the services of three young ladies, all ten or eleven years of age, to gather and account for the over seven thousand textbooks issued to and retrieved from over a thousand students on my campus. Unable to pay them, I made sure we took a break every morning and afternoon during which I plied them with snacks and sodas. During one of those breaks, I worked for a few minutes on a non-fiction book about Gaby Garza called <u>Chasing Horizons: Gaby's Story</u>. At the end of the break, the girls came into my office and asked what I was doing. After I answered that I was writing a book, they wanted to hear the story, so over the next couple of days during breaks, I told it. When I finished the story, they asked me to write a story about them. I did not know them well enough to write a non-fiction about them, but over the next few years, the story in this book came spilling out. I owe those girls for the inspiration to begin this work. It is not about them, but three characters in the book are modeled after their endearing qualities.

Acknowlegements

I would be remiss if I did not acknowledge my daughter, Tammy Harris for her encouragement and moral support and for reading and responding to the third draft with all its mistakes. In addition, I recognize Mrs. Rosa Trevino for enduring the first draft. Mrs. Jackie Humphries gave invaluable advice and support in the beginning stages of editing this work. My wife, Earlene Dufner listened to and reacted to many parts of the book, offering encouragement. Mr. Andrew Downing has given me a great friendship and supported and encouraged my efforts to write. Mrs. Esperaza Torrez listened to the gist of the story long before it was finished and gave me a thumbs up, which was a great encouragement. Mrs. Christie Williams, my partner teacher for a time, has offered many suggestions and worked to help me find an illustrator.

About Esther Esquivel:

Ms. Esquivel is a high-school senior at this writing. She attends Manor High School in Manor, Texas. I have known her since she was a babe-in-arms. I was her Vice-Principal through elementary school. Most of her free time in school was devoted to drawing. Obviously, she had talent. She has won many accolades as an art student. When I was in need of an illustrator, I thought of her. I think she came through very well. She plans to attend the University of Texas at San Antonio beginning in the fall of 2015, to major in art.

This book is dedicated Blanca Ysenia Gonzalez Garcia, Asusena Diaz, and Jennifer Salgado who gave me the challenge of writing about the incidents in this book and whose delightful personalities I drew from to build characters.

Jimmy's Snake

our or five more stabs with the posthole digger could have finished the hole deep enough and had it clean enough to stand a post and tamp it in with a crowbar. The thin, reedy, cry from the cab of my old pickup stopped me in mid-stroke. Caryn needed changing, or feeding, or maybe just holding. *Could be she needs all three, I thought.* She had been sleeping for about two hours. *I guess it is time.* I laid the posthole digger on the pile of red dirt I had built from digging the hole, then walked around a large salt-cedar tree to the passenger door of the old truck.

Before opening the door, I glanced quickly at Jimmy who was just down the slope poking a stick down a rabbit hole under a stand of tall prickly-pear cactus. Waxy yellow and orange blooms were just beginning to open, and the nopales, young cactus leaves with undeveloped spines, were plentiful on this early spring day. The young, tender leaves cut into strips and fried, were a favorite food among my Mexican-American neighbors. I liked them also, but there were too many for me to make much of a dent picking and eating them. I invited my Hispanic neighbors to come and pick what they want, but most of them were shy about coming across the fence to pick the leaves, even when invited. I made a mental note to pick some to take to the neighbors before quitting for the day.

Bluebonnet plants had spread leaves out from the main stems that had survived the winter and sent up bloom stems, but they had not quite bloomed out yet. Soon, the bluebonnets and cactus flowers would be showing off their brilliant and contrasting blue, yellow and apricot colors that tourists love to get in their pictures. Brutus, my young, black tom cat that stayed with Jimmy whenever he was around, was rubbing himself back and forth against Jimmy's back, seemingly content with the world, and loving this child who paid him no mind. It was late in an early-spring day, warm, bordering on hot.

I shed my denim jacket and green John Deere cap before reaching into the passenger window to open the glove compartment for my camera. I zoomed in and took a quick, digital snapshot before attending to Caryn. *Great Kodak moment,* I thought as I watched the dark-skinned, black headed boy doing what comes natural to being a boy. The waxy, olive-drab cactus plants with their colorful yellow and orange buds formed a great backdrop. *Another week and I'll have to take the picture again to catch the bluebonnets,* I said to no one in particular because no one was around except Caryn who was far too young to understand or respond.

It took three hard jerks to open the door to the old pickup. The hinges on both doors on the ancient truck were so worn they sagged on the latches making them hard to open. The tailgate no longer closed, so I just left it in the open position held level with the bed by chains on either side. A Chevrolet commercial on TV lauded a scratch on a pick-up as "showing character." I was amused by that, because by that measure, this old dodge truck had enough character to run for office. The color was rust with small patches of army green. People told me I needed to buy a newer truck, but I just could not see spending the money as long as this one still ran. It did smoke a bit and rattled a lot, but there were a lot of memories floating about in the cab of that old truck having to do with a young wife and two growing children. Those memories and ghosts, I was reluctant to give up. I taught both my children to drive in that old truck. *Besides,* I reasoned, *I do not have the money.* Goats just did not bring enough at market to do much more than live a Spartan life and pay taxes.

Caryn was only two months old. Billie had expressed some milk for her before she left. I could see the little pink girl baby alternately sucking on her hands and crying, so I took one small bottle out of the ice-chest, lifted the hood on the old truck, and placed the bottle in the half-full water bucket resting on the manifold. Water in the bucket felt like it was still hot enough to warm the bottle in a pretty short time.

While we were waiting for the milk to warm, I began singing "Streets of Laredo" to try to calm her a bit. She stopped crying and listened briefly. My hands were hard, dirty, and calloused, but they worked quickly and expertly enough to clean the little girl and get her changed while she went back to screaming about being hungry. I had practiced the changing routine plenty of times when Jimmy was a baby. Of course, earlier in my life there had been my own two children, Ashley and Jake, whom I changed, sang to, rocked and fed most days when they were very young. I had just turned fifty, and Ashley would soon be graduating from college. Jake was already out and I had heard that he was soon to be married. Remembering my own children, I counted the five years since I had seen either of them, and I realized that I had heard Jake was to be married over a year ago. Changing someone else's babies seemed strange at first, but I had quickly gotten used to it. Billie left Jimmy and Caryn with me often. So often in fact, it seemed like she had forgotten they were hers and not mine. *Well,* I thought, *that fits with my former life, I guess.*

In a matter of just a couple of minutes, Caryn was snuggled in tight, sucking the bottle and loving being held and sung to. Twenty minutes later, I laid the sleeping girl down again, completed digging the hole and tamped the post in tight and straight. Six more posts and I would call it a day. I had already measured and sighted the next post when a movement down the hill caught my eye.

Jimmy had jumped back a step, then squatted down again still holding the stiff cedar stick, but there was something wrong with the scene. Brutus fuzzed up beside Jimmy. He looked the picture of the black Halloween cat with ears flattened on his head and his nose pointed at the ground in front of Jimmy. His hair stood on end down his back and all the way down his tail. I heard the tom yowl as only a tom cat can. But there was another subtle movement. It looked like the ground had moved. Squinting against the bright sunlight from the afternoon sun, I finally recognized what was happening. An icy hand grabbed my heart and squeezed as I recognized the shape, color, and movements of a large diamond-back rattlesnake as it coiled beside the rabbit hole, facing and licking the breeze that came to it from around Jimmy. Brutus hissed again and spit viciously, growling a warning.

A yell caught in my throat as the unseen hand choked off my breathing. Trying to move to save the boy, my mind raced looking for solutions. If I yelled, and Jimmy moved, the snake would strike for sure. Jimmy's best chance to keep from being struck was for him to remain perfectly still. Rattlers hunt by detecting body heat and movement. They have pits in the side of their heads under their eyes that detect the infrared rays of heat. Hence the name 'pit viper.' Their forked tongue flicks out the front of their mouth frequently, working much like a human's nose, detecting odors. They can detect size, and will not normally strike something they cannot swallow. However, they will strike quickly at almost anything if they feel threatened.

Vipers coil up like a spring and tense their muscles in preparation for a lightning fast strike to defend themselves or to strike prey to get food. This one was coiled and ready to strike at Jimmy. The black tongue flicked out, quivered briefly, then disappeared back inside the mouth again. About every three seconds the tongue flicked out then retreated. I wanted to run down the hill, but at first my feet would not move. Running toward the child and exciting him or the snake would not be a good idea. My whole body tingled like one's foot tingles from having the blood cut off for a time and the flow suddenly restored. Brutus walked back and forth, close to the snake seemingly trying to attract its attention; his ears were flat against his head and the hair on his whole body remained fuzzed up.

The snake's head raised about six inches above the ground and wagged back and forth with its tongue flicking, then stopped. It was aiming directly at Jimmy's hand, the one holding the stick. The head moved up and down slightly, then stopped. I recognized the targeting sequence some snakes use to determine where to strike when they are getting mixed messages from something that is still. The sequence was completed and Brutus was being ignored. The cat yowled again and spit. He feigned an attack, moving slightly forward then back and slapping at the air.

I forced myself to move. I dropped the diggers and started walking. Once I began, I quickly picked up speed and walked rapidly toward the boy who seemed intent on the snake. Jimmy watched the snake's movements, fascinated, seemingly mesmerized. He kept the sharpest end of the small cedar stick in his hand aimed at the snake's head; the other end was stuck in the ground. I purposefully began recalling the steps to offer first aid to a snake-bite victim. Ice, I needed ice. There was some in the freezer at the house a ten-minute drive away; *wait, there is a little left in the ice chest in the truck.* I had made ten steps toward the boy when I saw the snake strike. The flat, triangular head with the evil hooded eye, opened wide to expose needle-sharp, deadly, fangs and struck faster than my eye could follow. The boy's hand jerked backwards slightly from the impact as I had expected and another yell froze in my throat as I started running toward the boy. An aberration from the usual traveled down my optic nerves and poked at my brain. Something was different from what I expected. Something was not right. Maybe it was right, but not usual. The boy remained crouched and still. He did not react from pain or fear. I wondered for a moment if the snake had missed, but that hardly seemed likely.

Jimmy had not cried out or run away. He half stood, then squatted again and watched as the snake thrashed its head around and its body flopped clumsily back and forth, wrapping around its own head. Brutus sat down and wrapped his tail around his feet, moving his head to keep up with the snake, looking now, not from any malice, but with amused interest. I was running and almost to the boy when I saw what had happened. The sharp end of the stick was poking out the back of the snake's body about three inches below its head. The other end was intact and still in Jimmy's hand. The snake was impaled on the small stick and seemingly in its death throes. Jimmy sat watching the snake struggle with the stick in its mouth and through the back of its throat. The mouth opened then closed on the stick once again. The viper had not considered the sharp stick when it struck. It had struck at the boy, but impaled itself on the small stick instead. Jimmy seemed to know he was in no danger even while being attacked by a dangerous animal.

I took the stick from Jimmy's hand and stepped on the snake's head with my well-worn and scuffed right boot. Holding the snake's head against the ground with my foot, I reached with my left hand, pulled the stick out of the mouth that held the deadly fangs which had been aimed at the youngster I loved so very much. I grabbed the bleeding snake behind the arrow-shaped head then tossed it to the opposite side of the cactus patch where it continued for a while to writhe about the injured mouth and body. Gradually the snake relaxed, stopped writhing, accepted its injury, and slithered down the hill. With any luck, the snake would survive. I noticed a lump in the body about one third of its length from the head about the size of a rat or a small rabbit. I hoped it would live to continue eating a mouse or small rabbit a week. That snake would help protect my goat-feed supply.

All the excitement past, I felt the all too familiar sharp pain in my left pectoral muscle. *I have to talk to Dr. Pick about that someday,* I told myself for the nth time. The pain which started in the courtroom during my divorce nearly five years past, had come to visit more often lately. It always went away quickly, so I paid the pain little notice and forgot it as soon as it passed.

Still trembling and wondering, I took the boy by the hand and led him to the truck. After that excitement, I had had enough for the day. I forgot about cactus leaf gathering. Loading tools and children quickly, I drove them to my house and began preparing supper for Jimmy and myself as I continued to wonder at this remarkable boy. Soon I was rocking Caryn and Jimmy in the same old rocking chair I had used to put my own children to sleep at night many years before. The chair creaked familiarly from the years of use as I rocked. The regular creaking noise helped lull the children to sleep. This was a good and comforting feeling for me, but still, I missed contact with adults that I could talk to.

Billie Cloud did not come to get her children that night. I had to resort to powdered formula for Caryn, and I had to dress Jimmy in a tee shirt in place of pajamas when he was bathed and ready for bed. I fed and bathed Caryn, then wrapped her in a blanket and placed her in the mahogany crib I had built nearly twenty-five years before for my tiny son. The crib had lasted through Jake, my oldest, then Ashley, my daughter. A familiar twinge caught in my stomach, somewhat painful, but mostly a nostalgic feeling of things gone by when I thought of the good times I had with my own children. As the two babies slept, I washed their clothes in the sink, and laid them out to dry for the next day. The children were taken care of, so I was free to go to bed myself. Taking care of Jimmy and Caryn was fulfilling for me, but my fifty years were heavy this night. I slept soundly and got up early the next morning.

About noon the next day, Billie showed up to collect her children. She was almost silent as she gathered their belongings and clothes, then loaded the car and left. I didn't consider her thoughtlessness toward me. I loved keeping the children. They helped me feel not so alone. Billie often dropped them off without notice and seldom said "Thank you," when she collected them. Knowing her history, I could forgive the small slights. Actually, she seldom said more than was necessary to conduct the business of transferring the children. That was the way with most Cherokee. That was also my way, so it worked.

2

Girl on the Fence

n Saturday, two days after the snake incident, I worked in my kidding pen strengthening the fences against feral hogs. I was pounding stakes into the ground in the cold dawn before daylight. My
fingers were numb from the cold, but I knew the day would warm. Around
seven, Billie brought the children again. Two days was an average span of
time between visits. Tall, thin, and dark-skinned, even with a little baby-fat
middle still showing and breasts still swollen from producing milk, Billie
was still an attractive woman with her fine Cherokee features. She was con-
sistently a bit unkempt. Her dark hair was never quite combed and her
clothes always seemed a bit askew and a little slept in. I had always thought
that if she paid a little more attention to her looks, she could be a strikingly
attractive woman. She seemed to jump from job to job and even when well
employed, was always looking for the next place to improve her position or
earnings, or just move on. She seemed to make good money judging from
the quality of clothes she wore and the cars she drove, but I couldn't vouch
for it. I had baby-sat for her since Jimmy was less than a month old. I had
never been paid and seldom thanked. "I've gotta go. I can't take the kids.
There is milk in the cooler," was all she said as she placed Caryn's car-seat in
the cab of the old Dodge pickup. By the time Billie had placed Caryn in the
truck, Jimmy had already wrapped himself around my leg in a quick greet-
ing hug, and gone over the gate to the feed shed hunting for mice. Brutus
followed every move wherever the boy went.

I had learned the hard way that I must have baby supplies on hand.
In my house I had baby diapers, baby food, powdered formula mix, small
clothes, and a box full of toys for Jimmy. Absently I thought, *I have to get
some girl toys for Caryn. I'll need them before very long.*

"When will you be back?" I asked Billie as she climbed back in her
new yellow Suburban.

"Don't know. Maybe tonight, maybe not."

In a short time, I built a small wood fire beside the big rock in the
middle of the pen and placed a bucket with four inches of water in the bottom on a flat rock beside the fire, where the water could warm enough to
heat a bottle for Caryn.

Once again I busied myself with the fence. It was full daylight now
and warmer. I began to feel my fingers again as I drove a sharpened

stake into the ground. The stake was made from an eighteen inch piece of three-quarter inch reinforcing steel. I drove it into the ground next to a piece of two inch black pipe. Though I heard it, I didn't even look up at the noise of the suburban crossing the cattle guard at the outside gate. I was wiring another two-inch piece of black pipe to the bottom of pen posts and deep in thought about the snake incident, when the first "Hello, mister," came my way. I hadn't noticed the spritely girl climb onto the kidding-pen fence. Deep in thought, I registered a vocal noise from Jimmy and kept working. The "Whatcha doin'," that came next got through. My head snapped around involuntarily to find the source.

"Gee mister, I didn't mean to scare you."

Silently for a moment, I sized up the young stranger. She was small and much darker-skinned than I. I got the immediate impression of a young girl that spent a lot of time in the sun. Skinny and barefoot, she had long dark hair pulled back into a hastily wrapped pony tail that extended almost to her waist. Her plaid, knee-length shorts were faded from many washings, yet showed dirt from being worn longer than just that morning. The seat of her shorts was thread-bare to the point of being ready to tear at the first snag. Her faded yellow blouse was a little too big for her small frame and billowed in the breeze. There was a ragged hole on the left side of the blouse at her waist showing tummy skin that was only slightly lighter than her face. She had a pleasant face; pleasant with fine features, thin lips, dark eyes, dark complexion, and a slight, curious, sun-grin smile.

Her face seemed to be older than the rest of her. Looking into the dark eyes, I got the impression that the girl knew more than she should at her tender age, but there was also a spark of fun that glinted from her eyes. They shined with a spirit not reflected in her body language or her expression. Her bare heels were hooked through the tightly stretched fence and her small, left hand rested on a corner post for balance as she sat on the fence nearly four feet off the ground. She hunched her chest down to her thighs in an effort to keep warm. Her arms and legs were covered with goose bumps, but she did not shiver. She looked intently into my eyes as if searching for something she desperately needed to find. Something inside

me stirred. I did not know why, but I instantly liked the little waif auda-
ciously sitting on my fence like a curious crow. Like her or not, I was wary.
This girl looked to be about nine, still a little girl not yet ready to become
a woman, but I instantly recalled years before, being wounded severely by
a girl I liked instantly. I had loved her, wooed her, married her, then after
two children and nearly twenty years of being together, she had broken my
heart, broken me financially and killed the spirit of fun in me that I saw in
that girl sitting on my fence.

"Startled. You didn't scare me, you startled me," I instructed, "I was
thinking."

"What were you thinking about?"

I paused to think about this answer. The sun was well above the horizon now, and my red plaid jacket was no longer needed. My blue plaid
flannel shirt would be plenty until about ten, then I would take it off too.
My jeans had patches. Clumsy, uneven stitching held patches on both
knees and on the left side of the seat. I didn't know any seamstress that
would patch jeans, so I did it myself. My wide, brown western belt was
so old and frayed that the black paint on the letters, "VCT" tooled on the
back had worn to a shadow. The western buckle was pewter and at one
time, had had a brass roper on a horse roping a calf bradded to it. Now
there was a bit of brass rope left and holes where the horse and calf had
been attached. My boots were flat-heeled, round steel-toed, and worn
through to the steel on both toes. Soles of my boots were thin enough that
I avoided cactus and gravel. Conscious of my poor outfit, I stood and faced
the little girl before answering.

"I was deep in thought about times past and people in the past."

"What do you do here?"

"Well, I raise goats. I raise goats to sell. This is my farm."

"Why are you tying pipes to your posts?"

"Well child…"

"I'm not a child."

"Well, OK, fair enough, but I don't know what to call you."

"Bianca. My name is Bianca."

"OK, Bianca. What I am doing is trying to build something to keep feral hogs away from my baby goats. This pen is where I put the nanny goats when they are close to delivering babies. The hogs root under the fence. When they get in, they eat the babies."

"What is that?"

"What is what?"

"I know about hogs, but what is a feral hog?"

"Anything feral is wild. A feral hog is a wild hog."

"You mean like a javelina?"

"No, a javelina is wild, but it normally won't bother livestock. And, actually, the javelina is not related to hogs, they are more like a horse. A wild hog is one that is from those that got loose from a farm around here and lives in the woods over there and will eat anything. They will ruin almost any crop, tear up a garden, break in shed doors to eat sacked feed, break down fences, or seemingly do just about anything to take away a farmer's livelihood including killing and eating baby goats." The girl jumped down lightly into the pen and walked toward me examining the pipes already in place, standing with her hands on her hips.

"Wow, mister, you make them sound really bad. But, how does this help?"

"Well, I'm hoping they won't be able to lift or bend the pipe to get in, but also I'm driving stakes in the ground to stop their rooting under the fence."

"How does that help?"

"Well, again it is my hope, not something proven. I'm driving steel stakes in the ground because I think they can't pull them up and the top of the stake will have a sharp edge that I hope will cut their snouts when they try to root past it, and make them back off."

"That sounds pretty smart. Can I help?"

"Well, I would like the help, but first who are you?"

"I told you. I am Bianca. Bianca Alondra Gonzalez."

"Are you Abelardo's girl."

"Abelardo Gonzalez is my father."

"Does your mother know where you are?"

"She don't care."

"Bianca, that doesn't answer the question. Does she know where you are?"

"No. When she kicks Isidro and me out of the house, I go where I want to. Can I help you?"

"Sure you can help. What do you want to do?"

Bianca walked over to stand beside me. "I want to drive the stakes, but before I help you, who are you?"

"My name is Virgil Castor Trevor. I own this farm, well, me and the bank. Lived here…close to here most of my life. You want to try to drive a stake?"

"What kind of a name is that?"

"Which one?"

"Trevor. I never heard of that as a last name."

"It came from my grandfather's grandmother. She was Cherokee, but she was captured by a band of Cree Indians when she was a small girl. She was out picking berries when they got her. She would not tell them her name, so they called her Three Rivers for the place where they took her. It was not far from a place where two rivers came together to make one bigger one. When she was an old woman, her tribe bought her back with two horses, but no one knew her real name, so they kept her name as Three Rivers. That was an unusual name even for the Cherokee. When the Whites came to the reservation where she lived and signed her up as an Indian, they did not understand her when she told them her name. When she tried to say "Three Rivers," they understood Trevor. They named her Margaret Trevor. Back then, the Cherokee men took on the name of their wives, but now the wives take on the name of their husbands. Somehow the name Trevor was preserved."

"Wow, that's a great story."

Before I could respond, the familiar reedy cry came from the cab of my pickup. Bianca was immediately alert. "Who is that?"

"That is Caryn."

"Your baby?"

"No, my babies are grown and gone. She is Billie Cloud's baby. Her brother, Jimmy, is three. He's in the feed shed with Brutus the cat, looking for mice."

"Why doesn't your wife keep them?"

"I don't have a wife. At least not anymore," I answered as I put my hammer and stake down and started for the old truck.

Bianca followed me to the pickup and looked intently at the red-faced baby as Caryn began to get very serious about her screaming for help. I reached into the cooler for a bottle and handed it to Bianca. "Would you go put this in the water in that bucket over there by the fire, please?" Bianca looked at me with a question mark on her face, then took the bottle and put it in the bucket while I began changing a dirty diaper. Bianca arrived back at the truck while I was wiping the baby's bottom. I felt a little self-conscious in the presence of the half-grown girl wiping a little girl's bottom.

"What is in the bottle?"

"Milk from her mother."

"You milked her?"

"No. She...she..." I could not think of a better way to say it, so I continued, "she milked herself and put it in the bottle for later."

"That's gross," Bianca said with disgust apparent in her voice. "Mister Trevor," she asked without pause and with concern in her voice, "are you a babysitter?"

I answered without looking at her, "I don't think of myself as a babysitter, but I guess I *am* if you consider how long Jimmy and Caryn have stayed at my house under my care. Is that the question you wanted to ask when you found out Caryn wasn't mine?"

Bianca looked a little embarrassed. "Yes, babysitting isn't a man's job." I had to smile, "so you think if I babysit, I must not be much of a man?"

Bianca dodged the question. "My father says Billie Cloud is a slut. What does that mean?"

"That question is one you should ask your mother."

"I did. She slapped me."

"Well, I guess a slut is a woman who is not choosy about the men she associates with."

"You mean she has sex with lots of men, don't you?"

"I guess it could be that. I never really thought much about it. However, I wouldn't call Billie Cloud that."

"Why not?"

"Because I don't know that about her. I really don't know her very well lately. How old are you anyway?"

"I'm eleven. Did you ever have sex with her?"

"Is there any question you won't ask?"

"Have you?"

"Bianca. That is not a question that a young lady should ask. But no, I have never had sex with Billie Cloud. I take care of her children most days because I want to and I guess because they need someone to love them. Now, I will not answer any more questions about sex. Not about my sex life or anyone else's." The girl's openness and innocence made conversation with her easy. I liked that. Easy conversation was not usually easy for me.

Bianca walked beside me watching Caryn kicking and pumping the air with her fists struggling to be fed.

"What happened to your wife?"

I thought for a minute trying to decide how to answer then said, "She left." I was not surprised by the inevitable, "Why?" but I squirmed in discomfort as I recalled her leaving and tried to figure out what to say to this little girl.

Finally I said, "I don't know for sure, but I think it had to do with wanting more than I could give and thinking she could get more from someone else."

"Is she a slut?"

"No, Bianca. She is really a very good person. I just could not give her all she wanted." Bianca thought for a minute before asking, "You mean she wanted more money?"

"She wanted more things that money could buy, and she wanted more of me. She wanted more of me than there is of me, and more things than I could buy."

"I don't understand."

"Bianca, I don't either. That is one of my life's great mysteries. I often think about how I might have made it better…made her happy. I just don't have an answer."

I got to the big rock in the middle of the kidding pen and leaned back on it as I wrapped Caryn for feeding. I wedged the bottle nipple into her mouth and let her begin sucking down the milk. She drank hungrily and rewarded me with a 'coo' while she sucked. I smiled at her little noise, and for a moment, my world had narrowed to this little cooing girl and me. Bianca climbed atop the rock and positioned herself to watch Caryn suckle. She reached over and stroked the light-skinned baby's face with the back of her small, dark hand. I thought I knew the questions Bianca could think of were not all answered, but she honored a peaceful silence for a short time. She looked at the profile of the strange man she was beginning to learn and another line of questions formed.

"How many goats do you have?"

"Little girl, you make my head spin with your questions and changes of direction. I have about a thousand nanny goats, about a hundred twenty billys. Soon, I should have close to another thousand babies."

"I'm not a little girl. How much can you sell a baby for?"

"It depends on the market, but usually between thirty-five and fifty dollars each after they are weaned. Well-muscled billys will bring up to two hundred for breeding stock."

"You mean your wife was not satisfied with thirty-five thousand dollars a year?"

"When I was married, I had a lot more than a thousand head of goats. This farm was a ranch of over two thousand five hundred acres. I had four hundred head of cattle, and I raised horses and hay for sale also. Even with four hired hands, we cleared much more than thirty-five thousand dollars a year."

"What happened to the ranch?"

"Over two thousand acres and most of the livestock were sold to pay credit card bills, a lump settlement to my ex-wife, and an expensive lawyer. When my wife decided to get a divorce, she ran up some incredible bills, then she hired a lawyer, a very high-dollar lawyer, and sued me for everything that was left." I was talking very quietly. Bianca did not interrupt with another question. It probably seemed to her that I was not finished and she sensed I would continue unbidden.

"I could have fought it," I said distantly, "but in the end, she would win or give it all to lawyers, so I settled. What I have now is what is left after selling another ten acres for a stake, then rebuilding a piece of my life on a small corner of what used to be my ranch. The larger ranch was left to me by my grandfather. You know the big house on Highway 80 toward Wilton?" I continued without waiting for a response. "That was my house. She lived there for a while after the divorce, then she sold it to the Bakers and moved on. It took about a year for her to run out of money again, then she sued again for more money. She lost that time. Even her expensive lawyer could not pry more money loose. He didn't know he was going to, but he worked on that little deal pro bono.

She lost because she had already taken most of what I had, and she had signed a paper agreeing to not sue for more and her expensive lawyer was busy running for the legislature. I have a much smaller house now, but it is all I need. I built it myself. To me, it is much more satisfactory than the big house on Highway 80. I still have the same truck I bought used not long after we married. Now, that will be enough about my life. Maybe someday I'll write a book and you can buy one and read all about it. But that is enough for today."

"Mister Trevor?"

"What Bianca?"

"I'm sorry."

"For what?"

"I'm sorry you are so hurt."

I had not talked to anyone since the divorce like I had talked to this little sprite of a girl in the past few minutes. Her innocent and pure sympathy caused an unexpected and unwelcome reaction. Immediately upon her statement of sorrow for me, a lump came to my throat. I hoped for no more questions for a while. I did not want to give my emotions away to this little girl who had dug into me so deeply and so quickly.

"Mister Trevor, I think it is time."

"Time for what?"

"Time for a new truck. That old one is a wreck."

The lump left my throat. I laughed it out. The tears could easily have been tears from laughter. Bianca had meant the statement to be serious, but she was at the age when anything could be funny. She laughed along with me for a while, then sat thoughtfully for another few minutes while Caryn finished her bottle and fell asleep.

"What does it mean to work pro bono."

"Well, Bianca, that means to work for no pay."

"You mean like you do raising goats?"

"Not exactly, but that is a great analogy."

"I know what that is."

"You mean you know what an analogy is?"

"Most of the time when you use "like," you are making an analogy."

"You mean like when you say, 'A girl who asks too many questions is like a squeaky wheel'?"

"Exactly." Her 'exactly' was matter of fact. She seemed to get the example without the point.

"Well, not to strain at a point, but when you use "like" to compare two very different things, you are making a simile. Analogies usually require three components."

Bianca looked at me with a sun-grin and without commenting further.

3

The Rope

I stood with Caryn in my arms and started for the truck. "You don't know much about babysitting do you?" Bianca didn't seem judgmental, just stating what she understood as a fact.

"Maybe not. What do you have in mind?" I was a little put off, but decided to listen instead of react.

"She will sleep better in the fresh air close to where you are working. The noise will not disturb her."

I looked around at the pen, bare except for the large rock in the middle, and tools and materials. "I'm listening. What do you think I should do?"

Bianca smiled at being asked. "Take those three longest rods, drive them in here, leaning like this, here like this, and here like this." She had walked an equilateral triangle with sides about five feet long and marked each vertex in the dirt with her toe and directed me to drive the stakes in at an angle leaning out. I handed Caryn to her and followed her directions. Handing Caryn back to me, she walked to the pickup cab and brought back a blanket and a roll of heavy string. I watched silently as she tied the string to the top of one stake, then ran the string from stake to stake stretching it tight between and tying it to the top of each. She draped the blanket over the string making a rough tent. "Shade," she said simply as she turned back to the truck, brought back the old quilt I had folded behind the seat, and spread it under the shade. She indicated with her hands that I should lay Caryn down on the quilt, which I did.

"Good," I said as I patted Bianca on the shoulder. She shied away at my touching her. I noted but ignored her reaction, "Ready to drive a stake?"

"Yes, I believe so," she said looking at her handiwork with obvious pride.

I picked up a stake and started it with a couple of taps then drove it with the ten-pound sledge. Bianca watched, then after picking up the sledge, asked, "Do you have a smaller hammer?"

I considered the girl couldn't weigh more than seventy-five pounds, and the handle of the big hammer was almost as tall as her shoulder. "Yes. I think I have something that fits you better." I walked to the truck and came back with an old two-pounder and a length of rope. I laid the rope down and handed her the hammer. It was an old hammer. The handle had been splintered before, probably several times and wired and taped together. "Hit the top of the stake gently at first. Get used to the distance before you try to hit it hard. Be careful of the handle of the hammer. If you over-shoot the stake and hit the handle, it will probably break. Watch again." I demonstrated and explained each step and swing as I drove a stake with the small hammer. "Now, you try." I handed the tool to her.

Jimmy came running around the corner of the feed shed with a paper feed-sack in his hand. Brutus was running close behind meowing expectantly. Jimmy climbed the gate and ran to the middle of the kidding pen not far from the fire. "Look, Trevor. I got three!" Jimmy opened the mouth of the sack and shook it until one big rat ran out and scampered toward the feed shed only to be caught and quickly killed by Brutus. The big cat let the dead rat lay and readied himself for the next one to escape the sack. Twice more the drama was played out. The result was the same each time to the delight of the small dark boy. "I get more," Jimmy said as he grabbed up the sack and ran back to the shed. "C'mon Brutus." Brutus picked up one of the rats and carried it with him.

With the exuberance and confidence of youth, Bianca grabbed a stake from the stack and the hammer to begin her challenge. I watched the first few strikes, then picked up the rope to tie to one end of another couple of lengths of pipe and drag them to the next opening. Just as I picked up the rope, I heard the crack that meant Bianca had swung hard and the handle of the hammer was broken. When I glanced up Bianca was trying to stick the head of the hammer back on the handle.

I tried to be comforting when I spoke. "It is broken. Too bad. We can't fix that. I'll have to get another handle or a new hammer."

With sorrow showing on her face, and her mouth open to speak, but no sound coming out, Bianca looked up to see me holding the rope in my hand and probably a frown on my face. She dropped the hammer head and handle and ran for the gate. She cleared it in two steps and was gone. I watched her leave not understanding at first what made her bolt. But when Bianca climbed the gate, I noticed a deep bruise on the back of her right calf. It was a bruise that could only have been made by a rope or electric cord, or even a buggy whip. Several more bruises told more of the story. The lump returned to my throat at what I knew she must be thinking, but I knew that any protest would be useless.

***

Bianca hit the gate at a dead run and in the wink of an eye was over it and running for the woods. She was small, but very fast. She looked back and was a little surprised to see Mr. Trevor standing in the middle of the kidding pen with his head down. *What does that mean?* she wondered. *Would he really hit me? Just then he looked like Tio Flaco. Tio always hits me. I never broke anything of his and he still hits me. When I run, he chases me down...or one of his men. Mr. Trevor seems nice, but why did he pick up the rope?*

Watching from the wood, Bianca saw Castor tie the rope to a couple of pipes and drag them to the next opening to be reinforced. For the next hour, she watched him as he worked. Occasionally, he stopped to go check on Jimmy and play a bit with him, then he checked Caryn, changed her, and fed her again. Occasionally, the man shaded his eyes and looked toward the woods. After a while, Bianca began feeling a bit foolish. She guessed this man would not hurt her, but how could she begin again after the unspoken accusation? *Maybe,* she thought, *I should just not go back. That will be easier. I won't have to explain.*

Human beings choose their own teachers and mentors. Children do this in an especially pointed way. Often children that turn out to be 'teacher's pets' are simply children that see in an adult, something they want to emulate or learn. The children probably cannot state this; more than likely they don't even know it. They follow and serve the mentor until the child gets his or her questions answered, or learns the thing they are after, then they move on to another mentor or become more independent for a while. The chosen mentor often does not understand what is happening and resists, complains, and drives the child away. Occasionally a mentor will misread the intentions of the child, attribute adult motives or feelings to the child, and cause harm by acting on their assumptions. Clearly, Bianca was in the process of choosing Virgil Castor Trevor as her mentor. Castor did not have enough information or experience that could tell him what was happening or how to react.

4

Next Saturday

One week after the first meeting, close to noon, on my way back from town and the hardware store in the rattling pickup truck, I saw Bianca walking in the direction of her house beside the dirt county road that also ran by my house. She was on the left side of the road walking with her head down in the way a youngster walks when they have no purpose, but are deep in thought. Her clothing was the same as the previous Saturday. She didn't look up when I slowed, so I called her name. She jerked her head up with a look of mild surprise and curiosity on her face, but no welcoming smile. "Bianca, look. I got a new hammer. This handle won't break. At least that is what the clerk at Home Depot said." I held up the two-pound hammer with a yellow fiber-glass handle. "If you want to try again, I will be working on the pen in about an hour." She looked at me with what I took as suspicion. "Look. Bianca, I know it looked like I might be mad at you and I think you thought I would hit you with that rope. I saw the bruise on your leg. But really, the hammer was old, that handle was first broken by my grandfather before I was born. It was not your fault. It would have broken with anyone. That was not your fault. Even if you had broken it on purpose, I would not hit you. I would never hit you with a rope, an extension cord, a paddle, my hand or anything else. You don't hit friends like that."

Through my speech, Bianca did not move to speak. Gradually, she lifted her head and took on a sun grin. After I was quiet, she looked down at the ground and spoke softly, "About an hour?"

"Yes. I need to get a bite to eat first." At that moment a bit of understanding of her situation hit me, "Where are you having lunch?"

"I, I, I'm not very hungry."

"Tell you what. Meet me at the kidding pen in a half-hour. I'll bring lunch for both of us, then I'll see if you can break this unbreakable handle. See you then?"

"What about Caryn and Jimmy?"

"Billie is bringing them over now. They will both be there soon. You already know I'm not much of a babysitter, so I do need some help."

"OK, what do we eat?"

"Buttermilk and pretzels."

"You are saying a joke, right?"

"Show up and find out. Go ask your mother's permission."

***

IN THE WOODS

Bianca turned into the woods and walked around for a bit. She kicked dirt into piles, then kicked the piles down and smoothed the ground with her feet. She climbed a tree and looked over into Mr. Trevor's place. He had built a small fire in the kidding pen and propped a blanket up for a low shade just like she had shown him the week before, only he used four stakes instead of three. She could see bright wrappings from food on top of the rock. To herself, *I guess Jimmy and Caryn are coming soon. I am hungry. I can't go home, Tio Flacco is there, at least his truck is there. So, the choice is stay here hungry, go home and get beaten or go to Mr. Trevor's and eat. Okay, anyone could make that decision.* She climbed down and walked through the woods, to the gate and over into the pen.

***

LUNCH AT THE PEN

I was feeding a second round of mesquite sticks into the small fire in the pen when Bianca climbed the gate. "Why you building a fire?" I looked up and smiled. I was happy to see her. I had not noticed her accent before. She had a heavy Spanish influence in her pronunciation, sentence structure, and in her speech cadence.

"Well, we are having hot dogs, beans and smores. All three of those things require a source of heat, and I have to heat Caryn's bottles. I'm using mesquite for a good smoky flavor for the food. Do you like hot dogs?"

"Mr. Castor, I like hot dogs but I was wondering what buttermilk and pretzels would be like."

"Well, Bianca, if you like, next time we'll try that meal."

Bianca had a worried look on her face. I showed off my sparse Spanish, "Que piensa? What are you thinking?"

"Oh," she answered, "I haven't been home since about nine when my mother told me to leave. I need to go to the bathroom. Maybe I should go to the woods over there." I thought for a minute, then told her to go to my house and use the bathroom.

"Are you sure?" she asked with some worry showing in her voice.

"Sure. You need to go; the bathroom is sitting there idle. Go on." She still looked doubtful, "Where is the bathroom?"

"Well, go in through the kitchen door under the car port, straight through to the living room. Opposite the kitchen through the living room is a short hallway. The door at the end of the hallway is to the bathroom. If you get lost, just keep hunting and opening doors 'til you find it. It is a small house and none of the doors are locked. You can wash your hands and face while you are there."

"Is my face dirty?" She involuntarily scrubbed at dirt she could not see.

"No, it is not dirty, but I always wash my face before eating to...well, to feel better. I feel refreshed. Although, sometimes I need to wash off dirt also."

By the time she got back, I had the hotdog package open and sticks sharpened to hold wieners over the fire. The big rock had ketchup, relish, chopped onions, mustard, a half-loaf of bread, four bottles of green tea, and salad dressing all set up on the flat top. I had emptied two cans of pork and beans into a pot and placed it next to the fire to heat. Bianca stuck a wiener on a forked stick and began roasting it. Before I could get a wiener started, the big yellow suburban drove through the front gate and made its way to the pen. Billie got out looking as unkempt and worried as usual, grabbed Caryn's car seat, cooler, and diaper bag and set them down beside the suburban. Jimmy climbed out stepping over the diaper bag, climbed the fence, and ran to the fire.

"Stay away from the fire!" Billie's first words were directed sharply at Jimmy, then she immediately turned on me. "Trevor, why did you build a fire when you knew we were coming?"

"To roast wieners, heat beans and make smores. Jimmy has been around fire a lot more than you could know about, Billie. He knows to stay back. Heck, he can even build one. Bianca, would you help Jimmy please?" Jimmy already had a wiener roasting on a stick before I finished my defense. I climbed the fence, got Caryn and the diaper bag, set them over the fence, then climbed back in. Billie looked intently at Jimmy happily roasting a wiener. I could tell she was seeing more than just this event. She seemed to be reflecting on something she wished she could experience or something she missed; something from the past. After an audible sigh, she came back to the present and spoke.

"I have to go. There ain't much milk. I think I'm drying up. Who is your girlfriend?" Billie's voice had made a sudden shift from informative to the use of an accusatory tone in her question.

Ignoring the innuendo, I said, "Don't worry, I've got a fresh supply of formula. Billie, meet Bianca Gonzalez. She lives down the road. I invited her over for lunch. How long you gonna be gone this time?"

"She is a little old for you to be babysitting, isn't she? I don't know, maybe just today, maybe a week."

Again I ignored her intended dig, "Like I said, she is here for lunch, then she will help me drive stakes. We will be fine until you get your business done."

Billie stepped back into the big car, "Yeah, I'll bet." Less than a minute later, she was driving out the front gate.

"She was trying to make you mad by saying something ugly about me, wasn't she?" Bianca seemed to be concerned.

"No, she is a suspicious woman. Suspicious about things which don't concern her. Come to think of it, I don't think there is any other kind of woman."

"To me, she was trying to say something bad about you, or maybe about me."

"Well," I answered indulgently, "she sure hinted at it, didn't she? Your hotdog is turning black. Maybe you have it cooked enough to eat. Why don't we just have a good lunch, do a little work and enjoy the time?"

"Okay."

By that time, Brutus had come out of his hiding place under the truck and was sitting expectantly beside Jimmy who promised him a piece of the wiener. Caryn woke up, rolled to her stomach, and cooed while she watched the fire. Shortly, I started her bottle warming in the bucket.

The afternoon went by fast. By the third stake, Bianca was driving them without a miss, but she had definitely tested the handle. It stood up well. She nicked it a couple of times, but caused no serious damage. I was glad I had remembered to get her a pair of goggles to wear. She did knock off a few sparks. I noticed that the girl was very strong for her size. She swung the hammer with both hands most of the time, but a few times when I looked up, she had choked up on the handle and swung it with only her right hand.

Late in the afternoon, it got very warm. We took a break to walk fences. I carried Caryn in the crook of my arm. She was alert and enjoyed the walk, looking unsteadily in every direction with her eyes bugged out and spittle drooling from the corners of her mouth. Jimmy ran ahead exploring anything that caught his attention. Two billys had stuck their heads through the fence and could not pull back through because their horns caught on the wire. Bianca asked why goats would stick their heads through the fence in the first place, when suddenly she jumped behind me and squealed. It sounded like surprise mixed with a tinge of fear. "What's the matter?" I was alerted, but could only see a small green-striped lizard that had run across the path.

"That!! What is that?" Bianca was pointing at the lizard. "Oh, that is only a striped lizard. He is out hunting bugs to eat. They are not at all dangerous. In fact, he is probably as frightened of you as you are of him. If you look closely you can see his ribs are sticking out and his skin is loose. He just came out of hibernation and is very hungry, but he wouldn't eat a young girl. Probably, too sour." Bianca smiled and hit me playfully on the shoulder.

"With all the time you spend in the woods, I am surprised you haven't seen one before."

"Oh, I have seen them, I just stay away. They look mean."

Close to dark, Caryn woke for the fourth time and cooed for a while, then got fussy. I began to gather my tools. "Time to call it a day, Bianca." She gave me the hammer with some reluctance showing on her face.

"Will your mother let you in by now?"

Bianca looked at me to see if I was serious or making fun. Seeing that the question was one of concern, she answered, "Yeah, I guess she figures she has to let me in about dark if Tio is gone. When can we do this again?"

"Bianca, I am out working most every day the weather will allow. You are welcome any time. I thank you for the help. You are a good worker."

Bianca looked at her feet and kicked in the dirt, "I guess I better go home," she said as she walked away looking at the ground. She climbed the fence and was soon gone toward the woods that were across the end of a neighbor's field and on the way to her house.

5

Caught Watching

Between the Trevor Place and the Gonzalez house was a wood broken by a field which had been planted in sorghum. The young plants were eight inches tall and dark green from the liquid nitrogen-rich fertilizer Kermit Herring had sprayed beside the young plants a week before. The Wednesday rain and subsequent drying had left a crust on the black-clay soil. The crust crunched a little under Bianca's feet as she crossed the field from one wood to the other. The warm and crumbly soil felt good on the bottoms of her feet. Once through the fields, she walked deep into the wood in order to view her house from cover. Squatting behind a large China-berry tree so that she could see but not be seen, she spotted the hated large black Ford truck; the one with four back wheels that never hauled anything. When she saw it, she got a little sick to her stomach. That truck parked at her house with the small, dark man leaning on it watching everything, meant her tio was in the house. Since he was there, she would stay away until he left. She knew if he caught her, he would beat her again.

She had not noticed the skinny, dark man with a black mustache, new jeans, green plaid shirt, and white hat off to her right and behind her. He had walked out into the wood to relieve himself, but now crouched low, all his attention was on her. Her attention was on the black truck. He moved silently until he was close enough she could not get away, then he ran in and grabbed her. Flaco would be happy with him. There would be a reward. *Too bad for the girl, though.*

Blanca screamed and fought as hard as she could, but she was badly overmatched. Realizing she could not get away, she screamed for help until a rough hand clamped down on her mouth. She bit him hard and screamed again until the hand slapped her then clamped down so that she could not bite. No one answered. Her screams had been muffled by the woods.

6

Third Saturday: Provisions

*B*ianca arrived at the Trevor farm around nine o'clock on the third Saturday morning. It was a warm, pleasant day. I had kept Caryn and Jimmy from the previous Saturday until late Friday night. It was increasingly hard to get much work done with Caryn. She was out of the stage of babyhood where all she did was eat, sleep, poop, and cry. She was much more active and demanding of attention. When Bianca arrived, I was twenty yards behind the house, on a little rise, close to a large Oak tree, digging a hole beside a small slab of freshly poured concrete. I already had the hole about two feet deep and was sweating profusely using a pick to loosen more rocks and dirt. Close-by, I had a stack of lumber and corrugated steel sheets, nails, two claw hammers, a carpenter's square, and a handsaw. Leaning against a small oak tree beside the hole, was a shovel and crowbar. Without

39

a word, when I stepped out of the hole, Bianca grabbed the shovel, stepped into the hole with her bare feet, and began digging out the loose soil and rocks.

"Good morning!" I broke the silence.

"Good morning. What are we digging the hole for?"

"We're building an outdoor toilet. Here, spread the dirt behind the hole. We want the toilet to be high ground."

"Why do you do this? You have a bathroom."

"Its not for me. I may use it occasionally, but it isn't for me."

"Who?"

"You."

"What for?"

"You get kicked out early in the morning. There isn't anywhere for you to go to the bathroom except the woods. I'm not always here on Saturdays for you to use mine. Well, now, after we get it built, there will be a place for you to…to meet your needs."

"Why do you do this for me?"

"You came to help me. Now, I will help you a little."

Twice during the morning, I walked down from the toilet job to the kidding pens which now had over a hundred nannies with kids. Around eleven, nails needed to be driven in the very top of each side of the structure to secure the short rafters. I could not reach that high and drive a nail, so I started off to get a ladder. "I can drive those nails," Bianca said confidently, "if you are strong enough to hold me up."

"OK, little girl, you are on." This time she allowed the 'little girl' and for the next ten minutes, Bianca stood on my shoulders while she drove the twelve nails needed. Then she climbed on top of the rafters to nail the two pieces of tin forming the roof in place. I was impressed with her skill with the hammer and told her so.

"Well, you taught me good," was her response. That made me smile.

A little past noon, the one-hole outdoor toilet was completed. Included was a piece of broomstick as a holder for toilet paper, a small shelf on which I placed baby wipes, and a medicine cabinet with a mirror and a lock which I told her would hold whatever she decided to put there, and she would be the only one to know where the key was. Bianca cried as she told me she had no other private place.

Ignoring her emotion, "There is more," I announced. "Come with me." Bianca followed me to the carport which I had built several years before on to the house over a rough concrete slab. She followed showing her curiosity about what the 'more' might be. When we got to the carport, she could see I had moved a table out of the house and set it up under the car port in front of my pick-up against the outside of the kitchen wall. On the table, there was a small refrigerator and a microwave plugged into new outlets set in the outside of the kitchen wall. I had been busy.

I opened the refrigerator showing her an assortment of fruit cups, puddings, sandwich fixings, soups and such. On top of the refrigerator was an assortment of plastic spoons, forks, and knives sealed in a glass gallon jar which sat on a pile of paper plates wrapped in plastic. Beside the microwave was a twenty-four pack of bottled water, a twelve-pack of green tea, and inside the fridge was a small assortment of sodas. "Anytime you are hungry and I'm not here, you can come here and get food. Even if I am here. It doesn't matter. If Isidro is with you, feed him too. Eat it cold or heat it. Up to you. Do you know how to use the microwave?"

I did not look at Bianca's face until I was finished showing her what provisions I had made for her. When I looked at her I stopped cold. She was standing beside the old truck with tears running down her face. I didn't know what to ask or do. Fumbling for words, I somehow asked what was wrong.

"I was just thinking that I thought you were about to whip me with a rope the first time I came over. Why are you doing this?"

"Oh, Bianca, this is not free. I expect you to work hard for these things. You can decide when you are paid up."

She looked intently into my face. "How do you know I won't steal from you?"

"Well, Bianca, you can't steal from me. Anything I have that you need, you can take. It's yours. I give it to you."

"You really would *not* whip me would you?"

"No, Bianca, I would rather cut my own arm off. Right now, young lady, you can start paying for the meal by pouring us each a glass of buttermilk and break out the pretzels over there." Bianca smiled and washed her hands at the hose, then busied herself following the directions.

"This milk stinks and it tastes bad. You need to take it back and get your money back." Bianca had taken a sip of the buttermilk after she saw me take a deep drink. I laughed at her ignorance of buttermilk. "No, child, that is what buttermilk tastes like. Try a couple more sips and, here," handing her a salt-shaker, "shake a little salt in it."

"I already told you, I'm not a child," Bianca's assertion was not angry or disrespectful, the tone was matter-of-fact; a reminder.

"I'm sorry, Bianca, you are probably right. Your age and your experiences are very disparate. How old are you anyway?"

"I told you the first day, I'm eleven…almost twelve," Bianca said in the same matter of fact tone with a little indulgent flavor to it.

"Eleven," I repeated thoughtfully, "you must be in the fifth grade?"

"Fourth. I'm in the fourth grade, okay? I failed a year. I took third grade twice," her tone was apologetic, defiant, and embarrassed all at the same time.

I had obviously hit a sensitive nerve. "I don't mean to insult you; I just want to know you better. Why did you take third grade twice?"

She looked down in something of a repentant attitude, "I failed the state reading test. I failed it three times in one year and again three times the second time in third grade."

"Oh. Well, how is it going this year?"

"OK, I guess, but not really. Reading is hard."

I changed the subject. "If you want something different or more to eat, you can fix it, but sometimes food that tastes strange at first begins to taste good when you allow it to become familiar. Here, try this with your buttermilk." I handed her an oatmeal cookie. She took a bite of the cookie and sipped the buttermilk nodding her approval. "Sometimes opposite flavors, like sour and sweet actually taste good together. It is like a war of flavors, but the result is pleasant."

"Kinda like an old man working and a girl working together to build an outhouse?"

I thought for a moment, "Yes, I guess that works."

After we ate, I showed Bianca where I hid the key to the back door. "You have the use of the house anytime you need it. The rule is that this is a privilege for you, not to be shared with anyone except your brother if he needs it too."

"You would let me use your house? Why do you do all this?" Bianca asked.

"Well, Bianca," I answered in a manner that indicated I really didn't want to have to explain, "I did not know how comfortable you would be coming into my house with me not here, or even with me here. I want you to feel safe to take care of yourself, whether inside or out. It isn't healthy for any youngster to have to hold off going to the bathroom, and it isn't healthy for you to go hungry. It isn't healthy for you to have to stay in the woods when the weather is bad."

Bianca walked the fences with me that afternoon. We were looking for goats that had stuck their heads through the fence and could not get back. If left alone in that condition, the goat would die a horrible slow death of dehydration in a few days. I showed her how to force a goat's head back and through the fence over their objections, to release them. One nanny was particularly stubborn and bruised Bianca's left hand against the fence wire. "I'll bring the saw in a couple of days," I said almost to myself. "She is a repeat offender and the next time she has her head stuck, I'll remove the reason she can't get back through."

Bianca was incensed, "You would saw her horns off because she is stubborn?"

I grinned at her anger, "No, that particular nanny has good kids. She is a strong producer. If she continues to get hung up, she will starve, and I will lose her. I would rather take off the horns which she only uses to get in trouble, than find her dead of starvation."

Bianca seemed satisfied, but thoughtful. "Does it hurt?"

"Yes, I think it does, but I think it hurts less than dying."

"Does it hurt to die?"

"You got me there," I said remembering sitting beside my grandfather's bed when he died. "I don't think it does. I think it is more of a release from cares." She thought about that for a while, but didn't say any more or ask more questions.

We continued the fence walk deep in conversation mostly concerning lighter things Bianca wanted to know and about which she could formulate questions. When we got back to the pens, I went to a nanny tied to the fence by her horns, with a kid standing close by. I untied her and released her so she could get to water and feed. Her kid followed her bleating.

"Why do you tie her?"

"Well, she rejected her kid. She wouldn't allow it to suckle. I think it must hurt at first. I tied her to the fence so she couldn't run away. See her bag? It is loose and not full. She has had to allow the kid to suckle and release the pressure. Her bag probably doesn't hurt anymore and she should remember that the kid sucking milk is what released that pain. They should be okay now, but I'll keep them in the pen for a couple more days to be sure."

Before Bianca went home, I went back into the house and brought out a copy of the book, "The Traveling Musicians" and handed it to her. "We will talk about the story when you come again. Bianca opened the front cover as she walked home and read written inside the front cover, "To Ashley, my darling daughter."

7

Spring Break

March was a busy month for goat kidding at the Trevor farm. By the fifteenth, the kidding pen held over five hundred nannies, half my herd. There was little room to get around, but newborn kids ran and played everywhere in the pen through the day, and bedded down at night, sleeping next to their mothers to keep warm. Throughout the day and night, more kids were born. A flock of about twenty vultures lined the pen roosting on the fence standing ready to clean up the gore left by births. I did not bother the vultures; they were a part of the process.

The side of the pen that faced the woods was the part of the fence that I had reinforced using pipes and stakes. Each night, hogs attempted to dig under the fence. Each day, I repaired the damage. So far, there had been no breakthroughs. I was satisfied that the precautions were effective.

Saturday would have been a long, hard day even without the break-in. The hog had to have been huge, and judging from the tracks, it was a sow accompanied by as many as six half-grown shoats. The year-old piglets had followed her into the pen, then joined her in eating kid goats. I could find pieces of remains of four different kids. I couldn't tell if the fifth nanny's kid had been eaten or was one of the twelve stillborn kids that I had disposed of the day before. Daylight found me examining the bent pipe and deciding what to do to stop this brute.

Blood on the ground indicated the huge sow had split her snout on one of the stakes, but still she came in and ate kid goats. I knew I would have to take more drastic measures. She would be back.

Somewhere in the middle of pounding the pipe back into place and adding another, Bianca showed up in plaid shorts and a yellow tank-top over a white T-shirt. I thought she seemed more serious and smaller than before. She was a tiny girl anyway, for eleven. I judged her height at four feet six inches and her weight at sixty-five to seventy-five pounds. She climbed into the pen and walked over to me looking at the carnage from the night before. She put her hand on my shoulder in a silent "Hello, I'm sorry for your loss." move.

"Quite a mess, isn't it?" I asked hiding my disappointment.

"Yes, this is very bad. How many?" she asked.
"Five, I think. I have to fix this breach. Then tonight, I will sit vigil."

"What is, 'sit vigil?'"

"Well, Bianca. Sitting vigil usually refers to someone sitting up all night with the body of someone who has died. It is normal in some societies for the body of someone who dies to not be left alone until they are buried. I'm not sure the reason. In this case, what *I* mean by sitting vigil, is that I will stay up waiting for the sow to come in the night. I plan to kill her. That is the only way I know to stop one that big and that determined." I looked at her for the first time realizing something was different in her manner, and asked, "Are you all right?"

"Yeah, I'm OK."

I did not dig for information. "Hand me those stakes, please," I said pointing to four freshly sharpened stakes laying to my right. She walked over and picked two up. While she had her back turned, I saw the fresh bruise on her left leg. It was a deep blue stripe halfway between her ankle and her knee. She was moving stiffly enough that I suspected there were more bruises on her thighs hidden by the shorts and probably on her back.

"Bianca, what happened to your leg?"

"It is nothing. I fell."

"Is that bruise on your leg the only one?"

"No, I fell on a chair. There is another one on my back."

"Bianca, that does not look like a bruise from a fall. Did you get a spanking?"

"It is none of your business," she said without looking at me.

"Bianca, you may be right. It may not be my business, but if someone is hurting you, it is everyone's business. I have been spanked, and I have been beaten. My grandfather. I think that is the reason he left this place to me. He beat me many times with a quirt. Left scars. Some scars are not just in the skin. Some are of the soul and heart. I don't want that to happen to you."

"Nobody's beating me. I got a spanking because I was bad, okay?" Her tone and her emphasis on, "okay?" indicated she wanted to end the conversation.

"Bianca, what I see is a bruise from a beating. No eleven-year old is bad enough to be beaten and left with those kinds of bruises." Feeling like I should do something, but not knowing what, I added, "If you ever have need of me, call me, or come get me. Don't let anyone beat you. No one has that right." I dropped the sledge and walked over to the truck to retrieve my camera. I asked to take a picture of the bruise on her leg. She allowed it after being asked repeatedly. When I asked if I could take a picture of her back, she refused flatly. I did not pursue it because I thought her refusal might have to do with modesty.

As the day wore on, Bianca perked up and became her audacious self again. She even accused me of being sexist with a twinkle in her eye when I asked her to go to the carport and fix us some lunch. She then quipped over her shoulder, "Ham sandwich, tea, and chips for me, pretzels and buttermilk for you!" She laughed out loud when I demanded equality, then ran to complete her task.

By the end of the day, we had walked the fences, released about seventy nannies with kids into the pasture, and brought nearly fifty more nannies that seemed ready for delivery into the kidding pens. We talked about the book I had loaned her. Bianca could recall very little. She changed the subject by asking questions about Ashley and Jake, and the nanny I had told her I would saw her horns off. I dodged the questions about my children answering only about the nanny. "Well, she hasn't gotten caught again. That was the deal. If she stuck her head through, then I would take her horns. I guess she heard how angry that made you, or maybe she understands that I will do it."

Bianca looked down and drew exes in the dust with her toe, "I've been thinking about that. I was wrong. I thought you were going to punish her for being bad. I am sorry for showing disrespect."

"Bianca, goats can't be bad. Hogs can't even be bad. They do what is normal to them. Unfortunately, what some animals do, hurt my ability to make a profit, so I must react. If you are worried about the hog, whenever I have to kill one, I butcher it out and keep some of the meat for myself, but most of it I give to the people who live along this road. I have given roasts, chops, hams and such to your family also. I just didn't know you then."

Bianca thought for a moment then looked up at me, "I know. That is why I thought I could talk to you. You seemed like a nice man."

"So, all this help you are giving me is just a ruse to get more meat?"

She smiled, "If that is so, that is very expensive meat." We laughed for a bit, more from the delight in each other's company than anything very funny. Shortly thereafter, she left to her house.

8

Sitting Vigil

I walked to the pens around ten that night. I carried the .270 deer rifle my grandfather left me, a freshly sharpened butcher knife, a three-cell flashlight, and a rope. I stationed myself under a small oak tree with a clear view of the point of entry from the night before. Around midnight, I climbed the tree and sat in a fork with what should have been an even better view. It would have been a better view except the night was almost completely dark. The moon was in the darkest phase. The only light was from stars.

I couldn't tell how long I had been asleep, but I awoke with a start from a noise I couldn't place. When I jerked awake, the motion almost jettisoned me out of the tree. The noise had come from the gate, not from the fence. Standing goats moved away from something moving through the pen. Most of the goats were white or had white markings, so I could see them move, but what they were moving away from was not white. I could only make out a shadow. I watched to see what it could be. It climbed the fence and stopped at the base of the tree I was sitting in. *Cougar, panther?* I asked myself. *No, not a predator. It would not come after me up here with all those tender little goats easily available.*

"Mr. Trevor," it was a quiet whisper that at first I could not identify.

Recognition came in a flash, "Bianca! What are you doing here?"

"I got home too late to get in, and under the house, I couldn't sleep, so I decided to come sit vigil with you."

A noise on the other side of the pen interrupted the questions I had. I climbed down quietly and squatted beside the young girl while we tried to see the hog rooting at the barriers we had put in place the day before. I handed her the flashlight, then instructed Bianca to wait for my signal then shine the light at the noise and hold it on the sow's head as long as she could.

By touch, I checked my rifle and clicked off the safety latch. Hearing the rattle of the pipe, "Now," I whispered.

Bianca clicked the light on and aimed it true. She took in a gasp of breath at the size of the sow. "Wow!" she exclaimed in an excited whisper, "That is one big pig!"

"Hold the light steady." The sow bolted before I could fire the gun. She ran a few steps toward the wood with the shoats following. "Man, they are all fat and healthy," I exclaimed admiringly. "They're done for tonight, but they will be back tomorrow." The hogs walked casually back to the woods.

"Bianca, what did you mean when you said you got home too late to get in? And where were you trying to sleep?"

"I can get in by now," she said, then left, walking toward her house in the dark before I could ask any more questions. I didn't know the circumstances, but I thought, *I'll bet you can't get in. I wonder where you will end up sleeping tonight.* The moon was just peeking over the horizon. The little bit of reflected light illuminated almost everything.

I had a very uneasy feeling about Bianca. I felt something in her voice, something fearful. Her body language belied worry as she walked to the white farmhouse just down the road from mine. My uneasiness grew as I readied for a nap, but I could not think what I should do. Sleep did not come easily.

9

The Crux

My young daughter, Ashley, stood across a fast moving stream. The ground she was on was sinking and the water was rising. I could see her and the trouble she was in, but I could not get across to help. I tried swimming only to be washed back and thrown on the safe shore exhausted. I ran to the bridge only to find it was washed out. Again, I ran back to the safe spot on the shore of the stream, breathless and struggling to move. Still Ashley beckoned, she called to me, "Mr. Trevor!" so I climbed a tree and tried to lean it across the stream. The tree broke and dumped me into the cold, rushing water. Once again I dragged myself out on the safe bank, but suddenly the bank began to give way, I began sliding into the rushing water..."

"Mr. Trevor!"

I was suddenly awake and sitting up. The dream had been vivid. At first it was very difficult to distinguish real from the vicarious experience of the dream. "Was the voice real? It hadn't sounded like Ashley's voice.

"Mr. Trevor! Wake up!"

"Bianca! I, I, I'm awake. What are you doing here? How did you get here?"

"I walked. You showed me where the key was hidden, remember. Mr. Trevor, I think I am hurt. I think I need your help."

Very quickly I was wide awake. I threw on a robe and turned on the ceiling light.

Bianca was sitting beside my bed on the carpet. "What hurts little one?" I asked before I looked at her back.

"My back and legs. It burns."

I looked at her back. Her shirt was torn in several places and she was bleeding under each tear in the cloth. Her long pony tail was soaked with blood from her back. There was blood soaking the back of her shorts and her calves had red whelps and some dried blood. The top of her bare right foot had a bleeding whelp. Immediately I was on the phone, "Dorothy, I have an emergency. I'm bringing a little girl to your house. No, she is not mine, but she still needs help. Someone has beaten her very badly. She is bleeding, hurting and shocky. Dorothy, I'm bringing her now! We will be there in fifteen minutes." I hung up the phone. "Bianca, I'm going to pick you up now and put you in my truck. You can lie on your side, or your stomach. This will probably hurt more for a little bit, but I'm taking you to the doctor." She started to object, but I ignored her and picked her up. She groaned in pain as I supported her weight on her injuries.

In the truck, I laid her across the seat on her stomach. She was short enough that with her knees bent up, she fit with her head on the seat leaving room for me to drive. I started the old truck and backed out quickly.

When I got the truck turned around and headed out, I met headlights coming in. *Billie was bringing the kids today*, I recalled. *It must be nearly six AM.* Billie had her window down and a cigarette hanging out of the corner of her mouth when I pulled to a stop next to her Suburban. "Follow me!" was all I said then sped away.

Thirteen minutes later I pulled into the circular driveway of Dr. Dorothy Pick's house.

She met me at the door as I carried Bianca face down to keep from hurting her further. I took her straight to the bedroom that had been remodeled to be an examination room, and placed her on the table. She seemed to be nearly asleep, but in so much pain she could not respond to anything else. "She is shocky," was all Dr. Pick said, but her expression told of her concern. Nearly an hour later, I was rocking Caryn back to sleep when Dr. Pick came out of her treatment room.

"She will be fine with a few days rest and some good food. Her wounds are superficial, I think. Someone really beat her up though. What did they hit her with? Who did this?"

I answered, "I don't know, but my bet is a rope or extension cord. I think someone in her family did this. By the way, the police are coming. I called them right after I brought her."

"Of course. Did you call Child Protective Services?"

"No, I didn't think to. Should I?" Before she could answer, Sgt. Correa knocked on the living room door.

While Sgt. Correa was talking with Bianca, I called Child Protective Services. After a long wait, I finally got to tell a Ms. Winston about Bianca. She said the case would be assigned and someone would be coming to talk to me. She could not say when they would come.

SUSPICION

Sgt. Correa came out of the treatment room with a look that could only be anger. "Mr. Trevor, did you whip that girl?"

"No, I did not!" I said emphatically, "She came to me about an hour and a half ago. Woke me up asking for help."

"Alright then, who did this to her?"

"Sgt., I don't know. She has had bruises on her legs the past three weeks that I know of, I suspect someone in her family is hurting her, but she wouldn't talk about it other than to say she fell. I think someone hit her with a frayed electric cord or something similar to cut her like that. Didn't she tell you?"

"No, she is very closed mouthed about who hurt her. Why did she come to you?"

"I already told you. She was hurt and wanted help. I had told her many times that if she needed me she could come to me and I would help her."

"Mr. Trevor, in these cases, most often the child will cling to the one who is hurting them…so you understand why I have to not believe you."

"I understand. However, I'm sure there are reasons why Bianca won't tell you who did this. She may be afraid you won't help and will give her back to the same person who whipped her like that. Then things could get worse."

"Suppose you tell me what you know…from the beginning."

I told him about the hints Bianca had given about being kicked out of the house, being locked out, and having to find a place to sleep. I also told him about her running away from me when I held the rope. He wondered aloud, "What happens now?"

"I called CPS. I guess they decide from here."

"Are they coming?"

"Said they would, but would not give me a time.

"I have a few more questions for you. Do you mind?"

"No, of course not."

The next thirty minutes was filled with explanations of the law, questions concerning my involvement in hurting the girl, and how she came to me. I was feeling like I had told the same story at least five times and was a strong suspect, when Sgt. Correa finally left. I was sure I would be arrested for hurting Bianca. *Well, I guess that's just the way it will have to be. I didn't do anything I wouldn't do again. I did it right! I wonder what they would have thought if I had not brought her to the doctor. No use thinking about that. She had to be brought. No use questioning myself, they seem to do that well enough.*

GETTING BACK

Caryn was cooing and laughing at being bounced on my knee when I called for Dr. Pick. She came in from the treatment room with a look of consternation on her face. "Castor, I gave her a sedative, so she will sleep for a while. I can keep her for a little while, but I have rounds at the hospital in about two hours."

Jimmy was outside leading Dr. Pick's dogs around the yard. He was looking at every bump and hole and digging into strange, dark places with a stick. Dr. Pick's two German Shepherds followed him with ears up and pointed forward seemingly wondering what the little human would do next.

I weighed the situation. "CPS will be here shortly. She will need clothes. I assume you cut her clothes off before treating her?"

Dr. Pick nodded and produced bloody size labels from her shirt, shorts, and underwear. "I thought you might need these."

I took the labels, almost retched at the blood, but held it in. "OK if I leave Jimmy here for about an hour? I figure Willow can get me a couple of sets of clothes together quickly. Should I get her some soft pajamas?" Dr. Pick said that would be very thoughtful and promised to look after the boy for a while, but that I had to take Caryn with me.

Sixty-five minutes later, I drove into Dr. Pick's driveway with two complete changes of clothes very much like the ones I had seen her wear, except new, a set of flannel pajamas, a soft, red, plaid robe, and a pair of fuzzy pink house shoes. CPS had not arrived. Dr. Pick was preparing to leave. "I've called CPS. I told them to go to your house. I'll get Bianca dressed and you can take her with you. She will be fine there until they decide what they will do." I quickly showed the doctor what I had bought and asked whether she thought they were OK.

"You are a knight in shining armor. She will love them. Listen, Sir Galahad, you are probably in for a rough time. I heard Sgt. Correa's questioning. Be very careful. I know Bianca will be in good hands with you. She trusts you, and so do I, but she also knows she has brought you trouble. I'll drop by your house to check on her on my way back home. She is not badly hurt, but she will be hurting badly for a couple of days."

Ten minutes later, Dr. Pick led Bianca out of the treatment room dressed in the fuzzy pink shoes and blue-flannel pajamas. I marveled at how tiny she was, and at the evil in anyone who could beat such a tiny girl. She walked very gingerly from pain and unsteadily from the sedative Dr. Pick had given her. Seeing the lack of room in my truck, Dr. Pick volunteered to drive Bianca to my house in her car. It was nearly eleven when the new grey Cadillac followed my rust-colored truck up to my house.

10

CPS

*A*fter I served Bianca and Jimmy soup and sandwiches, fed Caryn, and put her down for a nap, I got busy cleaning out the spare bedroom while Bianca slept on the sofa. Jimmy took Brutus to the feed shed to catch mice. The spare bedroom was not at all feminine. It was more a patchwork of things that did not fit elsewhere, but I made it somewhat comfortable in case CPS did not come that day.

Around four, Bianca was hurting again, and hungry. Following Dr. Pick's directions, I gave her two-hundred milligrams of ibuprofen and had her rest while I fixed pork-chops, mashed potatoes, gravy, a salad, and pork and beans. When I served Bianca, she sat up and ate hungrily declaring with a mischievous smile, this to be the best meal she had had that day. I felt some relief at the return of her sense of humor. I never asked her who had hurt her. I wanted to know, but with CPS on the way, I figured that was not my place. The police or CPS would get to the bottom of it. I tried to fill in as a nurse and care-giver while waiting for them.

Dr. Pick arrived at seven. She found Bianca sitting up playing checkers against me, but shivering. I had not noticed. Checking, she read a temperature of one hundred two degrees. She took Bianca into the bedroom and changed her dressings.

Before she left, she gave me a bottle of pills. "These are antibiotics," she said. "Bianca has an infection. Give her one when I leave, then one every four hours for the next three days. And this," she shoved another small bottle of pills into my hand, "is a mild pain killer. Give her one as an alternate to the ibuprophen, but only if she complains of pain. If CPS takes her, make sure these medications go with her." I nodded and thanked her, then asked her to send me the bill for her services. She looked at me with eyes narrowed, "What bill?" She then turned and left. "Oh, she needs to see someone to take stitches out next Monday."

Day by day, Bianca got physically stronger and seemingly happier. Billie picked up Jimmy and Caryn late Sunday night. She sniffed disapprovingly when she saw Bianca sitting in the living room. Her visit lasted only a few minutes. It seldom lasted longer, but this was especially brief.

Monday morning, I left Bianca sleeping while I went to check on the nannies. They were out of feed and the sow with six shoats had gotten into the pen again. I could miss thirteen kids. *Tonight, old girl. Tonight.*

When I started back to the house, there was a strange car parked in the driveway. It was a small Honda SUV. There were no people waiting outside, so I went inside.

Bianca was sitting on the sofa in her pajamas and robe crying softly. There were two strangers in the room. Standing with her hands on her hips was a tall, thin, middle-aged, red-headed woman dressed in a business suit complete with tie, looking very stern with her hair pulled back so tight it looked like it must cause pain, and might explain the sour look on her face. Sitting in my lounge chair was a younger Hispanic male, short, slightly overweight, balding, wearing a gray three-piece suit, white shirt, and blue-striped tie, and a black overcoat, and sporting a pencil-thin moustache. He was obviously the sidekick. Both strangers were facing Bianca who looked up at me when I walked in. Her look made me realize this was not to be a pleasant meeting.

"Excuse me, who are you? And what do you mean coming into my house uninvited?"

The red-headed woman stepped between Bianca and I and handed me a business card. "I am Blanch Hatchett. I am an investigator for CPS. Why is this girl with you instead of her family?" she asked. Technically it was a question, but it came out in the form of an accusation.

I looked at her card. "Before I answer any questions, I want to establish your identity. Please show me some identification." Then to myself, *Name fits the face. Hatchett-Face.*

"You have my card."

"Lady, I could have cards like this printed with *my* name on them. I need to see some identification, or I will call the police."

"Go ahead, call them. It looks like we will need them anyway," the woman said with a sneer as she handed me her picture ID identifying her as a CPS investigator.

"And yours?" I asked looking at the young man. The man quickly produced a picture ID with a similar title.

"Just a moment." I went to the phone and called the number on the sour faced woman's card. The voice on the other end identified both agents and stated that they had been dispatched to a complaint. When I asked when they were dispatched, she answered that they had been given the file the previous Saturday morning.

"OK, it seems you are who you say you are, now what do you want to know?"

"What happened to her?"

"I suggest you ask her. But before you do, I want to know what you have been telling her to have her crying. She was perfectly happy before you came."

"In any CPS investigation, all information is privileged. Since you are not a parent or guardian, you have no legal standing," the woman answered very directly.

"Bianca? What did they do to you?"

"They told me I had to go home."

"Do you want to go home?" I was not watching Bianca. I was watching Hatchet face.

"Don't answer his question. He has no right to ask you anything. Mr. Castor, we need to speak to you in the kitchen, please."

"It's Mr. Trevor. My first name is Castor."

ACCUSATIONS CONTINUE

In the kitchen, the young Hispanic man stood just inside the door holding it closed so Bianca could not hear. It seemed to me that the man was intending to block my access to Bianca. "What is this for?" he asked as he pulled a black, six-foot extension cord out of his pocket. The cord had weathered and cracked in several places and the female end was missing so that bare copper wire stuck out of the two leads.

I looked at the cord then answered, "I *don't* use that. If it were mine, I would throw it away. Why do you ask?"

"Did you throw it away?"

"No, that cord is not mine. Where did you find it?"

"I'll ask the questions. Is this your cord?"

"Mr. Juarez, why don't you quit beating bushes and ask the question you want answered?"

"Is this your cord," the man persisted.

"That isn't the question you want an answer to."

"When did you start beating Bianca with cords?"

"That question assumes guilt. Not a proper question. I have never laid a hand on that child. Ask her. And, keep in mind, she came to me asking for help. I helped her. Dr. Pick asked me to look after her until you guys arrived. That was Saturday, by the way. Today is Monday. You are two days late. If she had been in danger from me, she could be dead and you would have been in bed asleep." The bothersome pain began throbbing in my left pectoral. I rubbed the muscle absently.

"Do you realize we can have you picked up and held in jail?"

"Yes, I realize that. I also know CPS was called several times on Saturday, that you were given the assignment Saturday morning and did not come. You can have me arrested, but that does not make you right. If you want to be right, investigate her home. I have not suggested she go home, but I have not held her against her will either." With more passion, "If you send her back, you send her into what got her hurt in the first place, and she was hurt very badly. What I have done is what any caring human being should do." Almost screaming, "Now, it's your turn! Do what is right and keep her from getting hurt again!" I know I was red in the face and I was stabbing my finger alternately at the hatchet woman and Juarez. The pain in my chest intensified.

Hatchet-face returned to the living room telling Juarez to hold me in the kitchen. I went about fixing iced tea, slamming spoons, glasses, and the teakettle around, while Juarez stood at the door. When the tea was ready, Juarez refused a glass. "Would you take Ms. Hatchett and Bianca a glass, please. I will wait right here. Dr. Pick instructed me to make sure Bianca is well hydrated. There is possibly some damage to one of her kidneys," I lied. "It is time she had a drink of something." Juarez took the tea after I designated which glass was for whom. I did not relate that I had put lemon and sugar in Bianca's and a considerable dose of lemon juice in Hatchet-face's tea with no sugar

Juarez came back and suggested we step outside for a bit. I went, though I suspected while we were out of sight, Hatchet-face would take Bianca to their car. I hoped she would allow Bianca to take the clothes I had bought for her, but I doubted it would happen. I wondered if I would ever see her again. Flashes of scenes of the last time I saw Ashley passed through my mind as I led Juarez to the goat pens. "Are you going to have me arrested?" I asked knowing it was a real possibility.

Agent Juarez did not answer, so I simply took him on a tour of the kidding pens telling him about the barriers and the hogs. It looked as if about twenty more kids had been born that day, among them two sets of beautifully colored black and white twins. Three more nannies were down in labor. That done and nearly an hour past, I asked, "Don't you think they have had enough time to get away?"

Juarez looked toward the house and said, "Not yet. Tell me about that little house over there. It looks new." Figuring him to be a city boy, I assumed he did not know about outhouses. The assumption was correct. I took him to see the small building and pointed out the piece of broom-handle sticking out from a stud for toilet paper, the shelf for baby wipes, and the small cabinet I installed for Bianca to keep any personal items. I did not indicate the outhouse was for Bianca's needs. I did not see that as any of the little man's concern and could be a fact anyone could twist into something evil. Juarez's head jerked around at the sound of a car driving up.

"Let's go around to the carport. I think they are gone now."

Less than five minutes later, I was handcuffed in the back seat of the police cruiser on my way to the county sheriff's station. I spent a restless night behind bars wondering what I had gotten myself into. When my thoughts went to Bianca, I began feeling a little ashamed at my self-pity. Then I began wondering what had become of her. Feeling helpless, I prayed earnestly for her safety.

11

Arraignment

*T*uesday morning, I went before Judge Peterson to face charges. I had spent the night in jail, sleeping fitfully in my clothes. I am sure my appearance was unkempt and not made any better because of the handcuffs, and ankle chains. I must have made a sorry sight.

Judge Peterson was a big stocky black man over six feet tall with shockingly white hair and moustache. The man had a powerful but wise look about him. His court was sometimes a little more informal than some, but he got business done. He was a no-nonsense enforcer of the law. In the sparsely populated county, he was *the* County Judge and highly respected for his honesty and his fairness. Some had made the mistake of assuming his fairness made him ignore provisions of law. Where the law was clear, Judge Peterson administered it promptly with fidelity.

When asked about the pending charges, the prosecutor, Mr. Benjamine Foder, named several laws he said I had broken including kidnapping and assault. The judge asked me how I pleaded. I silenced the public defender I had been assigned and answered, "Not guilty, your honor." I started to explain, but the judge said this was not the time or place to prove my innocence. He asked the prosecutor for a run-down of the evidence his office had gathered. Hatchet-face joined the prosecutor's table and gave part of her story telling that she had found the extension cord under my truck and the prosecutor said the blood type on the cord matched that of the minor

child who had been beaten. The Judge asked if the prosecutor had asked the child who beat her. He said that her testimony was inconclusive.

"In other words," the judge said looking over his reading glasses at Foder, "the girl did not implicate Mr. Trevor in hurting her. Is that correct?" Mr. Foder shrugged. "That's what I thought. Get those restraints off the man!" While the cuffs were being removed, the judge gave the prosecutor ten days to come up with conclusive evidence or the case would be thrown out. Upon the suggestion of the court-appointed lawyer, the judge released me on what he called my personal bond.

ENTER OMAR AND LIZBET

Finally free from the court, I went to the strip mall across from the courthouse and talked George Myers into driving me home during his lunch hour. George worked as a custodian in the mall. He had been a friend of my dad when they were both kids. His old Chevy truck seemed to just barely make it, but I could not recall when that truck didn't seem like it was on its last mile.

When we arrived at my house, just before noon, I invited George in for lunch. He declined stating he must get back to begin the afternoon's work. He left shaking his head causing me to wonder what the man was thinking. Using that mournful head-shake as a clue, I figured word had gotten around town that I was some sort of pedophile.

Down at the pens, I found fresh feed already put out for the goats. I was scratching my head wondering who had helped out, when I saw the pool of coagulated blood. It was outside the kidding pen amid freshly rooted ground. Drag trails indicated a very large animal had been drug toward the house. I followed the drag marks to the oak tree in my back yard. I threw rocks to run two vultures off the gore left by a butchering. It had definitely been a hog, but who had done it was a mystery for the moment.

Inside the house, I was amazed to see the house had been cleaned. The kitchen was immaculate, the living room was straightened and had been freshly vacuumed, and both bedrooms were vacuumed and the beds made. Laundry had been washed, dried, and folded, and the bathroom was shining better than it had at any time since being built. Again I was scratching my head. I was deep in thought when I heard the kitchen door open.

Senor, and Senora Buentello awaited me in the kitchen. I was still puzzled, but things were about to fall into place. "Omar, did you butcher the hog?" The old man was dressed in his worn blue overalls, brown work shoes, and ragged felt hat. He wore a thick gray handle-bar moustache. He was thin and bent, he seemed to be so frail and fragile that a good smack on the shoulder would turn him into a pile of dust. Senora Buentello, Lizbet, wore a dark purple dress overlain with a white apron bordered with lace, old fashioned black high-button shoes, heavy stockings, and a gray short coat. Her hair was held in place by an orange scarf that covered all her head except her kindly wrinkled face with dark shining eyes. She was almost as old as Omar, but she seemed a little more substantial, though she waddled a little when she walked. She held a covered ceramic dish in her weathered and crooked fingers. Those worn hands told of a life of hard work. The odor from that dish had to be among the best I had ever experienced.

"Some of the fresh pork," she said in Spanish as I took it from her. The dish was still hot enough that I soon placed it on the kitchen cabinet.

"Who killed the hog?" I asked again. Mr. Buentello took his battered hat off and held it in front of his chest as he told me in broken English that he had shot it but one of his nephews had butchered it out.

"Do you want some of the meat?" he asked.

"No Mr. Buentello, I don't need it. You fed my goats didn't you?"

"Si' Senor, I feed the chivos."

I regained my senses for a moment and invited the couple into my home. After they were sitting, and I was enjoying the caldo, I looked at Mrs. Buentello and said, "You, dear lady, cleaned my house. I thank you. I thank you, Senor for caring for my goats. I am in your debt."

It was Mr. Buentello who talked next. His voice cracked with emotion when he began, "No, Senor, it is we who are in your debt. You take good care of our great-granddaughter. Her parents do not care for her, and her uncle beats her, but you have done for our family a great service. I fear it has caused you much trouble. And your trouble is not over. So you see, it is we who are in your debt."

"Will you testify to the beatings?"

"No senor, I cannot go to court. You see I am not a citizen. I am in this country illegally for over twenty years now."

"Mr. Buentello, do you know where Bianca is being held now?"

"No senor, none of us know. The red-haired lady with the very sharp nose took her away ayer, yesterday. We have not seen her since. The red-haired lady came to my granddaughter's house asking questions, but Bianca is still gone."

"Why do you allow her to be beaten?"

"Her uncle is not of this family. He is a very powerful man and he is evil. He is of the devil. None of us can stand up to him. It is not because of him. He is a small man. But it is because of the gang to which he belongs. Los treses. The thirteens."

Mr. Buentello and I talked of many things past, present, and future as well as goats and other livestock, as I ate the rest of the caldo. When he was finished talking, I saw the old couple to the door, then went to walk the fences. I had heard a good deal of Bianca's family history, most of it in Mexico. There was much to think about. That night, I dreamed again of Ashley. This time the dream included Jake. Both children called for me from behind a wall of fire I could not see into and could not penetrate. I woke up as I had many times feeling exhausted, guilty, and helpless. Again in my dream I was not able to save them from the new disaster contained in the dream. The pain in my chest was sharp for a few minutes.

12

Return

hree days passed without incident and without any word concerning Bianca. On Friday, I moved all my goats to the pasture farthest from the woods. I was no longer concerned about the large hog, and in spite of the complications and losses, I had a good crop of healthy kids. There were only about fifty head still kidding. Early that day, Billie brought Caryn and Jimmy to stay for a few days. She said she was looking for work again.

I loaded the children into the old truck and made a trip to Lometa, Texas. I turned in by a sign that advertised Registered Boer goats. Another sign made of red paint on a piece of plywood advertised "Show Goats." After looking the stock over, I picked out a pair of Boer nannies, one two-year-old with a pair of twin kids, and a yearling not yet bred. I also picked out a well-muscled Boer Billy with a different blood-line.

While I was negotiating the price with Gus Lee, Jimmy wandered about going from animal to animal petting and talking to them. Gus didn't seem to mind and Jimmy had a way with animals I could not explain; I was not worried about him. As we agreed on prices and wound up the business, I wrote a check.

Suddenly Gus Lee broke into a run toward his pens hollering for me to come, "That boy's in the pen with Old Red!" I dropped my checkbook and pen and took out after him adrenalin was pumping and my head was trying to figure out who Old Red could be. I just assumed this was not good.

When I caught up to the owner, Gus was standing outside a fenced pen exclaiming, "Well, I'll be dipped in sheep snot!! Now, that beats all I ever saw!" I followed his eyes into the pen to see Jimmy feeding grass to a huge, old, red, Spanish billy goat. "What's that boy got?" he asked. "I don't even mess with Old Red. He's a good billy, but he is so mean, I have to bring the nannies to him. He butts and paws anyone or anything that comes into the pen. My dogs don't even go in there. Look at that! That old goat is following him around like a puppy! How'd he get in anyway?"

"There is no pen or shed on my place he can't get into and no animal he can't handle. Jimmy is just now four and all I can say is he has a way with animals that I can't explain," I said.

I told Gus about the snake impaling itself on Jimmy's stick while the man just scratched his head.

"Part Indian. He's got to be part Indian."

I laughed, "Well, he is Cherokee and not just a little part, but that don't explain it. I am part Cherokee, in fact, mostly Cherokee and I can't even get a woman to follow me around, much less a renegade animal."

Gus laughed and said, "That, my friend is too high a standard. If that one boy can figure out how to handle women like he does Old Red, well, then he is a master of all God's critters."

On the way back, I stopped at the Dairy Queen in Lampasas to eat and feed the kids. Jimmy knew exactly what he wanted. I ordered chicken strips and gravy and a small coke for Jimmy and a Hunger Buster and a root beer for me. While I ate my hamburger, I fed Caryn some pureed spinach and applesauce from baby-food jars then gave her a bottle. I noticed she had taken a jump in her growth. She hadn't looked that big before. On the way home from there, I made a last stop at a small farm just off the highway. The owner was an old friend everyone called Boss Dan, who had a litter of Border Collies. Jimmy walked straight to the puppies with a serious thoughtful look on his face and without hesitation, picked a young female that licked his hand and then followed him everywhere he walked. The rest of the way home, the little black and white dog with characteristically long hair, lay with her head in Jimmy's lap. After a while, Jimmy spoke, "Lucy. Her name is Lucy." That announcement was all the conversation we had for the remainder of the trip. We did have to make one more stop to change Caryn's smelly diaper and give her a bottle.

When we got home, I loosed the tied goats, fed and watered them, and gave them free use of a grassy fenced run beside the kidding pen. Jimmy took Lucy around the pens and house. Almost unconsciously, I looked around the place for any sign of Bianca. I wondered where she might be, and had to admit to myself that I missed her. I hated that she had been hurt, but I had enjoyed pampering her and seeing to her needs.

13

Runaway!

round ten that night, just as I was lying down for what I hoped would be a good sleep, Sheriff's deputy Bill Wagoner came by asking about Bianca. "She ran away from the foster home a little after dark. You mind if I look around?" I showed him around, then let him hunt around the house and outside for a while. Officer Wagoner left having not found Bianca. Before driving away, he warned me against harboring the girl and charged me to call if the girl showed up.

Late that night, I laid awake in bed wondering what was next in my life. I was confident I had done right by Bianca, but still she was with strangers, and now she had run away, and I was suspected of kidnapping her. *I guess everything will wash out,* I thought as I began to fade into sleep. That was one of the pieces of wisdom I had from my grandfather. So far, things did not seem to wash out right for Bianca.

I promised myself I would not be a bystander the next time she needed me. *This time, I'll fight for right. I just wish I could figure out who to fight. The only real villain seems to be an uncle. Overly zealous CPS workers and prosecutors will eventually be rendered ineffective, but the uncle? Could he be the one that threw that damning extension cord under my truck?*

In the middle of that thought, I heard the kitchen door open. With the uncle on my mind, I jumped up ready for battle. I always kept one of Jake's old baseball bats handy next to my bed. Donning a robe, and grabbing the bat, I walked silently and quickly to and through the living room. At the moment I got to the kitchen with the bat at the ready, the kitchen light came on. I could barely recognize her swollen face. "Bianca! What happened?!?"

DOUBLE THE TROUBLE

Bianca ran to me and held to my waist while she sobbed. "He hurt me again. I think he wants to kill me."

Dried blood indicated she had been bleeding from her nose and mouth and a cut above her hairline over her left eye was still oozing. Her clothes were wet and smelled of river. Her hair was still damp. Her face was bruised and her left eye was swollen almost closed. While she held on to my waist crying, I dialed Dorothy Pick's number. "Dorothy, I'm coming over again. I've got a youngster that needs your help. Yeah, it is Bianca again. I'll be there in a few minutes, I have to get Jimmy and Caryn up and ready. OK. Well, that would be great. I'll put some ice on the bruises." Hanging up the phone, I took Bianca's face in my hands, "Dr. Pick is coming over to see what we need to do for you. Meantime, let's get you on the couch and comfortable while I get some ice."

"Mr. Trevor?"

"Yes, Bianca?"

"Can I stay here? Can I stay here with you? At least tonight?"

"Bianca, you know you are always welcome in my house. I even like having you here, but that is not my decision, nor is it yours. I will have to call the sheriff's office and let them know you are here. My guess is that they will come and take you back to the foster home you ran away from."

"I don't like it there. I'm scared there. They have a really big boy that cusses and threatens me. He says he is going to do nasty things to me. I'm afraid of him. The woman is old and when she goes to bed, the boy gets up and goes into other rooms. I kept him out, by blocking the door with a chair, but he tried for three nights and cursed me when he could not get in. He tried again tonight. He banged hard on my door. I was so scared I climbed out the window to get away from him. I din't know where else to go, so I came here."

"Bianca, Mr. Buentello, your great-grandfather, came by. He told me about the uncle. But, who hurt you tonight?"

She looked surprised that I knew, but quickly answered, "It was him. When I ran away, I was coming here. I think the sheriff called my house and told them. Tio was waiting for me at the bridge. I think he knew I was coming here. He hit me with his fist and warned me to not tell. He said to tell everyone you are the one that beat me. Then he hit me again and again. It was like he could not stop. Finally, he knocked me in the water. I held my breath and stayed under and floated down away from him. It was dark. When I came up, I heard him calling me to come back, but he could not see me." I climbed out on the other side and walked through the woods. I saw lots of hogs, but they didn't bother me. My nose hurt so bad, and I couldn't see very good."

"Bianca, why did your tio whip you with the cord?"

"Because I didn't cry."

"What did he do to make you cry?"

"He slapped me, but I didn't cry."

"Why was it important for you to cry?"

"I don't know, except that he said something about my spirit. He said it had to be broken. He kept hitting me, but something in me wouldn't let me cry even when I saw the blood. I don't remember when he quit. I think I fainted.

"And I thought *I* was stubborn. Listen kid, I did the same thing with my grandfather. He beat me until he wore out. I just sat up and looked at him. When he finally quit, he went to bed. One night he beat me until he couldn't raise his whip any more. Then during the night, he had a stroke. He spent the rest of his life dependent on me. He was always afraid I would do something to him. He was afraid to eat or drink, and he couldn't sleep. I never mentioned the beatings, and I never retaliated, and I even told him he had nothing to fear from me, but he was always afraid. Hang tough, kid, there is an end to all this." Bianca smiled the smile of one who just found a long lost relative.

Dr. Pick's Cadillac pulled into my driveway within fifteen minutes of the call. When she walked in, I was on the phone calling the sheriff's office. She walked in without knocking carrying her bag and quickly got down to business, taking Bianca into the spare bedroom.

"Her nose is broken, and I think she has a fractured cheekbone. She should be in a hospital, but this time of night, you couldn't get anyone to do anything anyway. I prescribe that she not be moved tonight. She needs a bath, clean clothes, and rest." Dr. Pick seemed to be anticipating the sheriff's presence.

"Give me a minute, Dr. Pick. I'll draw a bath and get out some clothes that were bought for her. She can stay here, but I don't think the sheriff will go along with that."

Dr. Pick said flatly, "They won't have much choice. Let's get her in that bath before the sheriff gets here. She could use a good soaking in a disinfectant. Her sores and some of the stitches have been re-opened. Do you have any Lysol?" I immediately went about getting things ready for the doctor to bathe Bianca and dress her afterward.

Two minutes after I closed the bathroom door on Bianca and Dr. Pick, two constable cars arrived with sirens blaring and lights flashing. Caryn and Jimmy both woke up from the noise. Jimmy came out to watch, rubbing sleep from his eyes; Caryn started screaming. I held her close and talked to her as I answered the door before anyone could pound on it demanding entrance. With the sirens off, Caryn quieted, but she was awake and interested in everything. Her head snapped in every direction looking to see what was going on. Her eyes were wide open and bugged out at the strangeness of the unusual business. I placed her in her car seat on the floor of the living room so she would be out of the way of traffic but would still be able to see.

SHERIFF'S EDICT

Bill Wagoner seemed to be the senior of the two deputies and did the talking. "How did you get her to come here?"

I saw no future in answering that question, but tried. "She showed up maybe ten or fifteen minutes before I called you," I said quietly. She was wet from the river, bleeding from her nose, head, and mouth, and very scared. She told me she had been beaten again by the same person that has been beating her for a long time, only lately it has been getting worse. I know it flies in the face of what you have been told, but I didn't hurt that girl."

"Either way, we have to take her tonight."

"And do what with her. Jail?"

"That is not your concern."

"Officer Wagoner, I happen to care very much what happens to that little girl. I seem to be in the minority, and you are wrong. It is my concern. She has come to me twice because someone has hurt her. She didn't go to you, or CPS, or Judge Peterson, she came to me. She has a right to expect that I will do something to help her get away from the beatings. All I am getting from those who have the public charge of protecting her, is accused of hurting her myself, kidnapping her, and God only knows what else, along with being treated with great suspicion and disrespect. If you try to take her tonight, you will have to arrest me because I will not allow it." At the sternness of my voice, Caryn's face puckered up in a grimace in preparation for crying and Jimmy was listening closely and wide-eyed.

Bill and his partner were both the big-bellied stereotype of a deputy sheriff. Officer Wagoner grabbed my left arm with his right and pulled out his handcuffs, "I guess we will go ahead and do that then." He had no time to put the cuffs on, I jerked and twisted my arm away just as I had been taught in the military, but I did not attack as I had been taught.

"I'm in my own house, I've done nothing to be arrested for. Just calm down."

Bill waved his partner over to help. He came to me from behind in an attempt to pin my arms and subdue me. I felt him coming and at the right moment, dropped to the floor slipping through the constable's arms, and rolled to my right. Caryn screamed as if she had been hit. Bill saw the drop, and dove on top of me, full length. I was unable to move out of the way without rolling over Caryn. I took the full weight of the big bellied deputy in my chest and midsection. The wooden-frame house shook and windows rattled with the landing of the heavy man. I couldn't breathe. Caryn screamed louder and Jimmy went to comfort her. The deputy who had attempted to grab me drew his pistol, "Freeze! Stay where you are! Put your hands over your head!!" He did not seem to notice that he was pointing his pistol at me through Bill Wagoner. I groaned trying to get my breath, but put my hands above my head. Bill took out his handcuffs and put them on my wrists. Jimmy ran to the deputy who was holding the gun, latched on to his leg, and bit the outside of his thigh with all his might.

"Ow! You little…" He pushed Jimmy's head back tearing him loose from his leg. Jimmy did not release his bite, the flesh was pulled and pinched hard. The deputy hollered in pain again, "Aaaaugh! Stop it, you little devil!" Jimmy came back for more. This time, he bit the inside of the deputy's left leg bringing on another scream in pain and another push to get Jimmy off.

"You stop it!! Stop it, right now!!" Dr. Pick had come out of the bathroom. She had the look of a mother who had just caught her boys walking with muddy feet across her freshly mopped floor. "I have enough to worry about with that little girl in there without you busting each other up and making more work for me. Bill, why do you have him in handcuffs? Get them off him, right now!"

Bill Wagoner complained, "But Dr. Pick, he said he would fight us to keep the girl here. We are supposed to take her in."

"Well, it's about time somebody fought *for* this little girl instead of beating her up and taking her away from those who want to take care of her. He is fighting for something worthwhile, what are you fighting for? To keep your testosterone level up?" Bill opened his mouth to answer.

"That was a rhetorical question, Bill. It does not need an answer. I know the answer. The answer is, you don't know. You just follow orders." Bill ducked his head and took the handcuffs off. "Besides, Bill, there are two more children here that this man cares for. Have you noticed that? You have scared the living daylights out of Caryn. Can't you hear her crying?" Bill looked at Jimmy watching him still wrapped around the other deputy's leg with tears and a resolute expression on his face and for the first time, he looked as if he heard Caryn's screams."

"Now, Bill," Dr. Pick continued, "you get on your radio and tell your boss that I'm taking over. You will take orders from me or get out! That girl will stay here tonight. I don't know the extent of her injuries. We'll sort everything else out tomorrow. Right now, she needs some medical attention and rest, and she cannot be moved. One of you can stay here tonight to stand guard, or not, but that girl stays here. I'll be here for another hour, then I'm going home. Mr. Trevor will be in charge of her care until I get back tomorrow to check on her. If you stay, you take orders from him. You make the call to go or stay, then either settle in for the night, or get out! I'll remind you that I gave you your first smack on the bottom, and I tell you now, I can still swing hard enough to make you holler. Now, get busy." Looking back, it seems very funny now that the huge deputies were completely cowed by the tiny, seventy something year old woman.

Looking very sheepish, Bill Wagoner made the call to let dispatch know he was staying the night. I was still trying to fully catch my breath from being landed on, when I picked up the frightened screaming baby girl and held her close to offer her some measure of comfort. After I got her settled and put in her bed, I made sure of Bianca, and provided some covers for Bill who had settled on the couch. Then I made a pallet on the floor in my room for Jimmy who went over to Bill and hit him angrily on the knee on his way to bed. Bill flinched with a sheepish look on his face, though the punch by a four-year-old could hardly have caused pain. The kids and I settled in for a nap. Dr. Pick put Bianca to bed then left. Bill was already snoring with gusto when Dr. Pick walked by. "Fine lookout you'll make," she said shaking her head.

Bianca woke up in pain twice during the night. I got up when she called. I got fresh ice packs for her, and gave her a small yellow pill left by Dr. Pick. Caryn awoke twice, once for a change and feeding, and once for comforting. Jimmy woke up wet a little after midnight. A quick bath, fresh blankets and a dry t-shirt for pajamas was enough to get him resettled. Bill Wagoner slept soundly through the night waking at first light to the sweet, smoky odor of pork sausage cooking. Bianca still slept and the two little ones were not yet awake. It had been a difficult night.

14

Revenge of the Red-Head

atchet-face and Juarez arrived around nine. They walked into the house without knocking as Bill Wagoner was finishing the three-egg ham, onion, and cheese omelet with a side of sausage, coffee, and toast I had cooked. Caryn was in her car seat on the table looking around and cooing. I was already at the kidding pen feeding the new mothers and admiring their offspring. Several more were born in the night. Jimmy had eaten and was outside with Lucy teaching her to sit. Hatchet-face looked very disapprovingly at Wagoner, a disheveled deputy eating breakfast at the hand of the man she seemed convinced he should have arrested.

"Where is the girl?"

"She is in bed asleep and is not to be moved."

"You let her stay in the same house with the man that whipped her with that cord? What kind of lawman are you? She will have to be removed immediately."

"No, she stays right where she is until Dr. Pick says she can be moved. I got my orders."

"Stand down, deputy." Juarez injected himself with an air of importance and impatience, we'll take over now. What room is she in?"

"Mr. Juarez, I suggest you listen to what I just said," Bill stood and looked him directly in the eye with his right hand resting easily on his sidearm. "I'm kinda slow, but I learned something last night. We don't have a usual situation here. Castor Trevor is not the enemy here. That girl does not need to be rescued from him. She came to him for help. He helped her by calling a doctor and us. When we were going to take her last night, he was willing to fight to keep her from us. The last time you took her away, you put her in a foster home that was as dangerous to her as home with the uncle who beats her. Right now, you are the ones she needs to be kept away from. You obey your rules without heart and without listening. She begged you to let her stay here Monday and with your hearts and ears sealed up, you took her from safety and placed her in danger. In addition, you had an innocent man arrested. No Ms. Hatchett, Mr. Juarez, she stays right here until Dr. Pick or a court order says different." He stepped in the doorway filling it almost completely with his feet apart and his arms crossed.

Hatchet-face immediately replied with a smile showing that his speech had fallen flat. "A court order will be no problem."

Bill grinned, "It will be a problem if you are depending on Judge Peterson. He's fishing out in the middle of Stillwood Lake with the sheriff and both left word to not be bothered. Today, the bench is empty."

She smiled knowingly, "We'll manage."

When I came back into the house from feeding the animals, Wagoner, Hatchett, and Juarez were all sitting in the living room. Bill was obviously agitated. "Mr. Trevor, a Williams County deputy is on his way with a court order to turn Bianca over to Ms. Hatchett.

Looking at Hatchet-face's smug smile, I asked, "Haven't you done enough damage? You took her against her will, turned her over to someone who couldn't protect her in a house with a perverted teenager, and got her beaten up again. How much can one person screw up and still come back for more?"

"Mrs. Benson is a very competent caregiver. Bianca was in no danger at any time," Juarez stated flatly, "and as soon as the warrant gets here, she will be leaving with us."

Anger rose in my chest and almost throttled me when I spoke, "Bianca is in no danger if you totally discount everything Bianca has told me and Mr. Wagoner, and if you ignore her broken nose, black eye, bruises and other injuries. Have you even talked to Bianca?" My questions were aimed at Juarez.

"Ms. Hatchett interviewed the girl..."

My agitation was showing, "The *girl* has a name. Her name is Bianca. She is real flesh and blood. She is not a case study, nor a set of rules. She is a real live girl who has been abused all her life. Now that she is taking up for herself in the only ways she knows how, the ones she should be able to look to for protection keep stuffing her back into danger. This is insane! Where do you propose to send her now?"

Ms. Hatchett maintained her air of superiority, "I don't see that where she goes is any concern to you. Besides that is confidential."

I read something. I didn't know how I knew, but I knew. "You are sending her back to her parents, aren't you? Did you talk to them?" Hatchett and Juarez looked at each other seemingly to agree on what to say. That little glance told me I had guessed right.

"Mr. Trevor, there is no evidence of the uncle Bianca talked about. Her family is the best place for her."

"Wait a minute. I have something to show you. I went to the truck and brought my camera inside. I showed them the picture of Bianca's leg I took while we were building the out-house. "Someone at her house is beating her. If you persist in keeping your head in the sand, they will kill her." I started to say, "I won't stand by and let that happen," but thought better of it. Instead, I said, "Dr. Pick gave orders that she not be moved until she is examined today. You can't take her, at least until Dr. Pick gets here."

"Dr. Pick has no standing with the court," Hatchett asserted. Bill just shrugged.

AN ARRANGEMENT

I excused myself to go to the bathroom. No one of the three could have seen when I went into and through the bathroom and after closing the bathroom door, into the spare bedroom where Bianca was sleeping. "Bianca!" I hissed, hoping no one in the living room could hear. She was deep asleep. "Bianca, wake up!" I shook her shoulders hoping to wake her without hurting her.

"What?" she said sleepily through the pain-killer fog.

"Bianca, Hatchett-face is here." She is planning to take you to your family. She did not speak; the fear showing in her eyes spoke for her. "Bianca, sweetheart, I know you are hurting, but can you walk?"

"Yes, I can. What do you want me to do?"

"Bianca, what is your uncle's name?"

"Tio's name? Tio Flaco. "

"No, Bianca, Flaco means skinny. That is not his name."

"Wait, Mama said he was named after my grandfather, Rosendo. His name is Rosendo. I heard one of his men call him Rocio."

"Bianca, stay with me. What is his last name. Is it Garcia?" I guessed based on my limited knowledge of Hispanic names and naming practices. Bianca nodded, "Yes, Rosendo Garcia is his name. Why?"

"Never mind for now," I said with a slight tremor in my voice. "Bianca, can you climb out the window?"

"You might have to help me. But why?"

"No, it is important that you do it yourself. I'll move the stool over and unlock the window, but you must climb out on your own. Can you do it?"

"Yes, but why?"

"I can't let them take you back to your uncle, but I can't help you either."

"When I leave the room, get out the window and go to the feed shed. Burrow down under the loose hay and stay very still. If they find you, get out of your house and watch for my old truck on the road. I'll drive from here to your house back and forth all night if I need to. Once you are back here, we will figure something out."

I reappeared in the living room zipping my pants. Hatchet-face 'har-rumped' at the sight of me and Juarez looked disgusted. Bill looked at my face and read something the other two did not see.

THE WRIT

It was a few minutes after eleven that morning when the deputy from Williams County arrived. He delivered the order to Bill, then left. Bill looked at the court order and pronounced it real. It commanded any and all parties to turn Bianca Gonzalez over to Ms. Hatchett and Mr. Juarez. "*You* go wake her up if you must," I said, "but I have witnesses that Dr. Pick said she should not be moved. If you move her, I will make formal objections to your bosses however high I must go. I will also recommend that you both be subjected to a physical to assure there is life in your bodies. If there is life, I will report to the Guinness Record Book people that there are two people walking around working for CPS without the benefit of a heart or brain between them." Bill snickered and Hatchett turned a little red, but set her face expression at very stern and went to get Bianca.

"She's gone! She climbed out the window!" Hatchet Face walked quickly back into the living room and directed her attention to me, "You helped her go, didn't you!" She was seething, talking and spitting between her clenched teeth.

I shrugged, "I never had her in captivity. She has been free to come and go as she wished. You propose to capture her, which you will have to do because she doesn't want to go with you. You did not help her!!" I roared in her face, probably spitting with the 'c' in 'face.' "You would put her where she will be beaten or die. Maybe she heard what you had planned."

Juarez looked at me with a wondering gaze. "Where is she?"

"Mr. Juarez, maybe she got away and ran home," I answered with some measure of sarcasm in my voice. "Maybe she wanted to save you the trouble of throwing her away, and just gave up. Juarez and Hatchett immediately went back into the bedroom seemingly to look for evidence that would tell them where she went. Shortly, they searched the house, particularly my bedroom, then left the house and began searching outside.

Juarez went straight to the outhouse. The door was locked from the inside. Juarez knocked, then banged, then rushed the door crashing it in. Jimmy stepped out with a wry grin on his face. Juarez grabbed him by the arm and jerked him around grabbing both shoulders. "Where is Bianca?" It was not a violent shake, but it was a shake. Jimmy glared menacingly at Juarez and Lucy jumped him from behind. Juarez screamed as Lucy sunk sharp baby dog teeth into the inside of his left calf muscle. Turning around with a scream, the short man kicked the dog in the ribs. It was a solid kick. She rolled over twice, jumped to her feet and came back. Meantime, Jimmy attacked from the rear sinking his teeth into the back of Juarez's right thigh. Juarez grabbed Jimmy by the head and shoved him to the ground. The small dog came in again, but Juarez was ready. He kicked Lucy in the ribs again. She squalled and crawled over to Jimmy standing between him and the man. Brutus sat beside the splintered outdoor toilet door watching the drama with interest. His tail was flicking from side to side as if he were deciding whether to join the attack. Juarez ran from place to place almost aimlessly. He picked up the overturned wheelbarrow, threw tools and materials and repeatedly screamed, "Where is she? I know she is here. I know you let her go." At that moment, Brutus made up his mind. He climbed Juarez and sunk his teeth into the muscle between his neck and right shoulder. Juarez screamed again and grabbed at Brutus who turned loose and ran down his back disappearing behind the outhouse. I stood about ten yards from the outhouse watching the drama of a grown man going berserk. I wondered at the ease with which he had been pushed over the edge. Bill Wagoner had my video camera to his eye filming the scene.

CAPTURE

Eventually, Juarez made it to the feed shed. It took him a little time, but he found Bianca, grabbed her by the arm and jerked her to her feet. She yelled in pain, but Juarez ignored her protests. "Hide from me, will you? We'll see about that!" He was handling her roughly. My right arm felt tingly. I knew I was probably going to be in trouble, but I took two steps lining it up, then punched Juarez a hard right squarely on the end of his nose. Juarez went down like a slab of meat, hitting the ground with a grunt and lay flat for a moment before rolling to his right, bleeding from his nose into the gravel. The pain shooting up my arm indicated I might have broken a bone in my hand, but man that felt good!

Hatchett watched the drama with a look of stern pleasure on her face. She had that satisfied look that said, "Now, we have you."

Hatchett walked quickly to us, then grabbed Bianca by the shoulders and shook her. It was not enough to injure her, but it was a shake. I turned and saw Bianca being shaken, then forced my way between Bianca and Hatchett by pushing the surprised and indignant Hatchett back and jerking her hands loose from Bianca's shoulders. "Your display of anger toward Bianca is unwarranted and very unprofessional. You cannot..."

"Get out of the way, you pervert." "Move! Or I swear, I will shoot you." Juarez had gotten up and from behind Bill, pulled the deputy's gun. He had the gun leveled at my head while he walked around Bill. "We have a court order and we are enforcing it!" He was screaming, the pupils of his eyes were pinpoints, blazing with anger, his face red, and his nose was definitely out of alignment and bleeding profusely. I was amazed he could see with his eyes watering the way they were.

Hatchett and Juarez each took one of Bianca's arms and led her squirming and crying to their SUV. They put her in the back seat ahead of Juarez. The pistol was trained on Bill and I even as the SUV pulled out. Hatchett slid into the driver's seat and drove them out across the cattle guard. It was a little after twelve, noon. "Did you get all that, Bill?"

"All except for the part where Juarez pulled my gun. I was too focused on Hatchett shaking the girl."

I immediately fed Jimmy and Caryn then put them down for a nap. After calling to file complaints with CPS, I spent the afternoon sawing lumber, bolting pieces together, looking for parts, attaching rollers, and taking breaks to care for the children. Caryn was beginning to try to scoot around, so she had to be watched even more carefully than ever. Later, while I soaked my swollen right hand, I began reflecting that helping Bianca had turned my world over on its side. Never before had I even considered breaking a law, now I was possibly facing prison for what I did and was planning to do. The really odd thing was that it felt good. *It is that or let her get beaten up again. If I do the right thing, even if it is not legal, things will turn out right.* I convinced myself to continue what I had planned.

In the mid-afternoon, Dr. Pick came by to check on Bianca. She didn't say much when she heard the story; she just shook her head. After examining my hand and pronouncing it just swollen, she picked up her bag and left. I noticed a definite slowing in Dr. Pick's stride, then recalled she must be nearly eighty years old. *What a remarkable lady!*

ON PATROL

Close to dark, a heavy cloud-bank rolled in from the west, a cool breeze pushed the cloud bank and storm warnings went out. "It could be rough tonight," I told Jimmy as I buckled seatbelts for him and Caryn in the cab of my old truck. Around eight-thirty I drove out the gate and turned right toward the Gonzalez house. I drove slowly past the small, white frame house shining in the gloom of dusk backed by the dark woods. When I had passed the house and could not see it in the mirror any more, I turned the truck around and drove slowly back to my house. I waited a few minutes, then reversed direction again. There was no sign of Bianca or anyone at the house for five round trips.

On the sixth trip, a sheriff's deputy pulled me over. He kept the flashlight in my eyes until he saw Jimmy and Caryn in the truck. When I asked what the deputy was looking for, he dodged the question and wished me a good evening. Around nine-thirty, the wind came up again and the rain started. It was after ten and it had been dark for about four hours when I drove home to feed and change Caryn before going out again. I felt I must go out again. I could not put a finger on why, but I knew in my bones, something was happening and I needed to help. I changed the diaper and started for the door, but stopped short when I heard a key being inserted in the kitchen door lock. The door opened and Bianca walked in. She held on to the kitchen counter and stood looking at me. "I shouldn't be here," she said "I could get you in more trouble, but I have no one else to go to."

"Bianca, I may be in trouble, but no one will be beating me up. I will be alive and healthy and perhaps you will be also." I showed her to the spare bedroom and the modifications I had made to the bed. "Have you eaten?" She laid down heavily on the sofa reporting that she had not eaten since breakfast. The bruises around her eye and her nose had already begun to turn a greenish yellow.

Twenty minutes later, I took her scrambled eggs and toast and a bowl of tomato soup. "What happened today?"

"The Red-headed woman and the guy took me to town and asked me a lot of questions about you. They want to hurt you, I think, and they want me to help them. They asked some questions about nasty things. Later, they took me to my parents' house and left me. They warned my parents to keep me from Tio Rosendo."

"Did you see him today?"

"No, he is in Mexico on business."

"What is his business?"

"I don't know for certain. He goes to Mexico every week then usually returns by Friday." Bianca's voice was weak like she was drugged or in pain. "He stays at my house until Saturday night, then he goes out all night. Sometimes he does not come back until Sunday. I think he is the reason my mother doesn't want me in the house on Saturday. I think she doesn't like him beating me up, even though she will not help me. Mr. Trevor, do you have anything I can take. I'm hurting really bad in my nose and face. My back hurts a little too, but mostly it itches."

"Yes, I have one pill left by Dr. Pick to be used for pain, but the itching is a good thing. It means the sores on your back are healing. I don't know what I can do about the itching."

"That's OK. It feels much better than the hurting."

I took her dishes into the kitchen then helped Bianca into the spare bedroom and onto the trundle I had built that afternoon. I rolled it under the bed and let the edge of the covers down. The bedspread hung low enough to cover. The bed was a double, the trundle was a single, so there was plenty of room. The casual observer would see a tall double bed with a bedspread appropriately covering the underside. I placed a couple of boxes just under the edge of the bed so they would barely show to further sell the effect. "Bianca, if you hear someone come in, don't make a sound. Only make noise if I tell you that it is only me. Do you want a shower before you go to sleep?"

"No, Mr. Trevor, I just want to go to sleep."

Around two am, a deputy arrived with lights flashing. I got up dressed in my pajamas and let him in. "The girl is missing again, have you seen her?"

"Sure, deputy, I'm so stupid that I took her in again, come let me show you." I suddenly realized he was the same deputy that had been in the house with Bill Wagoner, Deputy Prewitt. "If you can find her, beat her up and arrest her again."

"Don't mess with me, Mr. Trevor. If you have her, there will be a boat-load of trouble coming your way."

I took him on a tour of the house. Jimmy was asleep on top of the bed in the spare bedroom. While we were in the room, Bianca moaned in her sleep. Prewitt didn't even pause. He seemed to ascribe the noise to Jimmy. "Where is the girl, Trevor?"

"Well," I said, "You can search the outbuildings, but the result will be the same as your search of the house. Would you like a cup of tea?" The deputy declined and prepared to leave. He reminded me of the laws concerning contributing to the delinquency of a minor among others.

"When you see her, I expect you to call me," he said as he left the kitchen on his way to his car. I started to tell him what I thought of that idea considering the outcome last time, but thought better of it.

"Billie? Billie, I'm sorry to call so late, but I need to call in some of my markers; I need your help... Well, Billie, I've been caring for your children for a long time now. I need you to care for Bianca for a few days...I understand, but put off the trip, Billie. This is more important. I'm trying to keep this girl alive...Billie, *you know* what it is like to be beaten when you can't protect yourself. I know about that because you told me. Help me with this please...OK, I'll see you about six. I need you to come before daylight."

At six am when Billie arrived, I had all the children fed and ready for transport. Bianca lay in the cargo area of the big suburban where she would not be recognized and could ride more comfortably. I thanked Billie over and over and assured her Bianca would be with her only a few days. "Bianca, you be good, like you are for me. If you need me, tell Billie to call or call yourself." Bianca nodded, then lay down again. It appeared to me that she was still in some pain.

Around eight that morning, I called Dr. Pick and told her what I had done. I was expecting a lecture, but she merely said, "Good. I'll go over to Billie's later and see about her. It is time for the stitches to come out anyway."

By ten, I was in Mick's Camera Shop. Rebecca worked behind the counter. She knew cameras and video equipment. Shortly I had a VHS copy of the contents of the camera. Rebecca and I looked at it together and agreed it looked bad.

By twelve, I was in the County Courthouse asking to see Judge Peterson. I had to wait for the judge to get back from lunch. It took about three minutes for the judge to order me out of his office telling me I was short-cutting the system. "You go from here to see an attorney. If you have a complaint to file, see the district attorney."

"Judge, is the system so blind and corrupt that the only way to get justice is to pay for it? My money would be much better spent caring for that girl, than trying to get the system to work properly," I was beginning to raise my voice.

"Look son, what you are proposing is so full of legal booby traps, that you need counsel. I suggest Don Stence."

I was calmer now, but pleading, "Judge, I don't know Mr. Stence. Add to that, I have no reason to trust lawyers or the justice system. I'm afraid I have to include you in that statement, Judge. So you see, I'm in kind of a dilemma. I know that girl needs your help, but so far, all the system has done is get her hurt worse, and all you have done is dodge the real issues." While I was talking and trying to control my temper, a familiar sharp pain struck in my upper left chest. I rubbed the pectoral muscle with my right hand, but gave no thought to the pain.

Judge Peterson sat down and in a fatherly tone said, "I understand your distrust. You got a raw deal in your divorce and it looks like the system is trying to place Bianca in danger that you think you know about. Just make sure you don't get sideways with my court. I will throw the book at a vigilante."

I looked him dead in the eyes, "Even if he is right?"

"Yes, Mr. Trevor, even if he is right."

"Judge," I said very directly as I walked out, "you are part of the problem."

"Just you mind what I have told you," he said as I turned down the hall.

15

Stence and Associates

*I*t was nearly three before I got to speak to a junior associate in Don Stence's office. By then the pain in my chest was constant, but I did not allow it to be a bother. I insisted that I needed to speak to Don Stence personally. The junior insisted that Don was not available, and that he was quite capable of helping no matter what the problem. Full of mistrust and frustration, I stood to leave when Don Stence walked through. Seeing a discontented patron, he asked the prospective client if he could help. I said I thought this was a bad idea and was sorry for disrupting Mr. Stence's day. I started to leave when Mr. Stence grabbed my elbow. "Come talk to me, please. It won't cost you anything to talk."

"Mr. Stence, lawyers are the main reason I have a five-hundred acre farm instead of a twenty-five hundred acre ranch. They used my marriage problems to loot my inheritance and leave me starting over. Lawyers on the side of the state are just about to ruin the life of a little girl, and I have no way to help without breaking the law. Judge Peterson sent me to you, but frankly, I don't put much store by him either."

My tirade had released some of the pent-up anger. I didn't know exactly why, but Don's calm listening caused me to feel like I had a confidant. The pain in my chest lessened. "OK, if you don't charge for talking, let's talk."

I went through all the events relating to Bianca. I told Don everything, down to the provisions I had made for her to eat and have a place to go to the bathroom, and the hidden bed.

"Mr. Trevor," Stence said, "They will try to make it sound like you are trying to entice the girl to come to your house…that you are grooming her for sex. The hidden bed and the outdoor toilet should be kept between us. Do not rebuild the outhouse…at least until all this is settled."

"Mr. Stence, is there anything I could to for the girl that they can't twist into something perverted and evil?" I was bewildered by the potential attacks on what I had provided for Bianca's health and well-being.

"No, there isn't. We have an adversarial justice system. That is the way it works. The prosecutor has to make you sound like a child-molester to make his case against you. You have to show that what he is saying is false."

I was puzzled. "What happened to simply telling the truth?"

"If everyone told the truth, there would be no need for my services. Unfortunately, truth seldom has anything to do with court decisions. Mr. Trevor, what do you want?"

"What do you mean?"

"When all this is settled, what will it look like if it turns out right for Bianca?"

"She will be living in a safe place with people who love her and can provide for her and will protect her from her uncle."

"Where will that be? And with whom would she live?"

I realized with a rush that I had put myself in a box. Blood rushed to my head and I attempted an answer, "I, I, I don't know. I, I guess a place she chooses and a caregiver she chooses."

"Would you be willing for her to go back home?"

"I don't think she would choose to go back home while there is a chance the uncle could come around. He has been beating her as long as she can remember. So, no. I would not want to see her go back; I don't think that is an option. Besides, where she goes is not my decision."

"Where do you think she would choose to live?"

"At my house...but, but, Mr. Stence...I, I didn't even do a good job with my own kids. If she really knew me, she wouldn't...the court couldn't...could it?"

"How much are you willing to commit to this girl's care and happiness?"

"Everything."

"Everything? All you have? What about your time? Are you willing to spend the time to teach her and take care of her?"

"Yessir. I am," I said with my mind racing. I was on the verge of saying, "NO!" when Mr. Stence asked, "Can you get in touch with Bianca?"

"What if I can?"

"Well, Mr. Trevor, I would be willing to represent Bianca pro bono."

"What does that mean? I mean what could you do for her?"

"That means I will handle her case in court and try my best to get her in a good place without charging anyone for the service."

"What if I could get her to come see you?"

"Do you have a dollar?"

"Yes, I have a dollar." Pulling a one out of my wallet, I gave it to Mr. Stence.

"You just retained me to speak with Bianca concerning the potential charge of kidnapping against you. While I'm talking to her, we can discuss your concerns and her future."

16

Dr. Pick Asserts Herself

"Pastor?"

"Billie! What is going on? It's three in the morning."

"Bianca got sick."

"What happened?"

"I don't know, she just started vomiting. I called Dr. Pick and she sent an ambulance."

Twenty minutes later, I was at the hospital asking about Bianca. "We have no Bianca registered." The candy striper at the front desk seemed to want to be helpful, but she seemed a few bricks short of a full hod.

"Well, has the ambulance brought anyone to the hospital in the last hour?" I insisted.

"Oh, yeah. There was one, a little girl. She would be checked in through the emergency room. We will know what room she is in tomorrow morning."

"Could you call the emergency room and find out now?"

"Oh, yeah. I could." I waited a moment, then insisted, "Well, would you please make the call?"

"Oh, yeah," she said as she dialed the number. "Room one thirty-seven."

Dr. Pick was in the room when I went in. She looked up smiling, "She's fine. Her cheekbone is fractured and that is giving her some nausea…and she may have a slight concussion. I think she needs several days in the hospital. I think also that this time, there will not be anyone to overrule me because her name will not be on the register. She will be a Jane Doe.

I told her briefly about my visit with the judge and with Don Stence. She listened thoughtfully nodding her approval at my alliance with Don. When I told her of the box Don backed me into, she said, "Sonny, you have been in that box for a long while. But like most men, you just didn't look into the future, or into this girl's heart. I believe you will do the right thing. Castor, you need to get Mr. Stence to start pushing the court date up. You will win, but until you get the court's decision, legally, I will have a hard time keeping her here if CPS or her parents find her and try to remove her. Medically, I will have little to stand on."

After the doctor left, I sat beside the bed while Bianca slept. An hour passed before she woke up looking wildly about her. I stood and before I could speak, she screamed in terror. "Bianca! It's me, Castor Trevor. Calm down." She stopped screaming but was breathing hard, still a little wild eyed, and looking from side to side when I put my hand on her head and smoothed her hair back, talking soothingly to her. "You are safe. You are in the hospital. You got sick. Do you remember?" Gradually she calmed and lay still. She was still breathing hard when the night nurse came in to see what the noise was about. I held Bianca's hand as the nurse checked her vitals and assured me that waking up frightened was not uncommon for children with a minor brain injury.

When the nurse left, Bianca spoke, "Yes, I remember. I was having a bad dream. I dreamed I was back home and Tio came in with the electric cord. I dreamed he swung at me and I fell down a dark hole. The hitting did not scare me, but the hole; the hole was very scary. When I woke up, I felt like I was still falling, then I saw you, but it didn't look like you, it looked like Tio Flaco. Mr. Trevor, I don't want to see him again. Don't let them take me back."

I thought for a moment then asked, "Bianca, did Mr. Stence talk to you?"

She looked at me with an unasked question in her eyes, "Yes, I talked to him."

"What did you tell him?"

"I told him the same like I told you. He told, uh, *asked* me what I wanted. I told him I wanted to stay with you, but I didn't know if you would want me. Mr. Trevor, I would clean your house, wash dishes, help with the goats...I...I could be good help...I could get a job when I get bigger and pay rent." She was looking at me with expectant and pleading eyes.

"Did he ask you that?"

"Yes, he asked me where I want to live, and who I want to take care for me. Did I do wrong?"

"No, Bianca. I don't know when I have felt more honored. But, you need to know, I did a very poor job raising my own children. I don't know very much. I don't know if I can live up to the responsibility."

Bianca looked at me with a hint of wonder in her eyes. "You are a good, good man. You have done more to take care of me than anyone since I can ever remember. You don't beat me, you talk to me. I have fun. I am not afraid when I am with you. You teach me things. You teach me little things I ask about and important things you think I should know. Maybe I can help *you* too. I know you would listen if I told you I thought you were making a mistake. I promise to listen to you, if you tell me I'm not doing good. I...I can help with Jimmy and Caryn too. I promise I will be good."

"Bianca, I have to think about this. Helping you out by building an outhouse and buying a few groceries is not at the level of taking responsibility for another person. That takes some thinking. That is a big commitment. I'm not really good at commitments. Maybe you should talk to my ex-wife before you decide."

"Too late. I made my decision." She crossed her arms and sank down in the pillow looking at the ceiling. Shortly she turned her head looking at my face in the half-light, "How long will you think before you decide?"

"I don't know. I want to...but I don't know. There are so many different...so many people who...I just don't know."

As I left the room, I stumbled over the fuzzy pink shoes I had bought for her a couple of weeks before. My head was spinning at the thought of trying to raise another child. I argued with myself about the question. When I got home around day-break, I fed the goats in the kidding pens, walked the fences as fast as I could, then went down for a nap.

DECISION

At eleven fifteen that morning I woke with a start from a bad dream I couldn't remember. I called Don Stence. Dr. Pick had told me, to try to push the court, but Don assured me the court would not be rushed. "By the way, just so you know, we are petitioning for you to have guardianship for Bianca. We are asking the court to make you her temporary guardian. It's pretty unusual since you are not related and single, but there is some precedent. I have statements by two sets of grandparents saying they think it is a good idea. All the grandparents commit to help, but they are unable to care for her themselves. Are you still on board?"

"Don, I just…this is a big…I need to…"

"Mr. Trevor, I need you to either fish or cut bait. You made a commitment to me that you would give everything to take care of her. Are you backing out?"

"Don, I would give everything I own, but do you realize the responsibility that I would be taking on if I took her into my home? What if I make a big mistake?"

"Yes I do know the responsibility Castor, and I promise you *will* make mistakes. It comes with the territory. However, do you realize what will likely happen to Bianca if you don't man up and do what you know is the right thing? That little girl sees you as her savior from a life among strangers, or a life of beatings. I can only imagine how she must be feeling now if you were this wishy washy with her. Whether or not you will make a mistake is not even a consideration. You will, and that is okay. They will be small mistakes you learn from. Castor, she has put all her hopes for a future on you. What are you going to do?"

Decisions at crucial points in everyone's life set in motion the events that determine the direction of the rest of their lives. Lives are enriched or devalued based on the quality of decisions made. I knew I was at a decision point and my stomach churned at the prospects. I knew the rest of my life would be different based on whether or not I did what I knew was right for Bianca. I also knew her life would be different as well. I could decide to involve myself to be a surrogate father and probably experience all the joys and sorrows of fatherhood again. But because I knew I would make mistakes that would possibly hurt her, I could also turn away and avoid all that pain and continue what had become comfortable to me: isolation and loneliness. But if I ignored the decision, Bianca's life was sure to be full of pain, both physical and emotional. It occurred to me that I could decide for, or against, or I could just not make a decision which was really to decide against.

I took a deep breath and sighed. A prolonged sigh at a decision time is a classic sign that a decision has been reached. "OK, Don, I know the right thing. I don't even know what I don't know, but I guess I just have to do it on faith. Go ahead with the petition. When do we go to court?"

"The hearing is Monday morning at nine, sixteen days from now."

"What happens to her in the meantime?"

"When she is released from the hospital in a couple of days, we should be able to get her placed with you. All we lack is a judge's signature. By the way, in the petition, you have agreed to have a female caregiver in the house with you at all times. I suggest her great-grandmother, Lizbet Buentello. She has agreed."

"I know Omar and his wife. They will do whatever they can. I have no doubt."

RELEASED

Afternoon visiting hours at the hospital began at four. I walked into the hospital at three fifty five carrying a bouquet of purple and white flowers with an acceptance speech all memorized. I did not pay attention to the name on the door when I got to room one thirty seven. I walked in interrupting Dr. Spivet examining a very large woman with emphysema. The room smelled of cigarette smoke. Embarrassed and confused, I went back to the Candy-Striper desk to ask where Bianca had been moved.

"Oh yeah, her parents came and got her."

17

Fully Committed

I wasted no time calling Don Stence. It took three calls but he finally answered. "Don, if we don't do something, her uncle will likely be at the house beating her tonight or tomorrow. I expect he will either kill her there or take her to Mexico and kill her. Don, what can we do? I've been warned by Judge Peterson to not take things into my own hands, but time is short."

"Mr. Trevor, don't do anything. You will jeopardize everything if you interfere. I will get hold of Judge Peterson and CPS. One of the two will come through."

"Don, you have two hours. If you don't get something done that takes her from that house, I will do what I must."

"Castor, if you mess this up, I will withdraw."

"Well, old son, you may have to withdraw then. Don, if the system will not protect her, I will step in. I can't guarantee someone won't get hurt, but I can't allow her to be held in that house another night, especially a Friday night with her uncle on the way from Mexico. It is now four. Six o'clock, Don. Get busy."

I hung up and went home. I drove by the Gonzalez house on the way. There was a small Toyota Camry and an old Nissan pickup in the driveway. *Neither of those vehicles match the truck Bianca described,* I thought. I was fighting the urge to barge into that house and carry Bianca out to safety. *I have to give the system a chance*, I said out loud, just as a bit of pink caught my eye. Upside down on the ground beside the Camry, lay one of the fuzzy house shoes I knew belonged to Bianca. "OK, I know she's here and I think the uncle is not here yet."

WAITING, PLANNING AND ACTING; SETTING THINGS RIGHT

My only shotgun was a four-ten automatic. That wasn't much fire-power, only six shots in reserve, but it was old and big and loud; the scare factor was all I desired anyway. There was no intent in my heart to hurt anyone; desire, but no intent. I cleaned it and polished the handle. Clean, shiny weapons are more impressive and imposing than old looking ones. After I had made the gun more than ready, I looked at the clock; it was only four-thirty. At five, Billie drove up with the children. I met her at the end of the driveway. "Billie, not today. I can't keep them today. You can bring them tomorrow early, but not tonight."

Billie gave me a glare. "This has to do with that little girl you have spoiled, doesn't it."

"Billie, you saw what happened to her. She is a long way from being spoiled by me or anyone else. Like I said, bring Jimmy and Caryn tomorrow morning at six, but I can't keep them tonight."

"Alright, Trevor. Six in the morning." Billie got in the Suburban, slammed it in gear, and gunned it out the front gate bouncing the front wheels off the ground as she crossed the cattle guard, kicking up considerable dust as she turned on to the county road traveling a little too fast.

I sat down at the kitchen table to write a letter. I wrote:

Dear Ashley,

I'm writing you this letter because I have to. There is no one holding a gun to my head, but this is a small payment on the debt I owe you and Jake.

Since your mother left and took most of the ranch, I have been very bitter and I know I have not been a good father at all. I wasn't much before the divorce, but I tried.

Something has happened to make me face up to the fact that I have been so full of pity for myself that I did not consider what I might be doing to you and Jake by becoming so isolated from you. My only communication with you for the past four years has been in the form of a check each month to help you with expenses. Although that felt like something, a check, no matter how large, is a poor substitute for a father. I want you to know I am sorry. I want to begin again if you will allow me into your life. If not, I will understand. I realize I do not deserve a good relationship with you because I threw the one we had away and treated you badly. I will hold no ill feelings if you do not respond.

Before I close, I want you to know that you and Jake are the best things that ever happened to me. I loved you. I love you. I will always love you. You are my daughter and he is my son. Until I lost my mind and pushed you away, you were also my best friend. I want that back, but whether we can pick it up again is up to you. If you can't find it in your heart to come back to me as my daughter, maybe you can find it possible to forgive me from a distance.

I love you,
Dad

I posted the letter to the same address I sent the check each month, then wrote a similar letter that began, "Dear Jake," and posted it along with the one to Ashley.

At five-thirty, I called Don Stence's number. No answer. Five fifty-five, I tried again to call Don. Again, no answer. I loaded the four-ten, one shot in the chamber and six in waiting, placed it in the seat of the old truck, then drove toward the Gonzalez house. My hands were sweating and I felt sweat running down my back. My stomach was turning, my heart was thumping hard on my ribs, and my mouth was so dry it felt like I was trying to chew and swallow cotton, and my legs trembled so badly I could hardly release the clutch to shift gears. These symptoms were vaguely familiar but I hadn't felt this way since before my first fire-fight in Viet Nam.

Shortly, I could see the house a quarter-mile away. I pulled my pickup off the right side of the road. I checked the shotgun again, then crossed the sorghum field on foot, and entered the woods. Daylight was beginning to fade as I walked deep into the thickly wooded area that ran behind the Gonzalez house. The trees and brush were good cover to within fifty feet of the back door of the small house.

Confrontation

The sun was setting behind the horizon as I approached the Gonzalez house from the woods. The reflection from the sun barely above the horizon made the white house shine brightly. Darkness would cover the land in less than an hour. I stopped just out of sight and knelt down to listen and plan. There was a solid wooden back door in the white frame house. It was closed and fronted by a screen door. There was a small heavily curtained window to the left of the door. The height of the window suggested a kitchen. It could be a window above the kitchen sink. From that distance and behind a curtain of plants, I couldn't see or hear anything from the house. I moved to my left and around the house still under cover of the woods to get a better view of the front. My breath caught and I froze for a few seconds when I spotted the big, black Ford dually Bianca had described as belonging to Tio Flaco. It was parked behind the Camry. At that moment, the big, black truck looked evil and angry.

There were two other trucks new to the scene, a bright red-and-white Chevy step-side, and an older blue and tan fleet-side Chevrolet both well-polished and shining in the fading light. Each truck was appointed with an expensive light-bar above the cab and fog-lights below the front bumper. One very thin man with a heavy black mustache and darkly sunburned complexion was leaning on the fleet-side truck watching the county road. Cigarette smoke curled up and over his ivory colored palm-leaf hat. He was armed with a big revolver pistol stuck in his wide, tooled-leather western belt. He was a dark man with a thin black goatee, wearing new jeans, black boots, and a black western shirt with white pearl snaps. A white kerchief, draped to the right of his throat and tied at the back of his neck, completed the outfit.

Each truck must have arrived carrying at least one man. That makes four men against my one, I thought. *The element of surprise may be my only asset.* Just at that moment, I heard a "pop" then a child's scream. It was Bianca. *No choices now. Time to man up. Let's roll,* I said to myself.

I crossed into the openness of the yard, approaching the house from behind and out of sight of the lookout. I tried the screen door, it was latched. Using my pocket-knife, I silently cut a hole in the plastic screen and lifted the latch. Another "pop" caused me to tremble as I worked. My militay training took over somewhat; I tried to not hurry into a mistake. Slowly and silently I opened the screen, holding my breath, then tried the doorknob. Another "pop" made me jump and my heart to hammer on my ribs. This time the pop was followed by a man yelling something I could not understand, but no child's scream. The heavy door was not locked. The door opened inward, so I pulled outward on the door as I turned the knob to avoid a click, then slowly pushed the door inside and open. Luckily someone had oiled the hinges on the door. Very little light showed above the horizon and night was creeping over the house, killing twilight, as I entered and stood very still for a few moments to allow my eyes time to adjust to the darkness of the room. The only light in the kitchen was from an incandescent bulb shining from the living room and a little fading sunlight shining through the heavy curtain over the small window. I heard some excited chatter, Bianca shouted "No! No! Por favor, no mas!"

"Demasiado tarde, mija. Aprende!"

I understood the exchange. Bianca was begging for someone to stop hitting her. The answer she got was "Too late, child. Learn!" Immediately, there was another "Pop!" I recognized the sound. I had heard it many times when I was a boy after my father had left me with my grandfather. Grandpa Trevor kept a quirt and a whip handy and used them often. The snapping sound was a whip hitting flesh. There was no further cry. I knew what was happening. Bianca was being whipped and she was determined not to cry anymore; she would not give in. I knew there would be no more begging for him to stop. I knew because I had done the same thing with my grandfather. Once I made the decision, no amount of beating would have made me admit defeat and cry. I figured if I didn't cry, I would win. I didn't cry, but I lost anyway.

"Dare iss no nosey gringos to be in the way at Mejico. I weel teash jou proper maneras." Another "Pop!" followed.

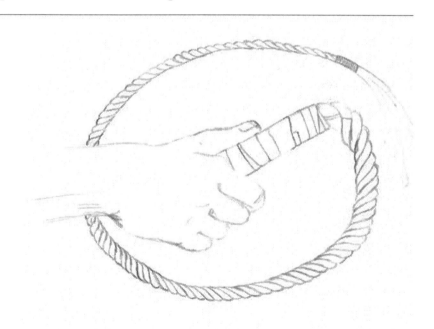

Quickly, I stuck my head into the light and withdrew. I wanted to see what I was up against, or rather *who* I was against. There were five adults I could see in the white room lit by a single bare light bulb in the ceiling at the center of the room. A man and a woman stood in the far corner of the room to my left at the end of the sofa holding each other. They watched the beating with some degree of fascination and fear. Recognizing Abulardo, I figured them to be Bianca's parents. A short stocky dark man in a black coat obscured my view of the sofa to my left. In the middle of the room, I could see a short, dark, and thin man with a very angry countenance popping the whip. *Tio Flaco*, I thought. *Skinny uncle, we will meet soon.* There was another man in the corner beside the front door almost hidden from my view. *Five adults, and no one to stand up for Bianca. All five standing around either beating a little girl or consenting to the beating.* I wasn't just disgusted, I was amazed.

I walked to the back door and closed it so it could be heard in the living room. At the click, I quickly and silently crossed the room so that I was still in the kitchen, but standing in darkness beside the living room door. I heard, "Anda a ver que es…" (Go see what it is.) The man in the black leather coat walked into the darkness of the kitchen. He walked toward the back window where the fading sunlight dimly shone. He walked toward the light without a glance to his right toward the man with an upraised shotgun. I hit him hard in the right temple with the rifle stock, knocking his hat back. I caught his arm to help him to the floor just inside the darkness without noise. Dragging him quickly and silently to the pantry, I placed him in a sitting position against some shelving then closed the door after delivering a hard shot to the man's chin for insurance. Another "Pop" and "Ella esta loca," was what I heard next, "She is crazy."

I've got to stop this. I said to myself almost out loud. The trembling and fear was gone. In their place was resolve and anger. *Bianca is taking another beating. Three men and a woman should be all that are left except for Bianca. OK, here goes.*

I stepped into the living room with the shotgun pressed against my hip at the ready leveled at Flaco's midsection. At that moment, the whip landed again with another loud "pop." Bianca was curled on the sofa with her face down into the cushion. She jumped from the sting but made no outcry. Bianca's parents were standing in the corner at the end of the sofa with expressions of wonder; they had spotted me but did not speak. The small, thin man was stretched out from delivering the blow. My, "Drop it!" was directed at the man with the whip.

Tio Flaco was definitely a Flaco. He still had his white straw hat on, his green plaid western shirt was only wrinkled around his waist where swinging the whip had caused it to pull out of his new Levis. His high-heeled riding boots were new with sharp-pointed toes and silver tip-protectors. His hair was longer than Bianca's and done in a pony-tail like hers. Bianca was to my left on a worn brown sofa. She turned her face toward Flaco harboring a resolutely stubborn look. Abulardo and a woman who I recognized as Abulardo's wife, were standing in the corner of the room at the end of the sofa. Tio Flaco was in the center of the room with a buggy–whip in his hand. The whip had a leather thong extension at the tip to cause even more injury and pain. He also had a pearl-handled, silver-plated revolver stuck in the front of his western belt with a tooled-silver buckle. Flaco had fine, sharp features that made him look evil, snake-like, and almost unhealthy. The other man, much larger than Tio Flaco, stood beside the front door. He jumped at my command and reached for his belt. I swung the shotgun to point at his belly and shouted "Levante su manos! Levante!" The man stopped his hand short of his pistol handle, and raised both hands above his head.

"Bianca, go get his gun." Bianca had been lying in a fetal position to offer a smaller target. She unwrapped herself and obeyed. Tears ran from both eyes in her paled face still set against pain. "From the side, Bianca. Don't get between him and me." Bianca retrieved the pistol and shot back to the sofa pointing the pistol at Tio Flaco.

"Now, Mr. Flaco. It is your turn. Su pistola por favor!" Tio Flaco obeyed, but he had a toothy smile on his face and watched me insolently through eyes narrowed so that along with his sharp nose, he reminded me of the rattlesnake that struck at Jimmy. "Get over with your burro!" The little man obeyed.

"Senor, jou don' know what jou are doing. Jou could be keeled. As a matter of fac', jou weell be keeled." Flaco spoke with a heavy accent and also with great confidence. There was wariness but no hint of fear in his voice.

"Mr. Flaco, you may be right. I may be killed. But I will die a man. I will not die a coward who only can fight little girls and then only with a weapon. You sir, whenever you die or wherever you die, you will die a coward, because that is what you are." The little man's face visibly darkened, the smile faded, and his eyes narrowed showing intense hatred.

Suddenly the front door opened and the lookout stepped into the room without looking first but with his gun drawn. My reaction was to shoot the hand with the gun. The man screamed and dropped his pistol at Flaco's feet, and retreated outside through the open door slamming it shut. Like a snake striking, Flaco reached for the dropped pistol. I let go another blast from the shotgun hitting the pistol and Falcco's right hand. A few pellets hit his sharp-toed boots. Tio Flaco screamed, then pulled his hand back moaning in agony. After a moment, he examined his hand and saw that although the pellets were painful, the damage was minimal.

"Birshot! All jou got is birshot? Jou maybe hurt us a leetle, but jou cannot keel us before we get to jou. Paco?" Flaco's evil smile had returned. Paco came around Flaco and started for me.

Before I could react, a pistol roared to my left. I jumped away from the unexpected explosion but kept my eyes on Paco and Flaco. Flaco fell back against the door, and Paco sat down screaming and holding his knee with both hands. Blood trickled between his fingers. Flaco stood with his hands above his head dripping blood on the crown of his hat. His well-pressed shirt was getting small spatters also. His face showed a look of fear for the first time. I glanced to my left and saw that Bianca held Flaco's smoking gun in both hands, a look of triumph on her face.

"Tio Flaco, you did not load your gun with birdshot, verdad? These are *real* bullets, verdad?" She cocked the pistol again.

I looked at Abulardo and his wife for the first time. They were both frozen with fear staring at their daughter as if they were seeing her for the first time. My mind came back to the problem at hand. I looked back to Flaco, and beckoned with my left hand. Flaco came to me with his hands still upraised still dripping blood on his well-pressed shirt. I grabbed him by the shoulder with my left and spun him around. I stuck the barrel of the shotgun in the back of Flaco's neck and grabbed a handful of his well-combed ponytail with my left pulling him firmly against the muzzle of the shotgun. "Now walk. We are going outside. If your man does anything foolish, I will give you a pain in the neck that you may not live through, so call him off. Even birdshot will do a lot of damage at this range. And don't do a lot of jerking around, I'm having a little trouble deciding which hand is which. Instead of pulling your hair, I might pull a trigger. That too would be tragic and messy."

Tio Flaco did not seem to be familiar with not being the powerful one, at least at this house. He walked slowly out the door and down the three concrete steps into the yard calling in Spanish for Benito to be still. I could feel him trembling through the tension I held on his pony-tail. Night was fully on us, but there were two rectangles of light shining into the yard from the door and a window. Bianca followed us out awkwardly carrying the heavy pistol.

"Call your man to come here. Do it now!" Flaco complied. The white hat appeared above the bed of the fleet-side pickup as the man stood. He walked around the front of the truck with a rifle in his left hand. His right was wrapped in a bloody undershirt.

"Tell him to put the rifle down here at your feet. Then lie down on his stomach with his feet over the rifle." I heard a pistol being cocked then the roar of a shot. Inside the open front door, Paco groaned and fumbled with the pistol he had recovered, then dropped it and grabbed his side. Bianca had shot him again. This time it looked as though he caught the .44 slug in the hip. "I'm sorry, Mr. Trevor. I forgot to get the other pistol. But, you came for me?"

"Yes, I came. Get the pistol now!" I ordered.

I gave a warning look to the man approaching. Benito held the rifle upside down and out from his body, then laid it at Flaco's feet. "Tell him to lie down with his feet on the rifle." Flaco complied, then Benito did as he was told. "Now you!" I held the shotgun against the little man's neck until he was flat on the ground. "Bianca, please, go tell your parents to come outside."

Once the parents were outside, and on the ground, I sent Bianca to call 911. When she returned, I sent her to my pickup to get rope, duct tape, and Vaseline jelly. Tio Flaco got his voice back "Senor Trevor, jou weel die very soon. I weel see to it."

I almost felt sorry for the little man, "I won't die at the hands of a woman. You better send someone else, someone closer to being a man, maybe a ten-year old boy. You couldn't get the job done without peeing your pants. Bianca, bring the whip!"

"Wha jou gonna do?" The whites of Flaco's eyes showed wildly as he turned his head to look.

"Keep your head down! You will know it well soon enough." Bianca dropped the rope, tape and jar of petroleum jelly at my feet, then went back inside. I heard Paco groan as he moved out of Bianca's way. I busied myself tying the three men and duct-taping the knots. I suddenly noticed the time lapse since I had sent Bianca inside the house. The man I had left in the pantry flashed through my mind. I picked up the shotgun and ran inside to secure him. It was too late. "Drop the gun senor." He had been waiting just inside the front door. Paco lay in the floor still bleeding and groaning. I turned to see the pistol aimed at my right eye. With my left hand held up in a signal of surrender, I bent down and placed the shotgun gently on the floor.

"Now Senor, back yourself out the door and untie my friends."

I walked a half-circle facing the gun, stepped over Paco, then began backing out the front door. "What did you do..." I stopped amid the sentence when I saw the leather thong wrap around the man's face drawing blood under his left eye. I jumped to my left as the man screamed in pain and fired the pistol. The bullet cut a swath across my right forearm then lodged in the doorframe. The bullet cutting through my flesh burned like a hot poker, but it did not slow me in the least. Before the gun could be fired again, I had covered the distance. I grabbed the man by the wrist with one hand and the gun-barrel with the other, twisting it upward and out of his grasp. The whip landed again lashing him around the throat. He gave up. He could not see, and now could hardly breathe. I gave him a sound right solidly in the nose then caught him by the collar and threw him out the door to the ground beside his tied companions. Very quickly I had the third man tied and the two burros blindfolded with duct tape. I had rubbed the petroleum jelly on eyelids prior to applying the tape to keep from pulling their eyelids off when the tape was removed. I didn't bother to blindfold Paco. He was well in submission, and I had another reason.

REVENGE

"Now Flaco, you seem ready to whip a young girl. How do you take the whip? I opened my pocket knife and cut a hole in the back of Tio Flaco's well-pressed but bloody shirt then ripped it open from the neck to the waist.

"Wha…Wha jou doing?" Flaco's voice was definitely an octave higher in pitch. He was on his stomach lying on his hands that were tied together at the wrist. I took the whip and laid it gently on the man's back, he jumped and began kicking his feet up and down when the leather touched him. I noticed some old scaring on the skinny's back.

"How does this go? Oh, yeah. Aprende, burro!" I drew the whip to full height and brought it whistling down on the ground beside Flaco who screamed as if fully hit.

"Oh, I'm sorry. I missed. Let's try again. Have you learned anything, Senor?" I brought the whip up again and whistled it popping it on the ground beside the man's back. He did not scream, but flinched violently.

"I learn! Senor, I learn!" Flaco's voice was shrill with fear and anticipation of the pain. I brought the whip up again. Bianca's mother got off the ground and ran to me speaking Spanish, but definitely begging me to not whip "mi hermanito." She inserted herself fully between him and me then fell to her knees begging.

"That is what I wanted to know." I said. "You did nothing to rescue your own daughter, from this despicable excuse for a man as he beat your own child." I heard sirens coming fast. "Yet you come between me and him begging for me to not hurt him. You do not deserve to have a daughter." I threw the whip aside. At that moment the yard filled with oscillating blue, white, and red lights. Three sheriff's cars slid to a stop simultaneously just outside the yard in response to Bianca's call. Six officers descended on the scene with pistols drawn.

AN ARREST IS MADE

"Get your hands up! On the ground! On the ground!" It took a moment for me to realize they were all pointing their pistols at me and ordering me to submit. This was all wrong! "Who is Bianca?"

"I am Bianca," a small voice spoke from the house.

At that moment an ambulance, with lights flashing, arrived followed by a fire truck which added to the light show and the confusion. Suddenly the scene was being trampled by about twenty public servants and I was on the ground being handcuffed. My protests went nowhere. "Bianca? How old are you?" The officer asking was Hispanic and not much over twenty himself. "I'm eleven. You should not put Mr. Trevor in handcuffs. He is the good guy."

"We'll be the judge of that. Where are your parents?"

"Over there," pointing to her mother and father huddled close to Tio Flaco, "but…" The officer cut her off and asked her parents what happened.

In Spanish, the mother began a very loud tirade about how "Senor Trevor" had broken into her house and shot three people, one her brother." She continued, "Then he tied these up and began whipping 'mi hermano' with the buggy whip."

Bianca stepped forward and between the officer and her mother, "She's lying. My uncle was beating me with that whip and Mr. Trevor stopped him. These men got shot by him and me because they were trying to kill him." The officer ignored the girl and continued to talk to the mother. He then began asking Tio Flaco questions in Spanish which were answered in Spanish. Sometime during the confusion of Paco being taken into the ambulance, the officers cutting Tio Flaco and company loose, and EMS workers treating two hands full of birdshot, all four pistols disappeared. Abulardo walked quietly around in the melee, collected them and deposited them behind a dead mesquite tree. When the officers asked about the weapons, all that could be found was my shotgun which was taken into custody. Deputies took statements separately from each person there except me and Paco. Of course they had been given the story by Mrs. Gonzalez's tirade and their stories collaborated her version. Bianca's did not, but that didn't seem to matter.

I saw Abulardo hide the pistols, and the direction things were taking. I called Bianca over. "Remember where you found me when I was hunting the hog?"

"Yes, in the..."

"Right. Your father has one that is loaded." She caught on that I was speaking in code and nodded slowly. "It should be unloaded and the fruit hidden carefully."

"OK, I will take care of it," she said.

"Oh, one more thing, you are welcome. Don't forget the rolling sleeper."

"Thanks."

Bianca seemed to understand that I was telling her to find the pistols and hide them, then get away to my house if she needed to. I had suggested that the trundle I had built might be a safe hiding place. One thing I knew for certain was that if Flaco got a chance at her, the beating she had gotten so far was nothing.

The deputy that put me in the back seat, slammed my head against the door frame, then apologized with a wink to his partner. Through the dizzying fog I noted his badge. It read 'Hammel' and the badge number was 8304.

19

In Jail...Again

"Trevor, git up! You have a visitor."

"Don, what are you doing here. I thought you would withdraw when you saw what a mess I made of things."

"Well, Trevor, I got a call from an eleven year old girl that changed my mind. She said something about being a man when it counts and not running out on friends. She told me what you did. I guess the point is that you stopped the beating she was getting, and I understand you drew blood from four assailants. That was a courageous thing you did when no one else would help."

"You give me too much credit. I was so scared, I almost wet myself, and I drew blood from only two. Bianca took care of the other two."

"The one that got shot twice seems to have a conscience. His story matches Bianca's in almost every detail. He said he is grateful you did not kill him and you got him medical help. He said something else that interested the police. It seems the seat of the Ford pickup was loaded with over two hundred thousand dollars in cocaine that could be cut and sold for many times that amount."

"Did the sheriff find it?"

"No. The dummies took statements and let the three men go. I suppose Bianca's uncle and friends went about making their deliveries then high-tailed it for Mexico. By the way, where is Bianca? I went to her house and no one was there."

"I have an idea, but I'm not telling unless you can get her in protective custody, and *not* with CPS. Child *Protective* Services? What a laugh!"

"Castor, a couple of bad apples does not mean the whole barrel is rotten. The director of that division is a friend of mine. I will get her taken care of."

"Don, I trust you, so call him now, right now, and get it set up. When you are satisfied that she will be safe, then I will tell you where to find her. By the way, can you get me out of here?"

"Not before Monday morning. I will tell you Judge Peterson will not be pleased with you taking the law into your own hands. Vigilante action is a favorite peeve of his."

"Don, if I had totally taken the law into my own hands, I would have killed six people: Rosendo Garcia, his three burros, and Bianca's parents. Don, look, I have never seen nor heard of such disregard of a parent for their own child than they showed last night. By the way, there is a small boy somewhere that belongs to them, Isidro Enrique. I didn't see him last night. Another by the way, Don, Bianca should have some evidence for you."

"You mean the guns?"

"Yes, did she mention them?"

"No, but it was clear that Paco was shot by something more powerful than your shotgun. Birdshot? Trevor, what were you *thinking*? Really? *Birdshot?*"

"What I was thinking was that I wouldn't have to shoot anyone. I thought the shotgun would scare them enough without shooting. Also, I thought that if I did shoot, I didn't want a dead person on my conscience, no matter how bad they may be."

"At least that will be in your favor in court."

"Let's see what happens Monday."

Don made the call to arrange for Bianca's safety. There was to be a police escort to pick her up, then she would be secretly placed with someone whose identity would remain known to few people until Monday morning when she would be needed in court.

BEFORE JUDGE PETERSON AGAIN

"So, Mr. Trevor, you could not take my advice I see."

"No your honor, your advice would have left a young girl beaten or dead. I could not allow that."

"Mr. Foder, what are the charges."

"Judge, there are several pending, but to start with, attempted murder, breaking and entering, reckless endangerment of a child, aggravated assault with a deadly weapon, and attempted kidnapping."

"Mr. Trevor, how do you plead?"
Don stood with me, but I had told him not to speak. He was to simply give advice.

"On which charge, your honor?"

"Break it down for me, Mr. Trevor."

"OK, on the breaking and entering, your honor, I am guilty. On the rest, not guilty."

"Your honor, may I talk?" A small voice interrupted the judge's train of thought.

"Who are you?"

"I am Bianca Alondra Gonzalez, your honor."

"Oh, yes, the girl in question. Why are you wishing to speak?"

"Because I think Mr. Trevor is not guilty of anything."

"Interesting. Please go on."

"Well, your honor, I invited Mr. Trevor to come to my house."

"Really?" the judge asked, doubt tinting his voice, "How is that?"

"Well, your honor, my uncle beats me almost every Friday and Saturday night when I don't get away. I could take it when it was only a spanking, even when it was for nothing, but for the last couple of months he has beat me with a rope, an extension cord, and Friday, he brought a whip from Mexico to whip me. I told Mr. Trevor about the beatings. He has taken me to the doctor twice and hidden me from my uncle to keep me from being hurt. I asked Mr. Trevor if I could come live with him. When he came to my house, he was answering that question. He was coming to get me to live with him."

"Faulty as your reasoning is, I think I see what you are saying. However, you don't have the option of just changing parents."

"Your honor, it wasn't only my decision. My parents also had a choice to make. They could tell the truth and have Tio Flaco arrested for beating me and for selling drugs, or lie and have Mr. Trevor arrested. They chose to lie. So you see, your honor, no one cares enough to stand up for me except Mr. Trevor. He did not break into my house, I invited him."

"Mr. Foder, have you spoken with this young lady?"

"No, your honor. I wasn't aware of her involvement in this case."

"You are a liar too!" Bianca blurted angrily, "I call your office and you refuse to talk to me!"

"Your honor, I never..."

Don Stence stepped forward, "Your honor, if I may. As an officer of the court, I feel I must come forward. I was present when Miss Gonzalez attempted to talk to Mr. Foder. She is telling the truth." My eyes must have gotten as big as a saucer when I realized Don Stence had set this up! Mr. Foder's mouth hung open and he started to speak, but the Judge held up his hand for silence.

Judge Peterson was incensed. "Mr. Foder, this young girl just caught you lying to the court. Just hold still for a moment. Mr. Trevor?"

"Yes, your honor?" "Mr. Trevor, I understand there is another matter pending before this court. The matter of custody of this young lady..." "Yes, yo..."

"Be still, Mr. Trevor. I will make a decision on that matter in thirty days. The reason I pick thirty days, Mr. Trevor, is that is the time you will be in jail for contempt of court. I specifically told you to let the system take care of the girl. While you are in county jail, you will complete the Foster Parent Training course offered by the county. Bailiff, see that Mr. Howard is informed that he has a student in county jail. As to the matter of other charges pending from Friday night's fiasco, the charges were brought by one whose veracity is suspect, therefore all charges except contempt are dismissed pending further investigation.

Now. Mr. Foder, you have the same thirty days to bring before me any proof that you may conjure up to convince me that you should not have disbarment procedures brought against you. This court is adjourned. Bailiff, deliver Mr. Trevor to the constables."

While the bailiff was making his way over to handcuff and deliver me up, I leaned over to Don, "You are a crafty son. How did you know Foder wouldn't talk to Bianca?"

"I didn't. But when he wouldn't, I figured he would lie to the court. Two things I know in your favor. Judge Peterson has an affinity for little girls. He has four of his own. And I know he cannot abide dishonesty in his court. See you in thirty days, right here. The judge may have to punish you for not respecting his directions, but he also has to respect what you did for Bianca."

"What will happen to Bianca during the thirty days I'll be in jail?" "Don smiled and said, I have talked with Kay and Mr. Howard. She will be a guest in my home for the duration. We'll bring her by to see you once in a while."

I clouded up for a moment, "What do I do with the video of Hatchett and Juarez on their rampage?"

Don smiled, "I have already given it to their boss. Mr. Howard is not a happy man. I expect he will be sharing some of his unhappiness about now. I expect them to be looking for employment outside of the arena of child care. Now go and do your thirty days…have a good time."

"Don, that isn't good enough. They belong in jail. Get them put in my cell. Justice will be served."

Don smiled indulgently as the bailiff put handcuffs on me and led me through a side-door to the basement of the County Court House where the jail was located. Stence hurried out talking to himself with a list of to-dos on his mind.

20

Thirty Days Hard Time

onday afternoon on the third day of my thirty days of incarceration in the county jail, Judge Peterson gave me credit for
Saturday and Sunday, a social worker, Ms. Stephanie Gomez,
came to see me with two hours of instruction. Her charge was to teach me
the law concerning foster care, housing, care and feeding of children, dos
and don'ts of discipline, education, medical care, and so on, for children to
be placed in my home. After the instruction was completed and at the end
of the thirty days, she was to give her opinion to the court as to my fitness
to be a foster parent.

When she walked in for the first time, I was almost happy to be in
jail. Sparks flew for me. Ms. Gomez was a very attractive and attentive
woman, but it was more than just seeing a pretty face. She had an aura
about her, like a light shining behind her and framing her face and body,
an aura that only I could see. It was very difficult for me to listen to

what she was saying because I was so taken by her presence. I was happy because the training she provided represented the chance I was being given to get Bianca out of her situation, but being in the presence of this enchanting person for six hours per week was a definite bonus. There were many times I avoided looking at her because of the roller-coaster feeling I got in my stomach every time I looked into her eyes. I could not look at her and concentrate on the studies at the same time, and I knew I had to pass tests.

On Tuesday, Kay Stence brought Bianca to see me. The news was mixed. Bianca was excited that Don had provided a horse and saddle for her to learn to ride and Kay was teaching her to cook simple meals. They were also making sure she got to school and did her homework, and studying. They had made a visit to my house so she could show Don the provisions I had made for her, but the house and my truck had been completely burned. Evidently, there had not even been a fire reported. The house was completely destroyed except for the rock wainscot on the outside, which they said was the only thing left standing except for a couple of water pipes. I did not have to wonder about who set the fire.

Wednesday, Ms. Gomez made her appointed visit. For two hours, I couldn't have told you about the fire. She had all my attention. I discovered I had to stay about two feet away from her because when I caught a whiff of her perfume, I temporarily lost the ability to breathe. I won't say I was infatuated, but *I was* quite taken. The appointment was for two to four in the afternoon. I was a little irritated with Don Stence when he brought Frank Castillo, a local builder, by to begin discussing building a new house. I was irritated first because he showed up at three forty-five, Ms. Gomez graciously left fifteen minutes early. Secondly, I could not figure how I could make a large mortgage payment. I thought about maybe selling some more land, but I was using every acre. Frank was a nice man and ignored my concerns showing me some suggestions that might work, knowing I would have a permanent guest and a female caregiver, both of whom would have to be quartered separately. I did not make a decision, but asked Frank to come back the next Tuesday so he wouldn't interfere with Ms. Gomez' visit and so I would have time to think and talk to Frank Perkins, the agent who had all my insurance policies.

On Thursday, another Stence initiated visit brought, Tommy Franklin, the local Dodge dealer with some pictures of choices for a new vehicle. We finally picked out a used red, single-cab, half-ton truck that looked like it would meet my needs for a while. After Mr. Franklin left, I felt like I was drowning in debt again. The house, contents, and pickup had been insured, but I was certain the replacements would cost much more than the insurance would pay. There was also the matter of the mortgage remaining on the old house that was burned. My old truck couldn't have been worth more than five hundred dollars, little more than what I could get to sell it as scrap metal.

Frank Perkins came by on Friday at ten in the morning. It seems Don Stence had alerted him and told him of my predicament. He came by with two checks, one for fifteen hundred dollars for my truck and forty-five thousand dollars for the house and contents and the remainder of the mortgage. It seems I had mortgage insurance I didn't know about. Both checks were for much more than I anticipated, but still even after that money was paid out, there would be huge debts. The used truck was over six thousand dollars by itself. My goat business did not leave much money for building houses.

Ms. Gomez came at two and stayed through four fifteen. That was an unexpected bonus and made me a little suspicious, and hopeful, that Ms. Gomez might be enjoying the visits also. I gained a lot of respect for Ms. Gomez because she never made reference to my being in jail, or to the charges against me. I could have been in her office or in a school classroom so far as she treated me. I was an attentive student, doing all the readings and assignments she gave me and asking many questions. I understood everything just fine, but I asked a lot of questions so I could listen to her talk. I liked her voice. She also convinced the constable to bring me a table with a drawer, and a lamp so I could have a place to study and stow my materials.

On the second Tuesday, Frank Castillo showed up with some alternatives to plans we had discussed. One alternative he suggested was to build the house so that adding on a room or rooms later would be more cost effective. By the end of his visit on Thursday, we had a good plan, but the mortgage would still be very large. Ms. Gomez continued meeting the appointments that week and even began extending the time a little just talking. I figured out she knew a lot about kids, even though she had none of her own.

Kay Stence brought Bianca to see me every other day. I learned from Kay that she and Don were receiving training as a condition to their keeping Bianca during my stay in jail. Ms. Gomez had visited her on five different occasions to explain the rules of foster care.

The second week of my incarceration was testing week for fourth graders in the State of Texas. Bianca took the reading and math tests given all fourth graders. When I questioned her, she was not confident that she had passed either.

The second Saturday after my incarceration, Bianca told me that over a hundred of my goats had been shot and killed and several more wounded. She said she knew Tio Flaco or some of his men had done it, but of course, none of it could be proven. There had been an 'XIII' spray-painted on my mail-box the next day after my house was burned. The sign had been refreshed and another painted on a second post after the goats were killed. Bianca explained that the 'XIII' is Roman numeral thirteen. The thirteenth letter in the alphabet is 'm.' 'XIII' is one of the logos of the Mexican Mafia. They had left their calling card to let me know who burned my house and pickup and shot my goats.

On Friday of the third week, all the necessary people came to the jail to close on a new house. I was impressed that everyone treated me with respect. They used the visiting area to set up shop and never mentioned that they were having to do business in jail. It seemed almost normal. Frank assured me that his crew would begin clearing rubble and building forms for a concrete foundation early the next Monday morning.

After the first nine visits, I had completed the required course. The last three times Ms. Gomez came, we discussed Bianca, readings she had given me, my house, my goat business, and some topics that could only be called discussions on life. I looked forward to her visits and at the end of each session, I was left with a lingering feeling of warmth and anticipation for the next visit. Between visits, I dwelled on the memory of an all too short visit by a wonderful friend. I was also irritated with myself that I could not tell her what I was feeling. I wanted to. I just could not get the words out. Maybe I was a little embarrassed at being in jail.

On Friday during the second week of my stay, I began receiving a trail of visitors. Old friends, people I knew from church, and some I didn't even know. The message was almost always the same. They were proud of what I had done and wished more men were willing to stand up like that. One of my visitors was J.F. Andrews, a reporter from the local paper. The next Monday, The Express News carried the complete story. I was becoming a reluctant local hero, but I was still broke, and still in jail.

The Saturday of the third week was the most difficult day of my stay in jail. No one came to see me. I had no visitors and for the first time in a long time, I realized how much I had closed other people out of my life since my divorce. I missed the visits, and I missed Jimmy and Caryn. It had been a long time since I had seen them.

VISITOR FROM THE PAST

Wednesday of the last full week of my stay, Bill Wagoner got me up from reading to greet yet another visitor. Bill was being very secretive and I had a funny feeling about this one. I was especially suspicious and intrigued when the guard told me the visitor was a young and beautiful brunette from a college up north. As I walked into the visitation room, she was sitting at a table with her back to the entry door. I had a very strong familiar feeling as I approached her from behind, I knew I knew her, but it wasn't until I sat down that I recognized her. "Ashley! I jumped up over-turning my chair, grabbed her, and hugged her before I could remember I was not supposed to touch the visitors. Bill simply turned his back to not interrupt a tender moment with a broken rule.

"Daddy. I was so glad to get your letter! I have been homesick for so long! I went by the house you were building the last time I saw you, but it was gone and a new foundation is nearly finished."

"Yeah, someone burned down the old house, so I'm building a new one. I think I will be having another addition to the family. I'm anxious for you to meet her."

"Daddy, you are getting married?"

"Almost. But no, I'm trying to get a foster child. It is a long story, but she should be here in a little while. Tell me about you. I want to know about you, four...no, five years worth."

Ashley began at the completion of her junior year of high school when she left with her mother, and for the next hour hit the high points of her life for the past five years. I sat listening proudly to her story. Twice, I had to wipe wetness from my eyes. There were so many milestones I had missed. Ashley finished her story by saying that she had missed her daddy all that time.

"Why didn't you just come home?"

"Daddy, you were so hurt and I thought you blamed me for mom's leaving."

"How could you think that? You had nothing to do with it."

"Daddy, I was sixteen. I think every sixteen year-old believes the world revolves around them and every sour look or growl is directed at them. By the time I woke up and realized that the problems you and mom had were yours and hers, not mine, well, I thought it had just gone too far to go back. Your letter made me realize that you thought I blamed you for all the problems. I didn't and I don't."

I buried my face in my hands choking on sobs. "So much wasted time. So many hurts to overcome. Can you forgive me?"

"Daddy, haven't you been listening? I have nothing to forgive you for. All this time I thought I was the one needing forgiveness, but was too stubborn to ask. By the way, what is this about you rescuing a girl, but ending up in jail?"

Before I could answer, Bill interrupted. "I hate to jump in uninvited, but Castor, the *other woman* is here."

"Bill," I choked out, "meet my daughter, Ashley. She is just finishing up her college up north."

"Pleased to meetcha, maam." At that moment, the door buzzed and Bianca and Kay walked in. Bill made no objections even though two visitors at the same time was forbidden.

Bianca ran to me and gave me a hard hug talking excitedly about the horse Don bought and said was hers whenever she was at their house, and her new riding skills. She looked at Ashley, "I know you. "Your pictures are all over Mr. Trevor's house, well, they were before the fire. Yours and some boy's."

Ashley beamed, "I'm Ashley, Mr. Trevor's daughter."

"Really! When you were little, did he take good care of you?"

"Bianca, he was the best daddy anyone could ask for. You made a good choice. You did choose him didn't you?"

"Yeah, I picked him out. There wasn't many to choose from though. He was really scared at first, but he came through when it was important. Do you want me to tell you about it?"

"Yep! That's my daddy. Yes, I'd love to hear about it. How about I leave you to visit for a little bit, then when you are done, I will buy you an ice cream while we talk. Is that alright?" She was looking at Kay when she asked, but Bianca's nod preceded Kay's. "Goodbye Daddy. I'll come to see you tomorrow. Do you think you could put me up for the summer? Maybe we could live in a tent." Seeing her leave got to me. I couldn't talk. I just nodded.

HERE'S JAKE!

The next day, Ashley came again to visit. Only this time, she brought a couple with her. I recognized Jake, but he had changed. He was a man in size and manner. He was four inches taller and fifty pounds heavier than five years before and more than ever, he looked like his mother. The woman he had with him, he introduced as Margaret, his wife. I could see Margaret was about six months pregnant.

I sat across from my children feeling very uncomfortable and working hard to find something to say. Jake began, "Dad, thank you for your letter. I should have made the first move, but I was ashamed. It took me a long time to realize that during the storm between Mom and yourself, I heard a lot about how wrong you were and how right she was. I never heard you say an unkind thing about her even though she cost you almost everything. For a while, I hated you because I believed Mom. Lately I have begun to realize that she was the one who broke everything apart mainly through her spending and her irrational blaming everything on you."

I caught the scent of a little personal experience in what he was saying, "Ran up a credit card on you, did she?"

Jake ducked and smiled a smile that comes from enduring a shared pain, "I wish that was all. I started hearing all the same criticisms you endured. Only this time, the remarks were applied to me and to Margaret. That lesson has cost me dearly." He took Margaret's hand, "It almost cost me my marriage, but we have things going well now." Margaret smiled a knowing smile and briefly laid her head on his shoulder.

I found my full voice and spoke next, "Jake, Ashley, Margaret, I don't want to revisit all that. There is too much to look forward to." Jake looked a little puzzled, "Look forward to? Dad! Don't you know you are under attack by the Mexican Mafia?"

"Yeah, ain't it great!"

Jake was incredulous, "Great? Great?!? Dad! They will kill you if they can. How is that great?"

"Well, son, when you were little, and even when you got older, someone was constantly berating you. I seldom spoke up for you. I made the excuse that I had to show a united front…for your sake. Actually it was a copout. I was just afraid to confront her. I was afraid she would leave. Well, she left anyway. The Mexican Mafia is after me because I finally became a man able to confront when I saw abuse and injustice. It cost me thirty days in jail, over a hundred goats, my pickup, and my house, but I feel like a man. If they kill me it will be a bunch of cowards killing a man, not a sniveling coward afraid to stand up for principles. I'm not afraid of dying I think because I have just begun to live again. I don't want to die mind you, but now it would not be the tragedy it would have been three months ago. I have looked them in the eye and seen what cowards they are. They only fight from behind superior weapons and numbers, from behind women, and under cover of darkness. They are cowards whose greatest weapon is the fear in the hearts of others, and *their* greatest fear is that someone will stand up to them. One of them has been beating a small girl for a long time, trying to beat her into submission. He kept beating her because she kept her spirit. He broke her mother and father I think, but not her."

"Dad, you are not to blame," Jake and Ashley spoke at once. "Daddy, you are a great father. Don't throw it away."

"The die is cast," I explained. "There is no turning back now, they will come or not, but I will not run or yield. Besides, if I ran, they would just find me."

Over the course of the next two days, Jake and Ashley talked to me trying to get me to sell out and move anywhere the Mexican Mafia could not find me. Gradually, they changed their conversation to wanting to stay and fight with me. I had no plan they liked, but they finally saw I was serious and stopped trying to get me to run.

21

Out of Jail and Into Court

The Monday I was to be released was also the day for my appearance in court for the custody hearing. I was released at eight and was in court by nine wearing a new suit, white shirt, and tie that Ashley and Bianca had insisted was necessary. At Ashley's suggestion, Miss Gomez had come by to give me a haircut. I really enjoyed that! Mr. Foder was noticeably absent, but CPS was represented along with a string of public servants involved in child care. Don and Kay Stence arrived shortly before nine with Bianca in tow. The gallery was full of curiosity seekers and lots of people who had told me they would be there for support. Judge Peterson arrived wearing his usual judicial scowl. The judge asked the bailiff to call the next case. He announced the custody hearing and asked all concerned parties to come forward. The only members of Bianca's family that stood were Omar and his wife. I was proud of

Omar to be standing up for his great-granddaughter at what he thought
was the risk of deportation.

"Bailiff, ask Miss Gonzalez to take the stand." As Bianca made her
way uncertainly to the witness stand, Judge Peterson said, "This case is a
bit unusual so the handling of the case may be a bit unusual. There are
several things that may be overturned on appeal, if such an appeal is made.
However, Miss Gonzalez is almost to the age when the law doesn't make
decisions without consulting the child in a custody case, so I will be consulting her as I arrive at a decision."

Looking at Bianca, who was obviously intimidated by the imposing figure of Judge Peterson, and the number of people attending, Judge Peterson
asked, "Miss Gonzalez would you state your full name, your address, and
your age for the court?" "Yes, your honor." Her voice trembled at first then
got stronger, "My name is Bianca Alondra Gonzalez. I live at Rural Route
seven, box 196. I am eleven years old." Judge Peterson smiled, "Good.
Now what grade are you in?" "I am finishing fourth grade," Bianca was
gaining confidence and settling in.

"Bianca, where were you born?"

"In San Antonio, Texas, in Santa Rosa Hospital."

"Do you have a birth certificate?"

"Yes, your honor."

"What date does it say you were born?"

"October 29, 1980."

"Where were your parents born?"

"They were born in Mexico."

"Are your parents citizens of the United States?"

"No, your honor."

"Bianca, how are you doing in school?"

"Not too good."

"Explain what you mean by 'not too good' please."

"You mean tell you about school?" The judge nodded. "I didn't pass the reading and math test. I failed third grade, then I failed the reading test again in third grade, but I passed math. This year, I failed the reading test again, but I passed the math and writing."

"Do you do your homework?"

"Most of the time, your honor, but sometimes I don't get a chance."

"Tell the court about when you don't get a chance."

Bianca looked at me as if to plead, "Get me out of this!" I nodded and smiled, telling her to tell the judge everything. So she did. She told of having to stay away from home on Saturdays and sometimes Friday nights because Tio Flaco was there. She told of sleeping all night under the house so she could feel safe and he couldn't find her to beat her. She told of staying in the woods until he left, then going into the house to get food and a change of clothes. She told of occasions when Tio Flaco would come for a surprise visit during the week beating her and keeping her up most of the night. Her story changed to relating her meeting me and the things I did to help her. She told of going to my house in the night to get food and sleep in my truck, then leave in the morning before I came out. I was surprised by that revelation; I didn't know she had been sleeping in my truck. Then she told of the horrible beatings she received at the hands of her uncle and hurting so badly that she went to me to get help. She told of the CPS workers who kept telling her she had to stay at home and how they would not listen to her when she tried to tell them how bad home was.

Finally, she told of the night I interrupted the beating, then reminded the judge that he put me in jail because I got her away from the beating.

The judge shifted uneasily in his chair at that tangent accusation. Then she told of the past month in the care of Don and Kay Stence and how much she loved them.

"Bianca, when your uncle beat you, what did your parents say or do to help you?"

"Nothing. They never said nothing."

"Did they do anything to stop him?"

"No, your honor. They just stood there."

"Do you know why?"

"I think because he gave them money and made them afraid. One time, he said he gave them their house and their food, so they better sit still."

"Bianca, do you know where your parents are now?"

"I think probably in Mexico. They would sometimes go to Mexico when Tio Flaco was not coming for a week or when they thought they might get caught by immigration."

"Do you know why your uncle went to Mexico every week?"

"I don't know about *every* time, but one time I watched him take plastic bags from his truck into the house, then all day the next day, people would came and take away bags of white stuff, only they give him money and take little bags, then drive away. I think he was dealing drugs."

"One last question, Bianca. With your parents gone and maybe not coming back, you can't live alone and I must decide where you live, what do you think the court should do with you?"

There was no hesitation in her answer. Her face brightened, her voice lifted, and she glanced at me smiling, "I think you should let Mr. Trevor take care of me. He has a nice house, well, he had a nice house, and plenty of food, and he wouldn't let anyone beat me, and he likes me."

"What do you mean he likes you?"

Again her answer was immediate, "When I make a mistake, he talks to me. He doesn't yell or hit me or nothing like that. And when I was so sick, he fixed me soup and read to me. He made me feel safe and good. I think he would be good to me. He has rules that he lives."

The judge then heard from Ms. Gomez, the assigned social worker, then from Don and Kay Stence. Finally his gaze fell upon Omar and his wife. "And you sir? You came forward as an interested party, who are you and what do you have to add?"

In his broken English and in a voice that reflected his age, Omar identified himself as Bianca's great-grandfather, her oldest relative. He then said he believed Bianca should be placed with someone who cares for her. He volunteered himself and his wife to help with what they could if Bianca would be allowed to stay with Mr. Trevor.

WINDFALL

"Mr. Foder, please come forward and take the stand."

Don's face fell a bit, but he was curious as to what Judge Peterson could be up to now. After the swearing in, "Mr. Foder, have you completed the little task I sent you to do."

"Yes, your honor, I have the information concerning the property at Route seven Box 196."

"OK, Mr. Foder, please inform the court."

Mr. Foder seemed to be enjoying the attention and the drama and the fact he was being given a chance to redeem himself after the lie, "Your Honor, I found that the parcel is forty acres, valued at eight-thousand, five hundred dollars per acre. The boundaries have been properly surveyed and recorded, but the taxes have not been paid for the past twelve years. However, ownership of the property is a mystery. It seems it was owned by a couple with a Las Vegas address, but they have been deceased since nineteen seventy eight. There is a signed bill of sale and everything, but ownership cannot be established since the couple had no heirs and seemingly no living relatives at the time of their deaths."

"Is Randy Newman here?" The judge was looking over the audience.

A hand waved at the back, "Yes, your honor, I'm here."

"Well, Randy, then by now you have some idea why I asked you here today."

"Yes your honor, I will get on the sale of the property."

"Randy, pro bono, of course."

"Of course your honor."

"Don Stence, I see you standing with Mr. Trevor. Will you favor the court by handling the legal end of the sale of that property?"

"Yes, your honor. Pro bono, of course. What about the proceeds your honor, who do they go to?"

"Thank you, Mr. Stence. We will get to that in a moment."

"Now, Mr. Trevor. Are you quite finished taking the law into your own hands?"

Judge Peterson was smiling, but I was not. I thought for a minute, then I spoke my heart knowing I might spend another period of time in jail, "Your honor, I am a law abiding citizen, but I am also a friend and father. There are times when a man has to stand up and act. I may have gone beyond the minimum needed, but I believed Bianca's life to be in danger. Thirty days later, she has scars from that night, and the beating had just begun when I interfered. Your honor, out of respect for this court and you, I have to be honest. If the situation were to be repeated, I would try to get the system to take care of it, like I did, but if it failed, like it did, I hope I would have the gumption and courage to step in to protect someone from being harmed, even if it meant more time in jail."

Judge Peterson did not respond immediately. He thought for a moment drumming his fingers on the desk, then looked at Ms. Gomez. "Ms. Gomez, did this man successfully complete the course for providing foster care?"

Ms. Gomez nodded, "Yes, your honor." I was again caught up by the grace of this beautiful woman.

The judge then leaned forward and looked me directly in the eyes, "Mr. Trevor, are you ready and willing to take on the task of the primary caregiver for Bianca Alondra Gonzalez?"

I turned and looked directly at Bianca. I spoke to the court but did not take my eyes off her. "Your honor, I am honored that I am given the chance to care for this wonderful young lady. If the court will allow, I will do my very best to care for her better than I cared for my own children. I don't have a lot to offer, but what I have, I will share with her. I will see to her nourishment, her clothing, her sleep, her exercise, her education, and her spiritual and character growth."

Judge Peterson sat back in his chair and pounded his gavel. "So decreed. Mr. Trevor will be the primary caregiver for a trial period of ninety days. He is to have all authority to make decisions for her concerning health, welfare and schooling. At the end of that time, if no serious objections reach this court, permanent custody will be awarded at a hearing on that date. Bailiff, put that hearing on my docket. Ms. Gomez, would you get with Mr. Stence and draw up the paper-work for my signature?" Ms. Gomez nodded her ascent.

"Now to the matter of the proceeds of the real estate sale, after twelve years of back taxes are caught up and closing costs are subtracted, two hundred fifty thousand dollars will be set aside in an interest-bearing account for Bianca's college expenses." Judge Peterson pointed his gavel at Bianca. "That means, little Miss, that you will go all out and pass that reading test next spring. You are to bring notice to me at my office as soon as you get it." Bianca gulped but smiled, "Yes your honor." The judge continued, "The balance of the proceeds are to go to the rebuilding of Mr. Trevor's house and environs so Bianca has a fit place to live and Mr. Trevor will be able to pay the bills. That is, after the ninety day temporary placement. If the temporary placement is not successful, all bets are off and we will begin again.

Ms. Gomez, you will oversee this placement and submit a final report to this court at the end of the ninety days. Is there any other business that needs to come before this court concerning this matter at this time?" I raised my hand like I would have to get permission to answer a math question in fourth grade. The judge nodded toward me giving me permission to speak.

"Your honor, just so the court knows, my house and outbuildings were burned while I was in prison. In addition, the gang that Bianca's uncle belongs to took credit. Also your honor, the man threatened to kill me twice when I was messing up his fun whipping Bianca. If he shows up looking for trouble, and the sheriff can't get there, you don't want me taking the law into my own hands, so what do you suggest?"

Judge Peterson did not hesitate, "Make sure he is on your property and that he is a threat, then shoot him between the eyes, and not with birdshot. Court adjourned." Judge Peterson banged the gavel with a finality everyone understood, then left the courtroom to his chambers.

22

Back Home

ake, Margaret, Ashley, Bianca, and I all went together to Reuven's for lunch. I invited Ms. Gomez, but she declined, citing a large caseload. At the table, there was lively conversation, a number of funny stories from Jake and Ashley's childhood. Some of the stories pointed out some foolishness I had perpetrated. There were no mentions of my ex-wife. It was almost as if I had the children without her. I knew that Ashley probably had kept up with her, so I finally broke through by asking her and Jake how she was doing.

"Dad," Jake began, "I don't really know how to tell you except to just say it. She has remarried."

"Who to?" That was not welcome news at first and the question was partly out of a jealousy I didn't know I had. I had a ridiculous notion,

I guess, that she would have reacted to the divorce like I had. I guess I wanted her to be miserable without me like I had been without her.

"She met a divorced man in California about this time last year, and three months later, they married," Jake continued.

Ashley jumped in, "They ran off to Las Vegas over a weekend and got married."

"Dad," Jake added, he is very wealthy and she is happy. She is able to be impulsive and free." Suddenly I felt something I hadn't felt in a long time; suddenly I felt free inside. With that feeling came relief. Everything began looking differently.

"Well," I tried to end the conversation, "I hope she stays happy. She deserves some happiness. She sure never found it with me."

Ashley took my hand between hers, "Dad, last year Mom was diagnosed as an extreme bi-polar." Ashley held my eyes with hers as she continued. "I'm not sure exactly what that means, but she was hospitalized by the court for about three months for diagnosis after she spent some time in jail for passing hot checks, and then she was sent by the court to an institution for another month to get her medications regulated. If it is any comfort to you, her doctor told me no one could have made her happy until she got herself straightened out. You have to accept that it was not you that broke up your marriage, it wasn't even her, it was her condition. You were a good husband and a good dad." Looking at Bianca, "I think Bianca is one of the luckiest girls in the world to have your undivided attention. Actually, I'm a little jealous."

Ashley hugged her daddy and wiped away my tears with a table napkin. Bianca sat in wonderment at the love this grown woman showed her new dad. She wondered within herself if she would ever really have his undivided attention. She felt a twinge of jealousy herself. Margaret was in tears. Jake held her close looking on stoically.

After lunch, and after a stop for ice cream, we drove out to the Trevor place. Bianca and I both looked for life at the Gonzalez house as we drove by. The fuzzy pink slipper was still in the driveway, now a little flatter and muddy, but there was no sign that anyone had been there since the Friday night I broke up the beating. To Bianca, that night seemed to be ancient history. To me, it was as fresh as the morning sunrise. We arrived at the construction site, which had been my home, around two in the bright, hot afternoon. All was quiet, but the house was beginning to take shape. The frame was up, plywood sheets had been nailed in place at the corners of walls to hold everything in place, and the roof was covered with plywood and black tar paper. All that remained of my old house was a small pile of rubble off to one side, and a large pile of rocks that looked like they were waiting to be used again.

I went down to the kidding pen to get a look at the damage. Omar and his nephews had thrown up a makeshift shed for storing feed. They built it from the burned and warped tin and used lumber found around the place along with some left-overs from the fire, and scraps from the house construction. It appeared they had also restocked the feed supply to last for about another month. Omar's two nephews smiled and waved but did not stop their work. I could not help noticing the striking family resemblance between Bianca and one of the nephews. Speaking to Omar, I said "You must present me with a bill for the feed." Omar held up his hand waving off the request.

The watering troughs and feed bins looked in good shape. Going to the run, I was glad to find one of the Boer nannys and her young kid. Omar walked behind me and put his hand on my shoulder. "The billy and the other nanny were killed, he said. This nanny was shot, but we got out the bullet and she is healed now except for the limp. The kid looks very good; they didn't bother to shoot him. He is well muscled."

"Yes, he has really grown up in the month I was away."

The whole family walked back to the construction site. I noticed for the first time that in addition to the mobile home that served as a construction site office, there was a second, much larger mobile home moved in behind the office. I approached and found a sign on the door that read, "Mr. Trevor, This can be your house until the one you are building is finished. The furniture is yours. Let me know when you are through with it and I will pick it up." The note was signed John Clay Petit. John was the local dealer in Fleetwood mobile homes. We went inside to a fully furnished, and clean double-wide, including a well-stocked refrigerator and pantry. I held Ashley close as we explored the unexpected generosity of friends. "Well, Daddy, I guess you do have room for me after all."

"You would be welcome to stay if there were no room at all;" I countered, "somehow, I would make room."

It was shortly after four in the afternoon when Jake excused Margaret and himself saying they had to get back to their business and get ready for tomorrow. Bianca and I rode back into town with Jake to get the new truck which was still parked at the court house with keys in the ignition. Ashley stayed in the new mobile home planning supper.

"Well, kiddo, are you thinking this will work, or have you decided you made a mistake?" I asked Bianca as we started for home in the new, used truck.

"No, is not a mistake. It will be hard sometimes, I think, maybe, but not a mistake," Bianca answered matter-of-factly. "Can we get another ice-cream?"

"Yes ma'am, I think that is a great idea." We made a stop at Dairy Queen on the way home and laughing about it, got rid of all evidence on the way. When we got to the Trevor farm, Ashley had fixed chicken parmesan, green beans and mashed potatoes with gravy for dinner. Bianca giggled and looked at me with mischief in her eyes when Ashley complained that we were not eating very much. Ashley saw the conspiracy and guessed the reason for no appetite, but she allowed the meal to continue without comment, smiling to herself at the apparent bond developing between Bianca and myself. I congratulated myself on the perceptive daughter I had.

***

Wednesday, I went with Bianca to school to give them the paperwork ordering them to prohibit anyone except me or my designee to visit with

Bianca at school, or remove her from the campus during the day, or after school. I arranged to pick her up after school for a period of two weeks, then if everything went well, for her to ride the bus to and from school. She wanted to ride the bus immediately, but I was fearful. There were so many questions that I had to call Ms. Gomez to explain the situation to Bianca's principal and teacher. Actually, I was very happy to have an excuse to call her. Eventually, the school had the idea and enough phone numbers to contact me or Ms. Gomez if there were any problems or questions. The principal agreed to call the sheriff's office if Rosendo Garcia tried to contact Bianca or showed up at the school.

After homework and dinner, I instructed Bianca to dress for mid-week church services. I sent her back twice to change into more appropriate clothing. She complied and laughed at my nervousness. Soon we were on our way. We were both a little apprehensive at what we might run into at the gathering, but I figured we might as well get it over with. I had some tightness in my chest and some sharp pains in my left pectoral. I dismissed the discomfort as jitters.

People at church had lots of questions, most of which I dodged rather than say, "What you are asking is a little too personal." However, everyone's questions came from interest and support, not necessarily nosiness. Those who got to know Bianca a little, fell in love with her. I knew they would. Some had not seen Ashley for a long while and tried to catch up on five years in a few minutes. She had a lot of questions posed to her that she was not comfortable answering, but she was very gracious in dodging them. On the way home, we stopped at Dairy Queen for a dip cone. I needed another ice cream fix.

23

Return of Trouble

I smelled the smoke before my attention was attracted to the glow in the sky over my unfinished house. Fire trucks were already on the scene when Bianca, Ashley, and I drove up, but there was little they could do. The incomplete house was in full bloom, and the double-wide was a smoking ruin. Frank Castillo's yellow backhoe had been doused with diesel and was still burning after the fuel tank had exploded. Next to the double-wide, Ashley's Camero was a burned-out shell. I walked as close as I dared, staying just beyond being seared. Ashley and Bianca held on to each other crying. Frank showed up a few minutes after I did and walked up beside me. He was very philosophical about the loss. "Well, I wasn't pleased with the height of the roof anyway, and that backhoe has been worn out for over five years. Castor, we'll be here in the morning to clear this away and see what we can still use of the foundation. Then we will start over. Any second thoughts on the design?"

"Frank, can you do that? Can you just start over?"

Frank looked me in the eye, "If you want a house here, yes, we have to start over. This one is kinda fried. Is there anything we need to change?"

I was amazed and comforted at the same time by his non-emotional response to the situation. "Well, Frank," I grinned, "I guess we can give the women a chance to look over the plans. How can you be so calm about this? You know this fire was set on purpose, don't you?"

"Of course, Castor. Look at your entry post. The thirteens have left their calling card. But, everything was fully insured against vandalism and arson. You paid for the policy. It covers all the buildings and the equipment and cars, and our labor. By this time tomorrow, we can be in full swing again. We'll even throw up a new feed shed from new materials. Are you game?"

"OK, Frank get your crew cleaning it up first thing, then let's meet back here at four. Bianca will be out of school, and Ashley and I will have come to grips with this, and perhaps select a new car for her. We can look at plans then."

I walked to the kidding pens with a borrowed flashlight, looking through the pens and the run for any other damage. I found no dead or injured goats, so I busied myself putting out feed for the next day, then loaded Ashley and Bianca back into the pickup. We rented two rooms at Motel 6 just outside of town. I was soon asleep, but Ashley and Bianca were up very late first with fear-talk that eventually turned into giggling and girl-talking.

WHAT NEXT?

Six am found us having breakfast at the King Bee, laughing and planning the day. We arrived at Bianca's school at seven fifteen. By eight, I had paid two hundred seventeen dollars for books that had burned and gotten copies of homework assignments for Wednesday night, and make-up work for that which burned in the fire. Bianca's teacher wanted to excuse the homework, and Bianca was willing, but I would not hear of it. "We will have plenty of time to get caught up at the hotel tonight." Bianca pouted for a few minutes at my insistence on finishing all the work, but was soon resigned that I would not change my mind.

Ashley and I left the school and went straight for the car lots. By noon, we had made a deal on a used Pontiac sedan. After paperwork, we had a late lunch and Ashley went to the farm while I picked up Bianca at three thirty.

When Bianca and I arrived, we were surprised to see the burned-out mobile home with new tires installed and pulled to the side. A new double-wide was in the process of being set up. Ashley was talking to Frank over a set of plans spread atop a new stack of plywood. When we walked up, Frank grinned at me and lifted Bianca to the top of the plywood stack so she could see the plans. He said, "You made the commitment to allow the women to make suggestions; well here they are." I listened as Ashley described the house plan to Bianca. I was impressed that she could read the plans. The two females were soon engrossed and giggling about the "man cave" that I had chosen. An hour later, Frank scratched his head then rolled up the plans as we drove away to dinner, Motel 6, and a couple hours of homework.

"What changes did you make to the house?" I asked over hamburgers at Alff's. "Well," Bianca said smiling knowingly at Ashley, "We made the bathrooms, and living room smaller, the office larger so two desks could fit and added a window, and we made the workshop a separate building, taller and wider so you can cut an eight-foot sheet of plywood lengthwise. Aaaannnnddd," she stretched the next announcement, "we added a sewing room. I know you don't sew, but I want to learn and Ashley says she will come home some weekends and teach me…that is after you buy us a sewing machine."

I rolled my eyes, but smiled, "OK, how much extra is this going to cost me, Chifladas?" Ashley answered with pride, "Not much, Dad, about twenty dollars a month added to the mortgage. We gave up the outdoor toilet. Outdoor toilet? Dad!! What were you thinking?"

Bianca put her hand on Ashley's arm, "Please don't make fun of him about that. Building that outdoor toilet was very important to me. It proved to me that Mr. Trevor cared for me more than anyone else ever had. I love helping build it."

I was quick with a correction, "Loved." Ashley gave up the subject without a fight. "Let's talk about this 'Mr. Trevor' thing. I think you could call me something a little less formal."

Bianca spoke up, "yeah, I've been thinking that too, but what do you want me to call you?"

I grinned, "How about, 'Your Honor,' or 'Master,' or…"

"I see you not going to be serious," Bianca said with disappointment showing in her voice, "can we just drop it." My grin faded at the failure of my attempt at humor. I put my hand over Bianca's and squeezed lightly.

"Sweetheart, I'm sorry. I guess I'm just a little nervous. You can call me what you decide. Whatever name you give me doesn't matter, I'll do my best for you."

"OK, how about I just try out some names until I find one that fits?" She continued with a mischievous grin, "I've already got rid of 'Goat Man,' and 'Baby Sitter.'"

I corrected, "You have already *gotten* rid of…?"

"OK!" she said impatiently. "*Gotten.* I've *gotten* rid of 'Goat Man,' and 'Baby Sitter.'"

***

When I picked Bianca up from school the next day, she asked if Marianna Noemi Trejo could come home with us. I didn't know Marianna, but quickly called her mother and got an agreement, then had her mother talk to the office clerk so they would allow Marianna to leave with us.

Ashley had gone shopping for clothes and the girls were about the same size, so they were fixed up for one night. They just had to decide who wore which of the two outfits. When we arrived at the home place, the double-wide was completely ready. Ashley called Motel 6 to cancel the reservation.

Immediately inside the front door, there was a pile of clothes and boxes of food almost completely covering the living room floor. Among the pile of clothes, I found correct sizes for myself, Bianca, and Ashley. Under the clothes pile was a box of hand tools common to farm life, and a three hundred fifty dollar gift certificate to Home Depot to replace tools lost in two fires. All the clothes, tools, and gift certificate were courtesy of the church. They included a huge card with over two-hundred signatures and well wishes notes.

Bianca and Marianna modeled clothes for the next half hour with Ashley and I enjoying the show. A sudden thought struck me and suddenly I was very serious, "Dark of the Moon," I said with a finality one uses when a conclusion is reached or a decision made. Looking at Ashley, "Both times they came to burn me out. It was in the dark phase of the moon. I think they will be back at the next dark phase...I have to get ready." Immediately after that announcement, the mood changed. The reminder of bad people wishing us harm put a pall over the rest of the evening.

After delivering Bianca and Marianna to school Friday morning, Ashley and I drove to the Sheriff's office to discuss the matter. My theory fell on deaf ears. We then went to talk to Frank Castillo. He listened. "What do you suggest?" he asked.

"Give me a couple of days," I countered. "I'll have to study this." It had been a long time since my military service and tours in Viet Nam, but I quickly got into the waging-war and anticipating-the- enemy's-next-move mode. In Viet Nam, I was one of the few sergeants that brought all my men home, but still inflicted considerable damage on the North Vietnamese regulars. I will have to admit that some of my tactics were way outside of the regular army box, but I had a commanding officer that gave me a lot of latitude as long as I was successful.

THE VISIT

Late that night, I walked down to the kidding pens just to get a breath and think. The night was dark, but I knew my way around and navigated easily to the feed shed. Deep in thought, I walked through the run and checked on the Boer nanny and young billy, then turned to walk back to the trailer house. A scratching sound in the shed jerked me to full alert.

Thinking there must be a rodent digging into a sack of feed or a feral hog in the shed, I picked up a stick and banged loudly on the low roof. Nothing ran off that I could tell, so I stuck my head into the open door. Something I would never have done in Viet Nam, but this was my feed shed on my farm, which was a long way from Viet Nam. I could see nothing but I could feel a presence. It seemed to be something large. With hair standing up on my neck, I listened for a grunt that would tell me a wild hog had gotten into the feed, but no sound came. Still there was a presence, I could feel it. Wariness took over my mind and stopped my reasoning. If I had been reasoning, I would have backed out and come back with light and a gun, but instead, I took a step inside. Something was there, but what? Adrenaline began pumping and my breathing came faster, my mouth dried up, then reason began returning and I began backing out of the shed with the very definite feeling that I had been trapped.

Half in and half out, something suddenly shoved me inside and on my face in the straw on the floor. Immediately, something else landed heavily on my back knocking the breath out of me and cracking my spine. Hands from nowhere and everywhere grabbed my arms and pinned me down. I struggled for a few moments, but the hands were strong and practiced, and I was having trouble enough breathing. "I tol' jou I gonna keel jou," a heavily accented voice whispered in my right ear. I could smell his breath, heavy with cilantro, onions and cigarettes, I weel, keep my promise, but not this night. This night jou must learn to be afra'. Jou won't know when I weel keel you. It weel be all of a sudden. Until then, be afra'. I weel be watching jou." I had no breath to call out or answer. I had no breath to yell at the pain when I felt the blade cut through the skin of the back of my neck. "Nex' time, the knife weel go all the way through. I weel geeve jou head to Bianca. Thees time she weel scream an beg."

As suddenly as the attack began, it was over; they released me and ran. I heard quick footsteps heading toward the woods when I sat up. I staggered to my feet taking deep breaths and holding my neck as sticky blood ran down my back. I staggered toward the house where Ashley, Bianca, and

Marianna were having supper. Adrenaline was still pumping and I was full of rage, but not out of control when I burst in and ordered Ashley to follow me to the bathroom. Bianca and Marianna both screamed and began crying when they saw the blood running down my back. Ashley followed me to the bathroom without comment and began immediately holding a wash-cloth against the cut to staunch the bleeding. "Daddy, this needs stitches. What happened?"

I thought for a second before answering, then lied. "You know that shed Bianca's kin put up for me, well, there is a jagged piece of tin I did not see."

I should have known she was smarter than that, "Nice try, Daddy, this is not a cut from a piece of tin. This was done with a sharp knife. Who did you run into out there?"

"Alright! I ran into Bianca's uncle and his henchmen, but so far as the girls need to know, I was cut by a piece of tin. Call Dr. Pick and see if she can see me."

When Ashley got to the living room to make the call, Bianca was already on the phone to the Doctor. "She says bring him. She will be ready."

The bleeding had pretty well stopped by the time Dr. Pick looked at it, but sewing up the cut took a half-hour and eighteen stitches. Dr. Pick was still pretty nimble with her hands.

The next week was an uneasy time. Frank left two men over-night each night and three on Saturday and Sunday. They served as lookouts and for a presence of strength on the farm. We fed the men good and pulled them into the family routines. There were no incidents, but their presence gave me time and confidence to plan my next moves. At the end of the prescribed week, Dr. Pick took out the stitches and pronounced me healed. The next day, I began executing the plan. Since the attack, my resolve, not my fear, was more intense, and my fear dissolved into the commitment to fight them off, but time was short. That night I made a phone call to begin.

Preparations for the Next Round

I borrowed a two-horse, four-wheel trailer with divided stalls from Kermit Herring and pulled it to Mullin, Texas where I had heard there were donkeys for sale at a reasonable price. I knew donkeys made very good watch dogs and some were aggressive enough to be a great protection for any place. After hearing what I wanted, James Burrus, obviously a cowboy from way back, tipped his hat back, scratched his head and asked, "So, you want the orneryest mule I got?" I nodded. He pointed a crooked finger at a bony male standing off to the side in the shade of a tree with his head down. The donkey was not grazing, he just looked sad and lonesome. Mr. Burrus drawled, "That'd be Old Gus. I'll pert' near give *him* to ya 'cause I know you'll bring him back in a little while. I don't give no refunds. That donkey has made me over two thousand dollars since this time two year ago, because I've sold him about five times. One feller paid me to take him back. He causes more trouble with strangers than any animal I ever seen. If he's loose and don't know you when you come up, you are in for a time, I'll tell you right now. He squalls, then bites and paws and in the middle of that, he switches ends and kicks the daylights out of anything or anybody in the way. Onlyest thang you can do is squat down. He'll leave you alone then; 'til you git up. I seen him train more'n one good cowboy to squat and crawl."

I smiled and owned that there might be a time I would bring Old Gus back, but that donkey sounded like just what I needed at the moment. It took three cowboys four tries to get Old Gus roped and loaded in the trailer. Mr. Burrus stood to the side and laughed at the difficulties the hands were having with one old donkey. I was satisfied, so I wrote a check for two hundred fifty dollars, twenty-five more than he was asking. Looking at the check and still grinning at the fun, Mr. Burrus gave a last warning, "Now, remember, Mr. Trevor, I don't give no refunds, but I will take him back if you are ever of a mind to get rid o' him."

On the way back home, I stopped in Lometa to pick up the big red goat Jimmy and I had encountered earlier. Before the man, Gus, would sell the goat, I had to agree to sell him back at the same price before winter. Big Red was needed for breeding. While I was there, I showed the donkey, Old Gus to the man Gus. The donkey just stood in the trailer with his head down. Gus, the man, laughed and exclaimed that he had owned that donkey at one time, but had taken him back. He said he got bit and kicked, then the old donkey tore up his corn crib. We had a laugh about that, and the similarity in their names. He said when he had the old donkey, he could have sworn the name was not Gus, but Cuss.

***

Back at the farm, I backed the trailer up to the gate so I did not have to handle either animal and opened the trailer gates to turn both Old Gus and Big Red loose in the now barren kidding pen. There were two long and hot days before I offered to feed or water them. When they got their first small drink, they were too intent on the water to bother with me. Two days later, I came with a more substantial drink for them. They were getting pretty drawn, and were happy to see me. The next day after that, I provided a small amount of feed with the water and so on until at the end of ten days, they were getting a full ration of feed and water and were happy to see me any time I came to the pen. I started putting a little corn in the feed trough to put some weight back on them.

During the ten days, Jimmy and Bianca visited the two renegade animals many times. Jimmy never hesitated and the animals never threatened him. He walked around and under Gus leading Lucy and Brutus everywhere he went. Gus and Red followed him wherever he went in the pen. Jimmy was able to climb on the rock and then onto the back of the goat and ride. I laughed to see the parade. A little boy riding a huge red billy goat, followed by a raw-boned donkey, flanked by a border collie pup and a black cat. It reminded me of Aesop's "Traveling Musicians" fable. Bianca got in on the act when she got in from school by riding atop Gus. I made sure Gus and Red were familiar with me and Ashley, then turned both of them loose in the yard pasture every day after dark. Gus proved to be a protector of his new territory without parallel. No one came on the property without being challenged by Gus and Red. Lucy seemed to catch on and every time Gus set up a howl, she followed his lead with her barking.

***

OTHER PREPARATIONS

Shortly after bringing Gus and Red in on the problem, and while they were being 'seasoned,' I met with Frank Castillo about some equipment and materials. We agreed to split the cost of a diesel tractor with a shredder, blade, and backhoe, which would make Frank a profit after the insurance settlement on the old one. The agreement included my unrestricted use of the equipment after dark and full ownership at the completion of the construction of my house. We agreed upon a mid-sized John Deere with attachments, from George Roberts, the local dealer.

25

Becoming Dad

Tuesday evening after my trip to pick up Gus and Red, I sat reading with Bianca when a tendril of hair slid from her head to rest in front of her left eye. She made no move to push the hair back to its place, but kept reading. I reached up absently and with one finger guided the lock to a place behind her left ear much like I had done for Ashley many times when she was little. Bianca looked at me and smiled, then kept reading. When I looked away, she shook the lock of hair down again, and again gave it no attention. I knew this had become a test, so I pushed it back in place again. That time, Bianca just smiled to herself and kept reading. Ashley observed the entire process from the kitchen with a smile of understanding on her face. Later, after bedtime, Ashley had a talk with me.

"Daddy, she is flesh and blood."

"I know that. What are you getting at?"

"When you said 'good-night,' did you show her any affection?"

"I held her hand as we said our prayers."

"Daddy, she is a little girl. She needs you to caress her. Touch her with affection. Kiss her on the cheek or forehead. Do you remember when I was that age?"

"Yes, I do. But, Ashley, you are my flesh and blood. I don't know the boundaries with Bianca."

"Do you want her first affectionate touch to come from a boy that wants what boys want? If you let that happen, she will not know how to react. She must have a father who will treat her with affection and respect at the same time. Here, take this brush. Get her up and fix her hair, like you used to do for me. Start with that. I promise she will love that. She loves you, you know."

"Ashley, I have so much to learn. Things I won't even know to ask about. And besides that, I never did a good job on your hair. It was always crooked somehow." She just shooed me out with a giggled, "I know." I took the brush obediently and went to Bianca's room. I knocked at the door and Bianca invited me in. "Would you mind if I fixed your hair tonight?"

Bianca was already in her pajamas and looked at me with lots of questions in her expression. "I guess that would be alright, but...are you sure? I never had a man fix my hair. It's not easy as it looks. Do you know how?"

"Yes, well, no, I don't, but I would like to try. It's kinda something I think I should do or at least try."

"Well, if you should, I guess it will be okay." She got out of bed and stood in front of me as I brushed her course black hair. She giggled all through my abortive attempts to form braids on both sides of her head.

Finished, I apologized that I could not seem to get the two braids placed at the same level on both sides of her head. With shining eyes, she said it was OK, then kissed me on the cheek and hugged my neck. "Not bad for a beginner," she said. "We will just have to get more practice. How about tomorrow night? My father would never have done this for me. He would not think it was manly. I like you to brushing my hair."

Without correcting her English, "Well, young lady, there are a lot of things you may have to teach me as we go along."

Bianca was silent for a moment looking down at the floor, then looked up at me with black eyes shining and a furrow in her brow, "Mr. Trevor, do you think the judge will let me live with you forever?"

I paused not knowing exactly how to answer, "I think, Bianca," I said in a very measured manner trying to think ahead of my words, "that depends on whether or not your parents show up to fight for you."

"They won't," she said with finality. "They will be afraid of getting caught by immigration. How could they fight, they are not even citizens, besides, they would just let Tio Flacco beat me again."

"I don't know about those things, but if I were your dad, I would fight for you even if it meant...well, I just would." I thought better of saying negative things about her father. Every little girl should be able to think well of her father.

Bianca grabbed the brush and stood facing me directly, "OK, that settles it," she said with finality. "Since you have already fought for me, I will call you 'Dad.' Is that OK?"

"OK," was all I could say. I could not talk around that confounded lump in my throat. It amazed me how quickly she could melt me. I kissed her on the cheek, and squeaked out a, "Good-night," then walked into the living-room still carrying the lump and trying not to show it.

"Did it go alright?" Ashley asked hugging me.

"More than alright. It seems now I am 'Dad' again. Where did you get all this wisdom? We never talked about these things."

"No, Daddy, we did not talk about them. I grew up doing them. You taught me. You know the right things to do. You knew them for me, you just have to do what you know."

26

More Preparations

For the next three weeks, after homework, chores, supper, and reading, Bianca went to bed after some tender, dad and daughter time with me, then Ashley and I went to work. Without lights, using only moonlight, I dug trenches with the backhoe and covered them with three quarter inch plywood, then spread the plywood with a thin layer of dirt. During the day, Ashley planted shrubbery until most of the mobile home and the home under construction had a maze of eight-foot deep and six-foot wide trenches around them, all hidden by shrubbery.

The dirt from the trenches was used to build up the side of the trench away from the house. The trenches were camouflaged from anyone from the road or almost anywhere except right beside them, even then, one would have to be looking for something amiss to see it. Shrubbery was set on the edge of the trench on the house side. From a distance, it looked like a small rise on the road side of the houses and shrubbery close enough to the house to offer cover to someone approaching. By the time the trenches were finished, there were only three days left until the dark of the moon.

Hidden among bags of cement and concrete were two hundred fifty one-hundred pound bags of bentonite clay that I ordered from Arkansas. At the end of each night's digging, I spread about a six-inch layer of the Arkansas powder, often used to seal dirt tanks and ponds, into the freshly dug parts. What I wanted was a slick, mucky, surface at the bottom of the trenches.

Four times during that period, I cleaned 'XIII' or 'MM' off the entry post and mailbox to my farm. It seemed someone wanted to make sure I did not forget the threats against me and who made them. Each time the symbols appeared, I called the sheriff's office. Each time a constable came out to take pictures and log the incident.

A pair of eyes watched our every movement from daylight until dark. Once I spotted the owner of those eyes, but I felt them on me constantly. That ability to feel the presence of enemy had served me well in Viet Nam, and it was a skill being honed every day. Ashley felt the same presence. Once lights came on indicating the family was inside for the night, the watchers left. I saw a man dressed in black descend from a tree on the edge of the woods one evening about dark. I was very sure the changes around the place happened gradually enough that they went largely unnoticed and seemed natural.

Two days before the dark of the moon, I tried one more time to get the sheriff to listen to my concern about what I thought would be an attack on Bianca, me, and my property. The sheriff listened politely and promised to have a sheriff's car drive by three times each night until the dark of the moon had passed. Thursday, before the target date, I called Ms. Gomez. She came out to the farm that afternoon. "What do you want me to do?" she asked after she got a full account of what I was expecting and what I was doing to prepare. I blushed at not having a ready answer. What I knew, deep down, was that I just wanted to see her, but I could not say that to her. I had other legitimate reasons to make contact with her. "I just wanted you to be aware since you are Bianca's caseworker. We haven't talked much since I was given temporary custody. I have to make sure she is not here when they come."

Ms. Gomez blushed in the realization that there was more going on than I was saying. She blushed, I later found out, because the thought was not foreign nor unwelcome to her. She had had the same thoughts about me which I think I perceived, but she also kept them well hidden. After Ms. Gomez left, Ashley grinned knowingly at me as she cleaned the living room. "What?" with an exaggerated shrug was all I could muster.

"Daddy, you are not a teenager. It is very plain that you have feelings for Ms. Gomez. Why do you play the games? Why not just come out and tell her? It is just as plain that she has feelings for you."

"I don't know. It's too soon and it's complicated."

"Daddy, it's neither complicated nor too soon, but the first move is yours."

WHAT TO DO WITH BIANCA?

Thursday on the way to pick Bianca up from school, I asked Ashley about taking Bianca away for a few days until the Tio Flaco question was settled. Ashley refused,

"If you are staying, I am too!"

I was worried and I'm sure it showed, "You know they will come armed and ready to kill us."

"Yes," she countered, "but I have seen the preparations. I don't think they have a chance, but if any get through, facing two of us will be harder than one. Remember you taught me to handle a pistol and a rifle, and to stand up for myself. Also I took a class in marksmanship. I made an 'A.'"

"Shooting a target and a man are very different," was all the argument I could offer.

"I'm sure you are right. You have the experience to back that up, but I am just as sure that I could shoot anyone threatening me or mine."

I was still trying to figure out how to get Bianca out of the house for a couple of days when she came to my pickup after school. She was excited that Jasmine Diana Osornio had invited her, Marianna, and several more girls for a weekend sleep-over to celebrate the end of school. I thought since Bianca was a normal eleven-year old, everything else was forgotten when she got an invitation to be with her friends, at least that is what I thought. I agreed to drop her and Marianna off at Jasmine's house after school on Friday, then pick them up on Sunday afternoon. The dark of the moon was to be Saturday night. I was almost certain this episode would be history by Sunday morning.

JOY AND DREAD

Friday morning, I started hoses running in the trenches before delivering Bianca to school. I had her pack for the weekend and leave her suitcase in the pickup. Back at the house, I had Ashley drive her car into town and park it on the lot where we bought it. We had breakfast at Alff's and talked through the plan for the day. Around noon, Ashley and I met with Frank to get an update on the building and update him on the preparations. The meeting lasted longer than planned. I asked one of Frank's men to take Ashley to get Bianca. Frank already had instructed the man to take her to his house, disable the truck, and stay with her. With Ashley taken care of, I decided to get Bianca myself.

After they left, I jumped in the truck and picked up the girls. Shortly, I had them at Jasmine's house. When I dropped them off, I asked Bianca to promise to call to say goodnight. "Silly man," she responded giggling, "nobody sleeps at a year-end sleep-over, Da...Mr. Trevor...Dad, I'll call you tomorrow...after we wake up!"

I grinned all the way home. "She almost didn't call me dad in front of her friends. But she did!" When the farm came into sight, my mood changed immediately from light to dark. Suddenly, things were serious. It was still four hours until full darkness, and there were still a few things to be done. I worked quickly, but it did not seem to go quickly. There was an ominous dread settling over the farm. I could feel the eyes on me. Darkness would create a tension I would be able to taste.

When it was time for the building crew to go home for the weekend, Frank called me for a meeting. I went inside what was to be the living room of my new house where a crew of seven men sat waiting.

Frank began the conversation. "Castor, we know you had plans to face the 'XIIIs' by yourself, but we voted to stay with you, there were no votes against the idea. Tell us where you want us. Keep in mind we all lost time and had some of our best work destroyed by those monkeys. We all owe them a little payback. Four of us have military training. Beto and I are Marines, Glenn is Navy, and Toady flew a desk for the Air Force. Juan here, is an ex-member of the 'XIII.' He got out the hard way. Kenny is a black-belt, and Rufus lived the streets of Dallas for ten years. Altogether we are a pretty crusty bunch, and today we all came armed."

"I don't know, Frank," I began, "I don't want anyone killed. I don't even know if they will come, and whether it will be tonight or tomorrow. I don't know how many either."

"Six would be my guess, maybe eight," Juan spoke with some authority. "Six or eight... and armed. You can believe they will be ready to kill you. But...they will not be expecting any resistance. Gangs work off of fear more than anything else. They have to come because they threatened you. If they do not follow through, they will lose face. Also, I think they will come tonight. The weather is good, the night will be dark, and it is supposed to rain tomorrow. I think two will come through the kidding pens, two from behind the new house, maybe two from the west side, and two through the front entrance. They have to use the front entrance. A matter of pride. That is the direction the leader will come from. But this one is a coward. He will hope to keep you busy while the others come at you from behind. He will try to make it an old-fashioned type of shoot-out, but it won't matter to him that you are to be shot in the back."

Given this expert advice and information, I changed my mind quickly and welcomed the 'recruits.' I warned them against any shooting unless they were absolutely sure what, or who they were shooting, and the shooting was necessary to save themselves or someone else. I placed the men around the houses in locations that would be concealed after dark, but inside the construction fence because Gus and Red would be out on patrol. I did not want either animal wasting energy or time hurting one of the workers.

DARK OF THE MOON

Dusk came about eight-fifteen. By nine, it was completely dark and a cloud-cover was moving in. About ten, I had the men remove all the plywood that covered trenches and stack it at the end of the construction command trailer. Juan had indicated the XIIIs would probably show up at midnight or shortly after, so after releasing Gus and Red into the yard pasture around ten, we settled in for what could be a long wait. I allowed no showing of light from the men. No smoking, no flashlights, nothing that could reveal anyone's position. Around ten I turned on the security lights that illuminated areas around the houses. Dark areas between the bright lights lead directly to trenches. By that time, the bottoms of the trenches were muddy bogs.

A little after eleven I heard Big Red bleat from the direction of the kidding pens. I hadn't heard that sound from the big goat before, so I did not know what it meant. There was no commotion or noise to follow, so eventually I discounted it.

At exactly midnight, a lit torch landed on the new house roof. It had been thrown from the pasture behind the house. The man stationed on the roof quickly doused it and ducked down again. Another minute passed, then a lit match could be seen behind the house. Immediately another torch was lighted, but then the torch fell on the ground and a man screamed. Another scream came from someone else closer to the house. The noise stopped suddenly after a loud thump. Pained groans could be heard intermittently. The sounds were very much like someone trying to talk after having the breath knocked out. The still lit torch suddenly moved up and seemingly was being carried toward the house by a running man. After five steps the torch hit the ground and a man began screaming something about 'Diablo.' Men stationed in the house watched figures struggling in front of the torch which lay on the ground. Everyone watching got a brief glimpse of a profile of a man trying to rise from the ground and a horned goat head smashing into him. Small cloven hooves pounded the screaming figure on the ground which attempted to get up and run and was butted to the ground again. Eventually the downed figure managed to get to his knees crawling toward the house. An audible thump and the man went down again groaning. This time he stayed down and the pounding stopped. Suddenly, he jumped up and ran toward the house. After another breath stopping thump, his screams turned to cursing. The building crew began laughing aloud at the sounds like boots being pulled out of sucking mud. Old Red bleated pitifully as if asking the man to come out and play again. Silent again, the men could hear the first downed man get up. They could hear running footsteps then a thump and the scenario with "Diablo" began again with a different victim. Screaming and cursing and running ended with a splash, then the cursing started again and the laughter from the building crew. They could see very little, but the sounds and brief glances in the torchlight told a very humorous story.

After the scenario from the back of the house had played out to muffled cursing, rapid-interval pops sounding like a string of firecrackers being set off or maybe an assault rifle being fired suddenly grabbed everyone's attention. Flashes of light could be seen from the kidding pens. Darkness hid what else was happening. Pings and pops of something hitting the metal roof of the mobile home, the ground, and equipment all around, had everyone ducking for cover. Two thumps with sounds like someone being hit hard enough in the chest to force air though vocal chords, were followed by more cursing that seemed to come from the trench across the path from the kidding pens to the mobile home. More sounds of boots being pulled from mud reached the ears of waiting men who laughed out loud at the sound show.

Suddenly from the road side of the mobile home, a lit torch sailed through the air landing atop the living-quarters mobile home. I was ready with a running water-hose. The torch was not likely to cause damage on the metal roof, but I quickly doused it with a spray from the hose anyway. Suddenly, two more torches flew from the same direction. One landed atop the house, the other at my feet. I aimed the water at the torch on top of the house. That was a tactical error because the torch below illuminated my figure. I paid dearly for that mistake. Three shots rang out, from three locations in the dark witnessed by three different flashes and I went down, hit in the leg, and on the way down, I was slammed hard in my left shoulder. Two bullets had burned their way into me. The first hit my left calf muscle. The second set my left shoulder ablaze with pain. Still holding the water hose, though on my back, I aimed a stream at the torch on the ground. My pistol had fallen to the ground. Missing the torch with the water, I groped to find my weapon. Three more shots rang out, all three bore into the side of the mobile-home. The torch on the ground was still lit and blazing high enough to mark my position even through the screen of bushes. I rolled to my stomach and crawling on the ground using mainly my right leg and arm, I felt around for the stick end of the torch, found it, and rolling to my back, flipped it over the shrubbery into the ditch. It landed in the bottom and was quickly doused by the mud. Three more shots sent bullets whizzing over my position into the side of the mobile home. About that time, the adrenaline rush and endorphins released by my brain to soften the pain began to wear off. My leg and shoulder were raw and burning and I still had not found my pistol.

"Ah, Senor. Jou are wound, no?" I recognized the voice of Tio Flaco.

"Yes, you miserable fighter of little children, you cobardo (coward), I am wounded. I need someone to come help me up."

Flaco thought for a few seconds, then ordered, "Florencio, go. Bring the gringo. We weel deal con heem here in the light. Senor," he continued loudly, "jou need to tell the other helpers to stay away from this fight. Thees ees between jou an' me." Sounds of a man walking were followed by a scream of surprise and soft squishing noises as he slipped into muck at the bottom of the trench.

"Yes," I spoke loudly, "everyone stand down. This is between Flaco and me. By the way, Flaco, cobardo, you need to send a better man. The one you sent for me seems to be lost."

"I am not lost!" came a muffled voice from the trench, "I have fallen into a sewer pit. Flaco, I cannot see to get out. Send Rubio to help me, please." Before any answer could come, another man to Flaco's left screamed amidst dog growls and thumps that sounded like flesh being pounded. Suddenly all was quiet again.

"Flaco Cobardo," I chided trying to not allow the pain of my wounds to bleed into my voice, "It seems you are now alone. How about you come to pick me up to my feet? I am wounded in my leg and shoulder. I have only one arm and one leg to fight you with and you have a gun with three shots left. I probably have the advantage over the coward you are, but you can take your chances. None of my men will interfere. However, Flaco, I am in no shape to walk to you. You must come to me."

"No, Flaco! Don't do it!" it was the voice from the pit. "It is a trick! There is a big hole for you to fall in. Shoot him from there."

"Sure, Flaco Cobardo, be a man. Shoot me from there. I'm sure it wasn't your bullet that found me anyway. Your bullets will be in the dirt somewhere close to your feet, in the puddle you made out of your fear. Since I am not a little girl like those you are used to fighting, I'm sure you were shaking. Your pants are probably wet in front and your feet are also in that stinking puddle. The wind comes to me from your direction. I can smell the stench of your fear. You have already peed your pants from fear of facing a man whose only weapon is a water hose." Though I was in great pain, I continued to desperately grope in the dark for my pistol. I couldn't find it.

From the pit, Florencio spoke loudly, "Rosendo, perhaps it would be better to let him go. He has other men. And, Flaco, you are alone!"

But feeling the advantage, Flaco was not out of the fight yet, "Calletese, pendejo! Shut up and sit dow an' wash."

I watched through the bushes as Flaco stepped into the light with his pistol drawn pointed in my general direction. He was peering into the darkness which his eyes could not penetrate because he was standing in the umbra of a bright light. I spoke again. "I can see you shaking from here. I can smell your fear. The little girl you used to beat has much more courage than you. Actually, the little bird that flits off in the night at a slight sound on the breeze has more courage than you show."

I could see Flaco crouched, peering into the darkness intent on taking a shot. All his attention was focused on my voice. He pointed his gun first at one place then another as sweat poured down his face. "Keep callin' so I can fin' jou in the dark," he said. He sighted down the barrel of his pistol waiting for another sound to help him refine his shot.

The sudden bray directly behind him caused him to jump and turn in a reflex of fear. He fired the gun on the way around; his shot went into the dirt. There was no time for another shot. The donkey broke into the light as if jumping through a wall by magic, and with no hesitation, grabbed the small man by the right shoulder with his teeth. Gus lifted the little man off the ground and shook him side to side amidst his screams. The shaking reminded me of a dog catching a rat and shaking it violently to kill or at least disorient it. Flaco's pistol fell out of his grip hitting the ground muzzle first. The little man screamed a high pitched scream resembling a fearful sound from a small girl, and flailed his free arm and legs in a running motion. Gus shook him again like a rag doll.

With a feeling of relief coursing through my body and the pain fogging my mind, I realized I had gauged it correctly. Gus had been walking quietly in the dark to get behind the little man to surprise him. I watched the donkey attack, but something was different. Gus had a small rider. "Bianca!"

Talking softly to Gus, Bianca urged the donkey forward as Flaco screamed in such a high pitch it was almost silent. Yellow liquid dripped from his left boot, Bianca had Gus drop Flaco directly on top of his man, Florencio, in the ditch. Gus and Bianca were very familiar with the location of all the ditches.

27

Aftermath of the Attack

Seconds after Flaco was dropped into the pit, the entire unfinished farmhouse and grounds around were lit and Ashley and Bianca were at my side examining my wounds. Ashley put pressure on my shoulder wound and my leg simultaneously to slow the bleeding. I tried to sit up. "How? Why? You should have stayed away! Bianca! This is too dangerous!" I said that, then grabbed them both and pulled them down to hug them close.

Ashley spoke first, "Daddy, it's over and you need to just be still. Turn me loose! I need to put pressure on your wounds!" I turned her loose, she continued the pressure and the conversation, "Frank called for an ambulance," Bianca offered. "They will be here in a few minutes to take us to the hospital."

"Bianca, where are you hurt? Why do you need to go to the hospital?"

"Dad, really! Ashley is right! Sometimes you don't have a clue. I'm not hurt. I'm going so I can be with you. It's my turn to help *you*."

I sunk down flat, then tried to sit up again and couldn't. "Ashley how did you get here too!"

Ashley spoke as she tended my wounds, "Yes, Daddy, I'm here. Did you really think you were going to fool us away? Who do you think caused all the fireworks? Bianca and I hid in the feed shed and saw two of them go by us toward the house. They had pistols and rifles. When they were almost to the ditch, Bianca lit the firecrackers and I threw a couple of handfuls of gravel at them. Man, they must have thought we were really bad! They thought we had automatic weapons. You should have seen them run! What a couple of girls! They ran right into the pit you dug. They couldn't climb out and Frank's men made them throw their weapons out before they would throw a rope in to pull them out. Oh, and I joined Rufus in smacking Rubio around. He will have lots of little reminders of us. And, by the way, Jake is here somewhere." Ashley took over caring for my wounded leg which was bleeding badly. She directed Bianca to keep pressure on my shoulder. "Daddy, do you have your knife?" The knife was in my left back pocket. Since I couldn't reach it, Ashley rolled me to my side and took my knife and started, splitting the leg of my jeans. "Jake is here," Ashley repeated. "He thumped a couple of them."

"Ashley, those are nearly new jeans! Stop cutting my jeans!"

"Would you rather Bianca and I take the jeans off you here in front of all these men?" I gave up and lay still. The pain was taking over my body and muddying my mind.

About that time, Jake came into the light dragging two limp men with huge lumps on the side of their heads just in front of their right ears. Jake had the men's shirt collars in his big fists. "I found this one waiting in the pickup outside the front gate. And this one standing just inside the gate with a rifle. I think he is one of those who shot you. I'm sorry I didn't get to him sooner." As he finished his announcements, he threw Abulardo Gonzalez and another man in a black western shirt and pearl snaps into the pit beside Flaco and Florencio who were sitting in the mud against the side of the trench. Flaco was holding his broken right arm and whimpering. Bianca did not look up nor seem to notice her father was among the intruders. Abulardo did not speak.

"How bad is it?" Jake's question didn't get a verbal answer, just a nod from Ashley.

Juan took command of the scene at that point directing the other men. The EMS ambulance and a fire truck drove in the front gate stopping just short of the trench. In the confusion of flashing lights from two trucks, EMS workers taking care of me, and firemen walking back and forth checking to be sure no fires would start up later, Frank's crew gathered up the eight men. They quietly took the gangers over to the side of the buildings toward the kidding pens in the dark and away from the confusion. All eight frightened men were securely tied with strong cords. They continued asking what was going to happen to them until Frank went into the new house and brought out a roll of duct tape which he used to tape the mouth of each of the eight. "Don't worry," Juan said very quietly to each of them, "We aren't going to kill you, but before daylight, you may want us to. Juan said later, there were times the only thing that was visible in the dark was the frightened look of the whites of their eyes. Once they were secured, Juan and company threw them like so much cordwood into the bed of Flaco's truck which Beto had driven into the yard. At the same time the last man was loaded, it began to rain lightly. Lightning lit up the sky all around in intermittent flashes.

When the ambulance drove out to deliver me to the hospital, Bianca sat with me holding my hand and talking to me through the fog that was invading my brain. Ashley followed in my new used red truck. Juan drove Flaco's truck and followed Ashley to the front gate.

Taking weapons from the vanquished and casting about, the construction workers found seven pistols, one scoped rifle, and four assault rifles, all of which they hid in the new house under a staircase. As they were leaving, Juan and Beto in Flaco's new truck, met the two constable cars at the front gate, waited for them to enter, then quietly continued on their way. The police cars came in with lights flashing. At the intersection with the highway, the ambulance headed north to the hospital followed by my red truck; Juan headed Flaco's truck south on the way to Mexico with the bound and gagged cargo bouncing around and moaning in the bed of the truck. The rain began coming down in a heavy downpour giving the tied men even more discomfort.

AT THE BORDER

Just after daylight Saturday morning, Juan negotiated delivery of the eight men to the local XIIIs leader in a small sleepy village just across the Texas-Mexico border. He took them across at a designated point and paid a small mordido (bribe) to the border guard as directed. The young leader seemed a bit upset at the actions of his men. He kicked each one in the ribs as they were unloaded and spit on Tio Flaco. As Juan told it later, "He was not so upset that they were unsuccessful, but that they acted without his knowledge or consent." The leader also seemed grateful that none of his men had been harmed except for Flaco's broken arm and a few cuts and bruises. Juan perceived there would be some disciplinary measures taken. The gangster swore there would be no more attacks on Mr. Trevor by his men, and thanked Juan for splinting Rosendo's arm. He thanked them also for bringing the men back instead of turning them over to the U.S. police, who would have detained them for a while, then sent them back anyway.

The two tired men arrived at the local Greyhound bus stop late Sunday afternoon to the open arms of their worried families. They both insisted on going to the hospital to visit Mr. Trevor before going home.

AT THE HOSPITAL

In the wee hours of Saturday morning, Dr. Pick scolded Castor for taking things in his own hands again. She scolded Ashley and Bianca for not keeping him under better control, then she began the needed treatments. The wound to his leg was a through and through. An artery had been nicked which caused considerable bleeding, but Dr. Pick decided the wound just needed a good cleaning, draining and stitching. The bullet in his left shoulder was a different story. It had entered the fleshy part of his shoulder in front of the ulna knocking a small chunk of bone from his upper arm. It had continued through the flesh of his shoulder and into the scapula. The scapula was broken and the bullet was lodged in the bone so that it had to come out. X-rays showed the scapula was in two pieces that were held apart by the mushroomed bullet.

Dr. Pick called in Dr. Jacoby, a bone man, to work on the scapula after she handled removing the bullet and caring for the wound. They decided upon cleaning the wound from the front, and inserting a drain, then performing surgery from the back to remove the bullet. After the bullet was removed, Dr. Jacoby was to enlarge the same entry to pin and screw Castor's scapula together. Dr. Jacoby was excited by the challenge this injury presented to his skills. He was anxious to get started.

All the plans made, around four forty-five am Saturday morning, they administered anesthetics and began the process. Dr. Pick came out of the operating room around six-thirty to tell Ashley, Bianca, and Frank that the bullet was out, the wound was cleaned and a drain had been inserted from the front, and Dr. Jacoby had begun his attempt to put Castor's scapula together.

Dr. Jacoby came out at seven-fifteen still in his scrubs, to deliver the news that he was able to get the scapula back together with one pin and two screws. "A simple carpentry job," he quipped. He seemed delighted that he had been able to fit it back and secure it with a minimum of hardware. "The break was clean and it went back together just like a piece to a puzzle. He will be in recovery for a couple of hours and his pain will be fairly intense for a few days. That area of the body has a fairly dense set of nerves. You should be able to see and talk to him in about another hour. If all goes well, about ten, we will be moving him to a room.

He will be in the hospital for probably four days. If everything goes well from there, you should be able to take him home on Wednesday or Thursday. By then we should be able to tell if the pin and screws are going to hold and if he will be able to use a crutch to walk. We will need to sign him up for some physical therapy to begin in two weeks. Meantime, don't let him keep the shoulder immobile, but be careful to not put a lot of pressure on it. It needs to move even if it hurts. Motion is lotion."

Ashley and Bianca nodded understanding and hugged each other in relief. Jake hugged them both then walked down the hall to get coffee for them. Bianca sat down and now that the danger was past, cried bitterly for Castor's hurts more than she had ever cried over her own. Ashley laid the exhausted girl's head in her lap and stroked her hair." "You really love my daddy, don't you?" she asked quietly. Bianca didn't offer to get up,

"Yes. He is so good to me. He came and got me when I needed him, and I think he needs *me* now. I think he loves me too."

Ashley smiled the smile of the wise looking on and whispered, "You are right, he loves you very much. He loves you very much like he loved me as a child. He will show you often, but he won't say it often. You are also right that he needs you. He has been lost in his sorrow and bitterness for a long time. He chose to be alone, but you have pulled him out of that. I can see that his deepest wounds, those which cannot be seen, are being healed by his caring for you and Jimmy and Caryn." Ashley continued to stroke her hair and comfort her as she slept the hour until they could see Castor. Frank, who had been standing close enough to witness the conversation, hugged them both and nodded in his sympathy and gratitude that Castor would be okay, but left without saying anything. Finally, Ashley and Bianca were allowed to visit Castor in recovery. He was still unconscious, but Dr. Pick assured them he would be fine after some healing time.

Jake made his exit to go home without visiting with his dad. Margaret was due to have their baby soon and the pregnancy had its difficulties. Castor was now passed the time of danger, so Jake went home to take care of his wife. He cried some of his leftover hurts out before getting home to Margaret and her trouble.

28

Back at the Farm

onday morning, Frank assigned Beto full-time to fill in the trenches Castor had dug. He rented a small packing machine normally used to compress hot asphalt on highway construction. Beto pushed dirt into the trench with the tractor, leveled it then rolled it down tight, then repeated the process until the trenches were filled. In less than two days, all the trenches that took nearly two weeks to dig, Beto had filled in and packed tight enough for the mobile home to be pulled out when the time came. The new house was well under way. It was roughed in and sheetrock was hung. It was time to brick the outside and finish the inside. Ashley and Bianca visited the house daily to inspect the progress.

***

I was able to go home on Wednesday afternoon to the loving attention of Ashley and Bianca. I had gotten used to the crutch on smooth and level flooring; I had walked the halls of the hospital visiting other patients and pestering the nurses. Even though they said they would miss me, I think the hospital staff was happy to see me go. But now I had the task of using the crutch on rough or soft ground.

When I got home, the first thing I did was walk around in the yard for a few minutes. After I was sure of my skills with the crutch, I invited Ashley and Bianca to walk with me to the kidding pens. I had a pronounced limp and my left arm was in a sling, but I decided not to use the crutch, leaning a little on Ashley instead.

"Bianca, see that half-grown kid over there?" I pointed to the young Boer billy I had bought in the spring along with his mother.

"Yes, I do. He is a beautiful animal that I have admired many times and played with him some. What about him?"

"He's a show animal. He needs someone to train him and show him. Know anyone up for that?" I looked at Bianca who seemed deep in thought.

Finally she spoke, "If you win at a show, you get to sell your animal for a lot of money, right?" Bianca didn't shift her gaze from the goat.

That's right. College money." I kept my eyes on the goat, shifting occasionally to Bianca's face.

"OK. I'm up. What do I do?" Bianca still hadn't shifted her gaze.

"Well, you make sure he eats right. Lots of roughage along with a moderate amount of high-protein grain. I'll help you figure that out. Then you work him regularly to make sure he is getting plenty of exercise and learning the right stuff to show well."

"When do I start?"

I had to smile, "I've seen you out here playing with him. You started a long time ago. He trusts you. Now just keep on being a friend and teach him what he needs to know to show well. Talk to him using simple words and phrases and at least once a day, cup your hands over his nose and breathe in his nostrils so he never forgets your voice and your smell. Then start teaching him to lead with his head up. We'll see about getting you into the local FHA chapter. The lady who runs it showed animals as a youngster. She can help."

Bianca climbed over the fence, went into the feed shed for a short rope, then climbed into the run. Ashley moved close to me from the right, and put her arm around me holding on to my waist. "Daddy, I think my work here is done for a while. I think you are a great dad again; you didn't need me to tell you anything. I just had to push you to do what you already know to do. I have a job starting August fifteenth that I need to get situated for. I need to leave at the end of next week."

I looked into the face of the woman who used to be my little girl. I felt very proud of who she had become. I reveled in the wisdom of this child of mine. Then I looked at the young girl struggling to get a rope on a young show-goat and felt a mixture of pride in being selected to raise either and both of them, and sheer terror at what I still felt I didn't know. "I guess I can call for advice?"

Ashley laughed, "Of course, Daddy, any time. But your instincts are good and you love her. You need to tell her at times."

I got very serious for a moment. "I know the time to tell her about female things is not far in the future. I will need help with that."

"You are OK for a while, daddy. She's way shy of ninety pounds. Right now, she is still a little girl who needs a daddy to admire and take care of. And when the time comes, she will pin you down with questions. Do you remember when I asked you those questions?"

I grinned in remembrance, "Yes, I do. That is why I know I need help."

"Daddy, you did fine, and you will do well with her, but call me when you need to."

Jasmine and Marianna came for a two-day stay that weekend. Monday was a holiday from school. When Bianca told them about the goat, they both expressed the wish that they could raise a goat for show too. After the girls were finished giggling and bedded down for the night, I made some calls to their parents. Monday morning early, over Ashley's objections, I loaded all three girls into my truck and headed for Lometa pulling the borrowed horse trailer with Big Red in one side. I was driving with one arm so I steered and worked the clutch and brake and taught Bianca to shift for me when I signaled her. Very soon, she was very good at anticipating when to shift and made few mistakes with which gear. We stopped at the Dairy Queen in Lampasas for lunch and ice cream, but by dusk that same day, Red was back home with Gus the man, and three young girls were beginning a training regimen with their goats for the fall stock show. Gus, the man, was happy to trade even up Old Red for two more kid billys. When we stopped for the evening, I was in considerable pain from the day, but feeling good in my soul. The goats were expensive, but I felt they were worth the trouble. Ashley and I watched the three girls chasing their goats around having a great time. I said, "You know, there is nothing in this world that heals a man's soul better than helping a child."

Ashley hugged me and said, "You better be careful. You will end up with more kids than you bargained for."

"I'll deal with that better than I have with not having any kids around, I think. Bianca has shown me how much I have been missing." I held Ashley's face in my hands and looked in my daughter's eyes, "And you, you beautiful lady, you have reminded me how much fun I had being a dad."

A few minutes later, Billie drove up with Jimmy and Caryn. Billie was looking tired and haggard.

"I need some time alone," was all she said. Suddenly, I had six children and was all crippled up. Thankfully, four were old enough and willing to help with the two younger ones.

After supper, reading, and prayers, I kissed Bianca on the forehead, tousled two other wet heads and wished them all good-night then turned to leave. Bianca stopped me with, "Mr. Trevor...uh Dad, wait!"

I turned around facing three grinning girls each with wet hair and each holding a hairbrush out to me. "Okay. Okay. Into the living room, all of you." With one arm injured, brushing long, wet, tangled hair was a daunting task and pony-tails were impossible. Ashley agreed to join the party to do the hair arranging. Jasmine was first.

I brushed carefully pulling out tangles as gently as I could while Jasmine giggled at having a man brush her hair. "My dad would never do this," she quipped, "He would think it isn't manly."

"Ask him sometime," I challenged, "he might surprise you."

Something caught my eye that I wished was not familiar. Jasmine had head lice, a full nest of several behind her right ear. I stopped brushing and quickly checked Marianna and Bianca. They were all three infested with lice and nits, and all three had very beautiful, long, and thick black hair, perfect nesting places for head lice.

Ashley drove to town for the special shampoo, nit combs and a bottle of olive oil. She also woke Wilber Chainey to sell her three more sets of sheets, pillowcases and blankets. It was midnight before the girls and I finished stripping beds and placing all the bedding in plastic bags, while Ashley shampooed each head again and doused them with olive oil after they were dry. The shampoo was to kill the live lice. Olive oil was to keep nits from clinging to hair. If any more eggs were laid by a surviving louse, the glue the louse used to stick the egg to a hair would be rendered useless. Loose eggs would simply be combed out of the hair. Bagging the bedding was to let any live lice or nits live out their short lives and die. I warned the girls to be ready in the morning to wear plastic hair covers while they herded the goats and sprayed them for lice. "Training," I said with authority, "will be interrupted for three days while the spray works its magic."

It was after ten the next morning before I climbed out of bed. I was very sore and stiff from the wounds and from the renewed activity. When

I rolled out, I found myself facing three smiling girls waiting, fed, and dressed for battle in hooded plastic raincoats, and rubber boots. They giggled all through my breakfast and the delousing of the goats. After examining Gus, I sprayed him also. The old donkey stood with his head up, shaking his skin at the spray, but he offered no resistance. He seemed to understand that this was something done for him and not done to him.

None of the people delousing goats were aware of the dark little man with a black, pencil-thin moustache sitting on a mesquite limb just inside the edge of the woods holding binoculars in his left hand as he watched them working and playing. After the delousing was done, the girls went into the house for a bath and snacks. The little man winced at the pain in his right arm as he climbed down. He stood for a few moments as if deciding what to do next while he allowed the pain to subside. Seething in his hatred for a man and a little girl, he left, but vowed to return at a better time.

The remainder of the ninety days passed without incident.

29

Ninety Days Are Up

$\mathcal{A}$t the Ninety-day hearing, Judge Peterson heard from Ms. Gomez first. While she testified, she blushed every time she looked at me or said my name. Ashley's new boyfriend, Everitt, had driven her to witness the event and sat on Ashley's right. Bianca had asked to sit with me instead of with the social workers. I sat between Ashley and Bianca. Jake and his swollen wife sat on the audience bench directly behind us. They had driven to be with us even though the baby was due the next day. While Ms. Gomez was talking, I could not keep my eyes off her. Bianca saw the look on my face and I think, suddenly realized what it meant. She elbowed me in the ribs, and whispered, "Stop it. You are staring! And you are embarrassing me!" I looked at her and rolled my eyes. Billie Cloud, Jimmy, and Caryn were in the audience of about fifty people. Frank Castillo and his entire crew, except for three men left on guard duty, were there to witness. The house was within a month of being totally completed and landscaped. Since they were ahead of schedule, they had taken a day off. After they had helped ward off Tio Flaco, and since Bianca had become the sweetheart of the crew, Frank and his men felt they had a stake in this outcome.

After Ms. Gomez reported, Don Stence stood and reported to the judge that all the required paperwork was completed and that I had begun adoption proceedings. I started at that announcement. I almost stood because I hadn't talked with Don about adoption. Bianca poked me again and whispered, "I told him to start the adoption. I told him I wanted to adopt you, but he says it doesn't work that way. Do you mind?"

"Well, no, I guess it's OK, but shouldn't we talk about it first? Are you sure?" I stammered in a whisper but loud enough to get a glare from Judge Peterson.

"OK, let's talk later. And yes, I am sure! Keep talking and you will be contempted again. Behave yourself! I don't want to feed all those goats by myself!" I sat still through the rest of the proceedings with my head spinning at this new development. Ashley smiled at the friendly drama between Bianca and me, and at the whirlwind I had innocently walked into.

Judge Peterson asked if there were any present who had any witness to prevent me from being appointed legal guardian with sole permanent custody. No one spoke. His gavel fell and he pronounced the deal done.

"That sounded almost like a marriage ceremony!" I exclaimed to Bianca as we walked over to sign papers.

"Well, Mr. Castor Trevor, it is probably even more serious than a marriage. Do you know what kind of trouble you can get into if you don't take good care of me? I am just a little kid, you know."

"Wait a minute!" I countered, "If I can't call you a kid, then you can't hide behind it either!"

"Oh yes I can. I'm a female kid." Our laughter at something between just the two of us seemed a good omen to everyone else.

We signed papers and on the way out I caught Ms. Gomez by the arm and extracted a promise of help anytime I needed it. Bianca rolled her eyes at me and punched me in the ribs again. Ms. Gomez gave me her card then turned and left with a glance at me over her shoulder as she walked away. The glance built a fire in my insides and turned my face red. When I turned the card over, there was a private cell-phone number already written on the back with a message, "Please call." My bladder almost released when I realized what that meant. When I showed it to Bianca, she also realized what it meant and suddenly got quiet.

THE TALK

Goodbyes were said on the courthouse steps. Ashley and Jake both went back to their separate lives leaving Bianca and I alone with Lizbet. The ride home was very quiet. Bianca sat in the passenger seat without talking or answering. She seemed to be deep in thought, or angry. I could not figure out which. I tried a couple of times to get through the wall, but it stood firm. I continued to talk to her while I was wondering what her silence meant. With my ex-wife, silence meant she was about to give me a good tongue lashing. With Ashley or Jake, it usually meant they had a question they were figuring out how to ask. When we got to the mobile home, the walk inside was quiet also. Bianca's great grandmother welcomed us home. Bianca gave her a very brief account of the proceedings in Spanish. Lizbet grabbed Bianca and hugged her talking rapidly in Spanish. Bianca did not return the hug. She continued the silence toward me.

A few moments after we arrived at the house, Lizbet told me supper was ready. I called Bianca to the table and commented on the wonderful odor of caldo de pollo. When she was seated, I was ready with my speech and my questions, "Bianca, I promised the judge that I would take good care of you. I don't make promises lightly. I will take the best care of you that I know how to, but Bianca, I can't do my best work when you go hide from me. I think you have hidden away from me because I think I like Ms. Gomez and I let you see that. Maybe I shouldn't have let you inside my secrets like that, but Bianca, I don't plan to keep secrets from you, even when I enjoy a beautiful lady. I guess I should tell you right now, I am enjoying being with the most beautiful lady I know. I enjoy you. I love being with you more than anyone I know. Do you like being with me?"

"Yes, I like being with you."

"Are you afraid you will lose me, or that I will get rid of you if I fall in love with another woman?"

"No...yes...I'm not sure...yes, I guess I am. You see," she said suddenly looking me in the eyes, "I kinda thought...well, that you wait for me. You know, until I'm old enough."

I was trying to keep my voice very kind and serious. "Bianca, you honor me." My voice faltered a little then became very steady as I held both her hands in mine. "You asked me to be the one to take care of you, and now you have volunteered me to be your dad. Those things I can do...I think...at least I will try hard, but I'm thirty-nine years older than you. Even if it were legal, when you are old enough to marry...that is, after college, you will be twenty-three and full of the beginning of life. I will be over sixty and on the other end of life. As much as I love you, and that is a lot, allowing you to marry a man my age would be so unfair to you that as your adopted father, I can't allow it."

"Wow!" Bianca exclaimed with a frown, "I didn't know you were *that* old."

"Hey, hey!" I warned, in a much lighter voice, "I'm not ready for a wheel chair yet!" In a few moments, we were talking about other things, and laughing at the events of the day. Every little bit, Bianca would assume a pensive attitude, then return to the good time we were enjoying. Finally, she spoke after a pensive time, "I guess being your daughter is the proper thing for me. It is the best for both of us."

"Well, it will be much like a marriage. There will be good times and there will be hard times, but if we work together, we will thrill at the good times and make it through the hard ones in good shape."

I GET A NEW NAME

After the evening meal, Bianca stopped on her way to her room and came back. "Mr. Trevor?"

"Yes, Bianca."

She got a mischievous look in her eye, "You don't have to feel like you have to wait on me. I'll find someone younger, *much younger.*"

I grinned, "Keep in mind that I have veto power." Just as I turned around to go to my room, she tackled me knee-high from behind. I fell like a damp log and rolled to my back.

"I know what 'veto' means," Bianca said sitting on my stomach, "You do not have veto," she said tickling my ribs. Soon we were rolling on the floor like any father and daughter might. Bianca was squealing and giving the tussle all she had, I cradled her to protect her from bumping her head or getting hurt, like any good father would. We were laughing like two kids. Bianca stopped suddenly and sat up on the floor beside me, with a serious look on her face, "If you marry Ms. Gomez, what *will* you do with me?"

I smiled at her, "If I get married, and that is a big 'if,' I will still need a maid."

"Does that mean I will get paid?" There was mischief in Bianca's smile, "Or else I would not be a daughter. I would be a slave."

I answered on the lighter side of serious, "Well, little Miss Bianca, you are my daughter until death do us part. You will not be able to get rid of me even if you want to, and I certainly will not be giving you up for another woman. If it were to work out between another woman such as Ms. Gomez and myself, you have to approve, or the deal is off. Agreed?"

"No, that is too much on me. If you find another woman, and you want to marry her, I will go along. I just hope it is someone like Ms. Gomez because I do like her. Are we going to ask her out?"

"Yes, we are."

"Can I call you 'Papa,' now?"

"Wh..wha..what? Why?" I was suddenly confused by the question that seemed unconnected, "Is this a promotion? Yeah. Of course you can call me whatever you want, but please settle on something. What does this mean?"

"I don't know exactly how to say this in English, but 'Daddy' is the way little girls call their fathers the best name they know in English. It is closer than 'dad' or 'father.' In Spanish, the best name is 'Papa.' It is the most dearest name a girl can call their father in Spanish. It means 'love,' I think. You are the most dearest man. So, is it OK? I would like it. My real father was never a papa, not to me."

I bowed my head with my hands in my lap, humbled by this turn in the conversation. As much as I tried not to be, I was choked up...again. It was hard to talk with my throat closing. "Yes. I think that would be fine," I finally said quietly. "In fact, I like it. I like your explanation." My answer came out kind of squeaky. A little more under control, I continued, "You have changed my life. I didn't know I was so alone until you came along and broke into my solitude. You have made me so very uncomfortable," I said, stronger now, as I stood. "But, little mija, as much as it hurts, being uncomfortable has been and is good for me. I thought I was helping *you*, and taking care of you, but *you* are making *me* whole again. *I* am the one who is being helped." Bianca stood, hugged me around the waist and looked up into my face with a puzzled look on her's.

"What is that?"

"What is what?"

"That word you said, 'saltitute.'

"Sol-i-tude," I corrected, "it is very much like the Spanish word 'solo.' It means all alone. It usually means all alone on purpose."

"That's kinda sad."

"Yes, mija, that is very sad. But no more solitude. You have broken in and destroyed my selfish solitude."

"It's OK."

"What is OK?" I asked, again confused.

"You can call me 'mija.' It is a special name fathers call their little girls. Now, we both have special names."

Great-grandmother, Lizbet Buentello, stood at the door to the kitchen holding her hands over her mouth smiling at the word exchange she didn't fully understand, but in her heart she understood very well. She understood that Bianca and I were becoming a family. She smiled in understanding and approval.

Jake called the next day to announce the birth of Jason Edward Trevor. I noted the initials, JET. "If he is anything like his dad, he will live up to the title. How's the little mama?" Jake hesitated. Alarmed, I continued, "I can tell there is a problem. What is it?"

"Dad, Jason is very sick. Margaret is fine, but we don't know if Jason will make it."

"We are on the way. Is there anything I...uh, we can do?"

"Yes, I would really like it if you and Ashley came. The doctors say we will know more in the next thirty-six hours."

"I will call Ashley, and we will be there as fast as we can legally get there. What hospital?" After getting directions, I called Ashley. She said she was not very far, so she would meet me at the hospital. I told Bianca about the problem when we were underway. She wept most of the two hours we drove.

We met Ashley in the lobby of the hospital. Through tears and in a shaky voice, she said in the past two hours, the baby had taken a turn for the worse. The doctors did not give much hope. I ran to the waiting room to see Jake. He was in the infant ICU visiting with the doctor. After a few minutes wait, a shaken and pale Jake came to the waiting room and took us to see Margaret. She was devastated and had to be sedated. Jake and Margaret both had puffy eyes from crying.

Ashley, Bianca, Jake and I spent the night in tearful prayer at the foot of Margaret's bed. She awoke intermittently asking about her baby. Through the night, there was no news. No further deterioration in his condition, and no measurable progress. I was allowed to visit him briefly around three in the morning. He seemed peaceful enough, but appeared to be struggling to breathe. I could not shake a feeling of total helplessness in the face of the illness of this little boy that was my flesh and blood. Jake slept for a few minutes, Bianca slept for a short time on a chair brought by a nurse.

Around eight am, Dr. Ferguson came in the room. He spoke of the strength and determination of the little boy and announced a small improvement in his oxygen levels. He still gave little hope. We said a prayer of thanksgiving, then I took Bianca and Ashley to breakfast leaving Jake and Margaret to speak with each other privately. We brought Jake a plate of eggs and sausage from the cafeteria around nine. We also brought some strong coffee for both he and Margaret.

Ashley, Bianca, and I went to the waiting room to find a place to rest and let Jake and Margaret have their time. Jake woke me up at two pm with a smile and tears on his face. He told me Jason's oxygen level was almost normal and he was resting well. I had been very stoic and in control up until that point. When I got the news the baby was out of danger, I broke down into a weeping heap praying my thanks to God and comforted by my two daughters who wept with me. I think at that moment, the bridge between Bianca and I was totally crossed. I knew in that moment that we would be family, for better or worse until death do we part. My commitment was not one of finances, education, and physical care, it was one of love from the heart, love of a man for his daughter and a daughter for her father.

We met in Margaret's room for a celebration. Of course, the food chosen for celebration, was vanilla ice cream. Ashley, Bianca, and I checked into a motel for the night and slept soundly. The next morning we visited with Margaret as she nursed Jason for the fourth time. All the doctors could do is celebrate and pronounce Jason healthy enough to go home the next day. They had no explanations for his illness or recovery. With Jake's blessing and thanks, Bianca and I left for home. Ashley stayed another day to help with the transition home.

30

Homesick For Isidro

The second night we were home after returning from seeing Jason, a few minutes after midnight, Bianca awakened me sobbing. "I had a dream," she said when she was calm again. "My brother was lost and in danger. Tio Flaco was beating him. He was calling for me. I have been so selfish taking care of myself that I have almost forgotten him. Can you find him and bring him here too?"

"I don't know whether we can find him or not, mija, and if we do find him, I don't know what we could do for him. Did Flaco beat him when you were with your parents?"

"No, I never saw Tio Flaco pay any attention to Isidro."

"OK, we will see what we can do. Could we start tomorrow? I don't think we could get anything done tonight."

"Can I sleep in here with you tonight? I'm still a little scared, and I'm feeling lonely."

"Tell you what. I will read you a good book so you can fall asleep here, and then I will take you back to your room."

Bianca snuggled comfortably against my side while I sat up and read Aesop's Fable of the "Fox and Tiger." Shortly after the Fox stopped his trek through the woods, and asked whether the tiger was convinced that he was the most feared animal in the forest, Bianca was sleeping soundly. I found it difficult to leave her alone; it felt much like times that Jake or Ashley had bad dreams or were sick. I carried her to her room and tucked her in. She woke up enough to reach up and hug me. It wasn't much, just a hug, but it made me all soppy inside. I made a pallet outside her door so I could be close in case she awoke again. Shortly before dawn, Lizbet woke me on her way to fix breakfast. I went back to bed for a nap. When I awoke, a smiling Bianca and Lisbet had breakfast on a tray to serve me in bed. I thought, *I could get used to this very quickly.*

Later that morning, I called Juan, the former XIII member, to find out what could be done to find Bianca's brother, Isidro. "Let me see what I can do. I'll take a little trip. When I get back, I will give you a bill for my detective services." was all Juan answered.

Three days later, Juan called at the Trevor farm to report what he had found out. He said he found Isidro and his parents in the same little village to which he had delivered Tio Flaco. He said he had seen the boy, and it appeared he was healthy. He was a good student in school, and a favorite among all the mothers in the neighborhood where he lived. Juan reported seeing Isidro going from house to house with a group of boys on Saturday morning, being fed freshly made tortillas and tacos by the mothers of his friends, and playing soccer in the street.

Bianca was satisfied he was being cared for, but still she missed him.

31

The Date

wo weeks after the hearing, I still had not called Ms. Gomez. Finally, tired of the prodding of Bianca and the animated encouragement of Lizbet, I found the courage to call Ms. Gomez. Bianca sat on the couch so she could listen to the conversation.

"Hello, Ms. Gomez?"

"This is Castor Trevor, Bianca Gonzalez' guardian. I, uh, well, I called to ask you a question about Bianca." Bianca doubled her fist and shook it in my face. "Well, she's been wanting me to...actually, I've been wanting to call to...to...well to ask you to a minner and dovie." I sat down because of my trembling knees, and flustration. Bianca sat down mouthing, "Calm down." I was in too deep now to withdraw, so I continued.

"No, wait…let me try again. Would you like to go to a movie and to dinner…Why are you laughing? What? Oh, yes of course I would want to bring Bianca along…well because I don't trust a babysitter…actually, I don't know any babysitters." I knew that she knew this was a lie because Lizbet was living with us.

Bianca hissed, "Don't mess this up! She doesn't care about babysitters and I don't want to go!" She shook her fist at me again, but I turned away from her to listen, then back to face her. Lizbet stood at the door quietly watching and smiling as Bianca told her what was happening.

I covered the speaker end of the phone and whispered loudly, "You have to go. I won't know what to say!"

Bianca just shrugged and sat down on the sofa shaking her head and muttering, "este hombre, este hombre! Should we take Abuelita also, so you can feel safer?"

Quickly back to the phone, I realized I had covered the wrong part of the phone and Stephanie had probably heard everything. "Yes? Oh, great! How about Thursday night?...Oh, wait. That's a school night. Well, how about Friday?...Great, I'll see you then." I quickly hung up the phone and sat down relieved that the ordeal was over and that she had said yes.

"What time is it?" Bianca seemed to be trying to make a point.

"It's five thirty. There's a clock right there on the wall."

"What time is your *date*?" she asked emphatically.

"I don't re…wait, I should have set a time."

Bianca nodded her head and pointed at the phone. "Call her back. And calm down. She said yes! And, by the way, it is summer. I don't go to school in the summer. Where is your head?"

"I didn't remember how hard this could be! OK, I'll call her back." Pacing the floor with Bianca sitting on the sofa grinning at me, I redialed the number. "Ms. Gomez? Yes, it's me again. That's right, I forgot to set a time. Six will be fine; I mean, how about we pick you up at six? That will give me time to get the chores done and Bianca should be finished with homework. Supper will have to be a bit early but I can manage that..." Bianca rolled her eyes. "Oh, that's right. Where will we eat?...OK, uh, well I'll surprise you. Well, I'll see you at six on Friday, and thanks. Oh, wait, where do you live? 632 Redbrook Drive, apartment 107?" I was repeating for Bianca's benefit, hoping she could remember the information. "OK, I got that. We'll be there on Siday at Frix."

After I hung up, Bianca started in. "Honestly, you are about as romantic as Gus the donkey! I'm very surprised she agreed to see you. I still don't go to school in the summer and I don't have homework. We are going to have to work on getting you ready for this date! We are going to have to teach you to talk! Siday at Frix? AYYYYYY!"

After so many mistakes, I was resigned to being coached. I simply answered, "OK." Lizbet laughed out loud, then covered her mouth with her apron and turned to the kitchen. I noted that I had never heard her laugh before, actually it was more of a cackle. "I'm glad you see this as entertaining, Senora!" I was mixing embarrassment with just a little anger. I heard her muffle another laugh amidst the rattling of a skillet being placed on the kitchen stove.

***

Lizbet stood at the kitchen window waving her apron in a 'good luck, goodby' when Bianca and I drove over the cattle guard heading for town at about five-thirty on Friday. We appeared at Ms. Gomez' apartment at six sharp. When Stephanie answered the door, I was speechless. I just stood and stared at her face with my mouth not quite closed. Bianca had coached me about what to say, but try as I might, I couldn't remember Ms. Gomez being as lovely as she was at that moment. My tongue would not move. All I could muster was, "Hi."

Stephanie read my expression and asked, "What? Is my hair out of place?"

"N..no!" I replied finding part of my voice, but since my mind had gone numb, that was all I could say. She reached for my hand and took the bouquet of wildflowers that Bianca and I had picked from the farm and Bianca had arranged. She turned to allow me into the room, smelled the flowers and pretended to receive a pleasant fragrance. I knew the bouquet was very pretty, but I also knew her pretense at a pleasant fragrance was an act of graciousness. Most of the pretty wild-flowers in Texas do not have a pleasing odor. That knowledge of her grace in the moment gave me some encouragement and put my mind back into gear. Stephanie Gomez seemed very impressed that a goat farmer and a young girl could work together to produce such a pretty arrangement. Under pressure later, she admitted the odor was 'weedy,' but right then, she quickly put the flowers in a vase while I waited at the door gathering my composure and controlling my urge to kick myself or stomp on my own foot.

Bianca waited in the pickup shaking her head at what she saw and I think wishing she could be almost anywhere else at that moment. Then for a moment, she later told me, she remembered Tio Flaco and what I had gone through for her. She decided at that moment, maybe she was exactly where she wanted to be. It was obvious that I needed help. I escorted Stephanie to the pickup, opened the door for her and helped her in on the right side. When Stephanie saw the seating arrangement, she blushed, but took her place and went along.

Bianca welcomed Ms. Gomez graciously and smiled knowingly. "Couldn't talk, could he?" Stephanie smiled sympathetically and gave a knowing nod communicating in the unspoken manner women have. Bianca rode in the middle, and I drove somewhat uncertainly to the Alamo Draft House where we could watch a movie and order dinner at the same time. I was too nervous to think about going to two different places. All during the trip to the Draft House, I talked. It was a nervous, one-sided conversation about the farm, the truck, Bianca, my goats, Stephanie's dress, and many other unconnected things I connected clumsily into the lecture. Bianca rolled her eyes at the barrage, and Stephanie stole a look at Bianca and rolled her eyes causing both of them to laugh at what I thought must have been something I had said, but their laughter confused me because I could not remember saying anything funny.

It was 'Nostalgia Night' at the Draft House. The menu was old-fashioned hamburgers with French fries and a bottled coke, and the movie was "Rebel Without a Cause" starring James Dean.

In the darkened theatre, I sat between the ladies and still talked more than I really wanted to until our sandwiches arrived. Then I resumed when I finished eating. When the movie started, Bianca dug her elbow into my ribs and whispered loudly, "Shut up! Will you be quiet for just a few minutes so we can hear the movie? Honestly, you are so out of control!" I drew comfort from being given permission to be quiet.

After the movie, I drove them to Wendy's for a chocolate Frosty. I was finally composed enough that I was no longer jabbering aimlessly, but it was still hard to breathe properly. From the time I stopped talking so much, I think it was an enjoyable evening for all, full of light talk and some giggling between the ladies. Around ten, I took Stephanie home and escorted her to the door. She kissed me on the cheek, blushed, told me she had a wonderful time, then quickly went inside.

Back in the pickup, Bianca started in on me immediately, "Papa, I have never been so embarrassed. I don't want to go on one of your dates again! You need to settle down and stop being so nervous. You are sooooo out of control. We need more training!"

My cheek was still stinging from Stephanie's brief kiss and my legs were trembling when I got back to the truck. I said, "Well, did you see her. She is so beautiful! When I saw how lovely she was, I couldn't talk, then when I got started talking I couldn't stop. But," I whimpered, "I thought it went very well. She kissed me on the cheek, did you see that!"

"Papa, sometimes you don't have a clue. She likes you. She was embarrassed because I was along. When you ask her out again, leave me out of it. You are on your own! Except that we will go back to trying to teach you what to say and how to act." Bianca sat with her arms crossed in a "don't argue with me, the issue is closed," posture.

A little later, I asked Bianca if I should call Stephanie and apologize. "No. Don't apologize. Honestly! Just ask her out on a real date! You deserve a night out and she deserves a real date; you owe her a real date. But, before you go out, we need to talk again. I have never been on a date, but I *am* a girl. I can give you a few more pointers if you will listen. This time, listen! You forgot everything when she answered the door! You did forget everything, didn't you?"

"Yeah, I know. But Bianca, she is so very beautiful and gracious. I guess I mess up trying not to mess up!"

For about an hour every day that week, Bianca coached me about proper conversation and attentiveness to Ms. Gomez for the next date. Sunday, I called her and asked for another date on Friday. This time, I was very careful and used the words that Bianca gave me. Once again she said, "Yes."
Ashley came home that weekend. She and Everitt arrived on Friday. They stayed with Bianca while I went out with Stephanie. Bianca and Ashley both coached me for a few minutes before I left. This time, I ordered some pleasant scented flowers from Wendy's Fragrant Floral.

***

Bianca waited up for him to get home, much like a nervous father waits up for his daughter on her first date. She watched TV for a while, read without reading for a while, looked out the window often, and walked around the house. Lizbet came and sat down with her on the couch. After a few minutes of silence, she said in Spanish, "He will be fine!"

Bianca answered, "I know. But why do I worry? He is a grown man and can do very well without me."

"Mija, that is the problem, I think. Every little girl wants her papa to be only theirs. I think you are worried that if he falls in love with Senorita Gomez, perhaps he won't be your papa anymore; that in some ways, she will take over and you will have less of him."

"Si' Abuelita, that has been part of my thinking. But there is a loneliness in Papa that I think cannot be filled by a daughter, no matter how much she loves him."

"Es verdad, Mija. You are very observant and wise. Mr. Trevor is a good man and he needs a good woman to fill that loneliness. You cannot. A daughter has a different part of a papa's heart that cannot be filled by even a good woman. So, understand that when he finds that good woman and hopefully gets married, he will still be your papa. That will not change.

You have his heart as a daughter, and you will always have his heart, that part of his heart reserved for a daughter. Be calm and understand that. You are a very lucky girl to have the heart of such a man. Also, Mija, I think Mr. Trevor is a very lucky man to have such a good and wise daughter." Bianca looked into the eyes of her great grandmother seeing the wisdom of years of living and watching. The two sat in silence for a while lost in their own thoughts.

The spell was broken when Bianca saw pickup lights turn in to the farm gate and bounce up and down as the front tires rolled over the cattle guard. She jumped up and ran to the window. She watched him park then jump out of the truck and walk with a light step to the front door. When Castor came inside, Bianca hugged him and demanded a full report. At the same time, she noticed his clothes were wet. "Yeah, ain't it great! Was his response when she scolded him for his wet clothes. Lizbet, her job done for the day, ambled off to bed for the night. Her heart was full at the result of her talk with Bianca, but still sorrowful for all that had happened to her great granddaughter.

***

"Well," I began, when I was in the house and it was time for the report, "we went to a real restaurant with linen napkins and everything." I could not stop smiling. That seemed a little disconcerting to Bianca. "You would have been proud of me." I continued. "I was the perfect gentleman; I did everything just like you instructed me. Then we were going to go to a movie, but she suggested we just go for a walk instead. I didn't know what to do. That was not part of the plan, but I said 'Okay.' So, we went to the park down by the bridge, and walked along the river for a long ways and talked. You know, she can talk about almost anything except goats."

Bianca rolled her eyes at the mention of goats, "You didn't start talking about goats? Please tell me you did *not* start talking about goats again!! We made a list of what you were supposed to talk about. Goats were not on that list!!"

"Well, that is what I know best!" I defended. "Anyway," I continued, "we skipped rocks off the water for a while, and waded in the stream.

Down in water up to our knees, she slipped and fell down in the water full length. She got completely soaked, even her hair. When I tried to pick her up, she accidently kicked my foot. I slipped on a wet rock and fell in on top of her. I think she thought I did it on purpose. I swear I didn't, but she grabbed me around the neck and kissed me. Bianca, she kissed me right there in the water. I think I went numb all over, I'm still shaking. Bianca, that was exciting. She kissed me!"

"Papa, you still don't have a clue." Bianca shook her head and laughed as she explained, "She didn't fall, and she *pulled* you in. I think she was waiting for you to kiss her, and since you wouldn't, she set it up."

I had to grin, "I thought so too. I just didn't think you would know. Ain't it great? But how do you know such things. You have never been on a date, and you are just a young sprout."

Bianca smiled mischievously "I don't have the experience, but I am female. If I were a woman, I would do just what she did. I would want to be alone with you, and I would know that I would have to push you into kissing me." Bianca's face grew serious again, "How long will it take you to ask her to marry you?"

"Whoa, Mija. Let me enjoy the first gear before you throw it into overdrive. I like her. I like her a lot. She scares me, and excites me at the same time. That is good chemistry, I think. But whether she can fit this family is a different question. That's a *very* different question. Let's take it easy; we'll go one step at a time. I made a big mistake once and don't want to again. Oh yeah, she's meeting us at church and coming here for lunch on Sunday."

***

Ashley and Bianca fixed lunch on Sunday after church. Since Lizbet took the day to be with Omar, they had crock-pot roast with potatoes, carrots, peas, and onions left to cook while we were gone to worship. A fresh vegetable salad, iced tea, and hot butter-milk pie rounded out the meal. Everitt made the pie using his grandmother's recipe and raised his stock considerably with me. Ms. Gomez, Stephanie, brought yeast rolls, homemade.

We got a great surprise. Jake and Margaret brought Jason to see his grandfather. I got to hold him for the first time. I felt like such a baby when I started weeping again as I held that precious package. As almost every baby had done when I first held them, he pooped enough to leak stinky brown gel out the edge of his diaper. It was great!!

After lunch, we all took a leisurely walk down to the kidding pen. I wanted to check on the animals and everyone else wanted to shake lunch down. Ashley gave me an approving smile when I put my arm around Stephanie's waist on the way and we walked as a couple. After seeing to the goats, we took a walk through the unfinished house. Jake took his family home late in the afternoon. I felt a surge of pride watching him change a diaper before they left. Knowing Jake loved his son enough to do the dirty work made me understand that he would be a great dad.

32

Moving In

Bianca started back to school on August eighteenth. I met with the homeroom teacher on the afternoon of the nineteenth. She gave me a list of several things I could do at home, in addition to helping with homework, to expand Bianca's vocabulary and improve her reading.

Bianca's and my routine quickly revolved around the school schedule. Bianca caught the bus to school at six thirty in the morning and was usually dropped off with Jasmine and Marianna at three forty-five. After a snack, the girls put the goats through their paces and fed them until around five thirty. After training, the girls came inside and ate the supper Lizbet had fixed by then. They attacked their homework with my help until a parent picked up Marianna and Jasmine at around eight. By nine, Bianca had showered and we had had some quality time reading and talking before she went to bed for the night. School days followed that routine until we were able to move into the new house. Weekends were more creative and less structured but just as busy.

THE NEW HOUSE

On Wednesday, September fifteen, Frank turned the keys to the new house over and arranged for the mobile home we had lived in for the past few months to be picked up on Monday the twentieth. Everything had been completed on the new house except for painting the walls, ceilings, and trim. I decided to do that part of the finish work myself to save some money and give Bianca and I some sweat equity in the house.

We had five days to get the finish work done, and move out of the mobile home into the new house. I arranged with Frank for Juan and Beto to come on Saturday to help paint and move the big things, then I arranged with Jasmine and Marianna's parents for the girls to spend the weekend to care for their animals and help with the move. I thought boarding them would be easier and cheaper than taking them back and forth, and I knew they would work hard. Meanwhile, I attacked the trim painting and had it and the walls and ceilings of two rooms completed shortly after noon on Friday. I took the afternoon to shop for the supplies and paint I would need to equip six people for painting the remainder of the inside of the house.

Around eight that Saturday morning, Stephanie showed up in old jeans and a loose green t-shirt and her hair tied back with a red scarf. I had told her what we were doing and when, but I had not tried to involve her. For a moment, her presence scared me because I thought she might have come in an official capacity concerning Bianca. She soon convinced me she came to help. I was glad for the help, but more, I was excited to be around her in this more homey kind of endeavor and it excited me that she was comfortable enough to insert herself; it was like she felt she belonged. When Bianca saw her drive up, she looked at me with a knowing smile and gave me a thumbs up.

Jake and Ashley both showed up at about nine. I wasn't expecting either of them, but both brought extra hands. Margaret and Everitt also came ready to work. I was honored to be able to hold my grandson for a while, feeding and rocking him, and admiring him as he slept and the others worked around us. He was growing fast, and lucky for him, looking like his mother.

Shortly after noon on Saturday, the painting was complete. Lunch, and then moving small things began. Before six-thirty, the move was complete. Most of the items moved had found a place in the new house and the mobile home was ready for movers. I took everyone out for dinner to celebrate a job well done and quickly. When I asked the girls where they wanted to eat, they chose Louie's Steak House. The men and I were very happy their favorite eating place wasn't the Pizza Palace. Juan, Beto, Jake, Everitt, and I were ready for some real food, which to us meant beef.

Billie Cloud drove up with Caryn and Jimmy. She met us at the cattle guard just inside the front gate as we were leaving. She helped me load them into my pickup without a word. She did not speak or answer when I asked for details. I worried about her. I noticed the daggers she stared at Stephanie and wondered what that meant. I guessed she was afraid she would lose her babysitter if I got serious about a woman.

At Louie's we had a joyous time eating, telling stories, and laughing. I made sure of Jimmy's food, and Stephanie took over caring for Caryn. None of the stories got very serious. Everyone but me enjoyed the story Bianca told of my first date with Stephanie Gomez, but Lizbet laughed out loud again at the memory of my nervousness and Stephanie blushed at the accuracy of the story. Then Bianca told an embellished story of me threatening Flaco when Flaco was armed with a pistol and I had only a water-hose. Most everyone was mesmerized by the story, but saw little humor. Shortly before we left, the restaurant owner-manager, Louie Pedraza, came to the table to see what the noise was all about. Soon he was sitting with us, enjoying the tales and contributing stories from the restaurant. He did not allow me to pay for the meals. He said he had heard about the incidents with Flaco, but was glad to hear it from the actors themselves, and he wanted to thank the man who stood up for a little girl when not even her parents would. He said the stories were much better than he had heard second and third hand and asked if he could come to the Trevor farm and meet Gus. I readily agreed, but warned him that Gus did not like strangers, and added, "...and so far as I can tell, you are about as strange as they come." Everyone had a good laugh at Louie's expense, but Louie was very serious about the visit. Before dark, Ashley and Jake left to go back to their other lives. I was sorry to see them go, but still swelled with pride at the sight of my children.

Monday was usually a slow day at the steak house. Louie came out to the farm in the afternoon and admired Gus and the goats. He was very impressed with the work ethic of the three girls and complimented them profusely. He stayed long enough to take over the kitchen from Lizbet and fix a pasta dish for supper that everyone enjoyed.

33

CPS Comes in Again

On Thursday, the twenty-third, Jasmine and Marianna jumped off the bus at a dead run hollering for me. Alarmed at not seeing Bianca, and seeing their agitation, I ran to meet them. The girls were excited and scared at the same time. They both chattered at once so that I could not understand anything more than there was a problem with CPS and Bianca. I made them sit down on the ground and take a few deep breaths, then talk one at a time. The all-too familiar pain in my chest started again.

They told of a CPS worker meeting with Bianca and both of them at school, then taking Bianca with them at a little past noon. I immediately called Don Stence.

"Castor, what has happened? What could have stirred them up again?" I told him of the routine since school started and the move. He could think of nothing that could attract the attention of CPS. Don asked me to just wait for him or CPS to call back. For the next two hours, I paced the floor wondering what could be wrong and wondering where they could have taken Bianca. I helped Jasmine and Marianna take care of their goats, brought them sandwiches, chips and drinks at five-thirty, then continued pacing the floor and worrying. Marianna's aunt picked the girls up about six. The constable drove up at six fifteen. It was Bill Wagoner serving a warrant for my arrest for child endangerment.

Bill did not know anything except that he had a warrant and had to take me in. This time, he did not use handcuffs and allowed me to ride in the front seat. That told me what he thought of the charge. When we arrived at the county jail, no one would answer my questions about how Bianca was being treated or where she was. Using my one phone call privilege, I called Stephanie, told her everything, then asked her to call Don Stence. She put me on hold and called Don who recommended I serve the night in jail and calm down. He figured that way I would be brought before Judge Peterson the next morning first thing. The pain in my chest had radiated to my shoulder and jawbone.

The sharp pain in my chest stayed with me most of the night. Rubbing the pectoral muscles helped very little. I managed to get a jailer to give me an aspirin around ten that evening. That helped a little and I slept well.

Don was already in the courtroom when I was brought in. Judge Peterson came in with a scowl on his face at seeing me. He got right to business and asked for charges. I could not tell who the judge would be unhappy with. Assistant District Attorney Jackson read the charges of "Child Endangerment and lewd conduct with a minor." My mouth dropped open at the charges.

"Mr. Trevor, how are you this morning?" I still could not read the judge, "I'm very puzzled, your honor, and I'm worried about Bianca." The judge looked at me over his reading glasses, "How do you plead?" I answered quickly, "Not guilty, your honor."

"OK, Mr. Johnson, present your evidence."

"Your honor, Mr. Trevor has an open case with the Child Protection Service..."

The judge interrupted, "What? What child is named in that case?"

Mr. Jackson seemed to grow a bit and stood a little taller, "Why, the same Bianca Gonzalez, your honor."

"Mr. Jackson," the judge was waxing indignant, "you mean to tell me that CPS held that case open after it was dismissed in this court?"

"Yes, your hon…"

"Well, Mr. Jackson, you can just forget about that little piece of information, because it is inadmissible in my court!" He was getting loud and definitely speaking from indignation, "What other evidence do you have?"

"Well…well, your honor," he stammered, "it seems Mr. Trevor has had the girl in the presence of a known child offender, and he is accused of fondling her."

"Mr. Jackson, did you talk with the girl?"

"Yes, your honor, I did. I found the charges to be well founded."

"Let's start with the fondling charge. What evidence do you have?"

"The girl claims Mr. Trevor holds her hand, he holds her in his lap and hugs her, and in addition, he brushes her hair every night."

"Mr. Jackson, do you have any children?"

"Yes, your honor."

"Boys or girls?"

"Both, your honor. I have two girls and one boy."

"Mr. Jackson, may I assume that you never touch your children?"

"No, your honor. I mean, yes, I touch them."

"Mr. Jackson, have you ever bathed your little girls?"

"Yes, your honor, I have."

"So, you have seen your own girls naked?"

"Yes, your honor, but they are mine. They are my flesh and blood."

"Mr. Jackson, do you understand what full custody means?"

"Yes, your honor...I mean no...I mean I don't know what you are getting at."

"What I am getting at, is that your evidence so far, Mr. Jackson, is such that, if I accept it, you just convicted yourself of molesting your own daughters. Mr. Jackson, you are on very thin ice and it is a hot day."

"Your honor, the history..."

The judge was almost yelling, "I have already disallowed that history because it presents a false story! Mr. Jackson please present the rest of your evidence. The court's patience is running out quickly."

"Your honor, Mr. Trevor has taken the girl along with two other children, little girls, in the presence of a convicted child molester having lunch at Louie's Steak House. Mr. Albert Dunnaway also known as 'Beto' was convicted of having sex with a minor. He was present and sitting next to the child in question."

Mr. Jackson looked over at me, "Is this true?"

"Your honor, I don't know anything about the conviction, but yes, we had dinner with 'Beto' and another man. And yes, there were two other young girls there with us. We were celebrating the completion of moving in to our new house. Also, yes, Bianca sat next to Beto."

Don Stence stood. "If I may your honor, I can shed some light on the conviction of Mr. Dunnaway and we can dispense with this part of the evidence also."

"Please, Mr. Stence," Judge Peterson said as he glared at Mr. Jackson.

"Mr. Dunnaway," Don began, "*was* convicted of having sex with a minor. It was pressure by the young lady's father that brought charges to court. Mr. Dunnaway was nineteen at the time, and out of school. The young lady was sixteen and still in school. Mr. Dunnaway was convicted of statutory rape and sentenced to ten years in prison. He served five years in the pen and five more years on probation. He was twenty four when he got out of prison. The girl he was convicted of raping was twenty one when he got out. The day after he got out of prison, he and the girl were married. Nine years later, they are still married and have four children."

"Mr. Jackson, did you know what Mr. Stence just related to this court?"

"Yes your honor."

"Mr. Jackson, do you know what the word discernment means?...Never mind, I think I know that you could define the word without having the concept. Do you have any other evidence?"

"Yes, your honor, the girl told us Mr. Trevor holds hands with her regularly without her permission."

"Mr. Jackson, under what circumstances?"

Jackson cleared his throat and shifted nervously, "Wh, wh, When they are praying."

"When they are praying?"

"Yes, your honor."

"Mr. Jackson, do you have any evidence against Mr. Trevor that could not be brought against yourself?"

"Uh," Jackson scratched his head and looked at his list of charges and evidence again and adjusted his glasses, "No, your honor. It's just that this man has a history of abuse and this girl is not his."

"Mr. Jackson, are you a student of the law?"

"Yes, your honor, I am the Assistant District Attorney."

"You are an idiot. I find that there is no cause to hold Mr. Trevor in this matter. Case dismissed." The gavel ended the discussion with a bang. "Mr. Stence, I will entertain a motion to bring charges of false arrest against Mr. Howard and Mr. Jackson. Mr. Jackson, if you ever bring such a pile of innuendo into my court again, I will hold you in contempt of my court and you will spend time in jail. Do you get my drift?" Mr. Jackson could do no more than nod and wipe his sweating brow with an already wet hand-kerchief. He had no time to try to defend himself because the judge moved on. "Mr. Trevor, please feel free to go. And Mr. Trevor, please accept the apology of this court for this travesty visited upon you." In a much gentler tone, "Your little girl is in my chambers waiting for you. By the way, I think you are doing a marvelous job for her regardless of your history." The comment was definitely aimed at the Assistant District Attorney. Judge Peterson glared at the sweating Jackson as he raised his gavel again. This court is adjourned until one pm, at which time," he turned a withering glare on the prosecutor, "Mr. Jackson will bring a *real* case before the court or be in contempt!"

Mr. Jackson wiped his sweating brow again as he began looking through notes on his desk. I rushed to Judge Peterson's chambers with the judge following close behind rustling his robe.

After the 'hello' hugs and Bianca's excited report in which she said, "They asked me questions to try to make it look like you are bad."

I took her by the hand and said, "Come, Mija, let's go home." Judge Peterson stood by with a big smile and watched as we started out. "By the way, Judge," I looked him in the eye, "I understand you like to fish." The judge nodded assent. "If you are interested, sometime between my court appearances, I will take you to a place where there is a monster big mouthed bass that shows himself once in a while, but has eluded every attempt to catch him. He has a lot of brothers, sons and other kin-folk who are not so wily though."

The judge laughed and clapped me on the back. "You are on," he said, "if you can stay out of jail long enough for us to set it up!"

It was Friday about eleven am, so I went to the drive-through at Wendy's for a quick lunch for Bianca, then over her objections, delivered her to school.

Two weeks later, the local paper headlined the Director of CPS and the Assistant District Attorney jailed for false arrest. I was unaware. I didn't subscribe to the paper. Stephanie told me. On a Saturday early in October, Bianca and I took the judge and his older daughter fishing. He caught his limit amidst a lot of laughter and a good time. Judge Peterson took the time to visit the farm before going home. Gus ran to the fence threatening and stomping at the judge, but with Bianca's cajoling seemed to accept the man at a distance. The judge wisely kept that distance.

34

The Livestock Show

one of the three girls, had ever been to a livestock show before that late October. They were fascinated and a little frightened by the number of people and animals that all of a sudden were in a relatively small area and competing for a spotlight. All three girls got permission to go to the livestock show and compete as part of their schooling. They were away from school for five days and were not counted absent. All three were very happy with this unexpected freedom, but a little upset when I showed up with school assignments and books for each of them including a benchmark math test I would administer.

They spent their spare time during the days at the show wandering around to see the sights, currying and training their goats, watching the rodeo, and enjoying scary thrills from the myriad of roller coaster, ferris wheel, and whirling rides. Each day at eight to ten am and three to six pm, they met at the pens and attended to their school lessons with me supervising. I slept on a bed of hay in a borrowed horse-trailer in the parking lot of the Holiday Inn where the girls shared a double room on the fourth floor. Their window looked out over the parking lot where I slept. I made friends with the night clerk who promised to alert me of anything that might need my attention. I could see they didn't sleep much the first night, because when I woke them for breakfast at six am, they could hardly get up. Soon though, the excitement of the day to come took over and they began moving with a high degree of anticipation. They each showed their goats in the kid class on Thursday, but did not place. When the winners were announced, they had seen enough to know what they must do to do well the next year. None of the three agreed to sell their goats. They decided to show them the next year in the billy class and sell them after that.

BIANCA'S BIRTHDAY

That Thursday was the twenty-ninth of October. Bianca was too excited about the new adventure to recall that it was her birthday. Ms. Stephanie Gomez came to town and met us at Chucky Cheese carrying three large packages. The girls were having a great time teasing each other when the entire restaurant staff came to their table to sing happy birthday. I gave Bianca and her friends their presents in honor of Bianca's birthday. Each got two new pairs of boot-cut levis, a plaid western shirt with pearl snaps, a western hat, then a new pair of boots. Until that night, they had all dressed in the usual knee-length, ragged-out, denim shorts, muscle t-shirts, and tennis shoes. They wanted to wear flip-flops, but I just could not see it. Three giggling little girls went to the bathroom to change and came out cowgirls. Stephanie had packed a suitcase so she could spend Thursday and Friday nights with the girls. All three girls slept in one double bed giving Stephanie one by herself. The change and the excitement of the day caused another night of giggling by the three girls. All four ladies were puffy-eyed and still giggling at six am.

Luckily, Friday was a cool day and all three girls had completed the showing. The girls wore their new uniforms that afternoon while Stephanie and I escorted them around the fair grounds to look at everything they had missed during the week.

ESTHER

Late in the afternoon, we ran into Esther, a black girl who had come to the livestock show looking for her father. The girls had befriended her several times during the week when she did not seem to have money to buy food. She seemed to be in a state of desperation. They invited Esther to join us. She seemed happy to find a friendly set of faces.

Esther seemed to be a bright girl of twelve with a continuous sad look on her face. She seemed sad even when she smiled. Her sadness, her demeanor, and her clothing told Stephanie's practiced eye that there was trouble in her past and that she did not feel good about her prospects for the future. Stephanie invited Esther to walk around with us and have dinner. She shrugged and accepted with a muffled thanks. When I asked who she was with, she just shrugged again and said, "Nobody."

Stephanie sat Esther beside her and began a conversation that soon revealed what she suspected. Esther was almost alone and troubled. Her father, whom she had never met had been a cowboy, a bronc rider, in his younger days. She came to the livestock show in hopes he would be there and she could spot him. All she had was a picture of him taken fourteen years earlier. He was a tall, handsome man wearing a grey wide-brim Stetson hat, he was very dark and well built, with a smile that lit up the picture and seemingly, the young woman at his side. The young woman in the picture was Esther's mother who had died two months before of a gunshot wound. She had gotten caught in the crossfire between two warring gangs on the way home from grocery shopping. Esther was now living with an older sister who had three small children and did not really want Esther around. She had all she could handle with her own three children and a minimum-wage job. Stephanie gave Esther her number to call if she needed to talk, and the number of a social worker in her town who might be able to help. In addition, she called the social worker and left a message with Esther's name, address, and a little information. Since she had no place to stay for the night, Stephanie rented another room and let her stay in the room with Bianca, Mariana, and Jasmine. Again, there was little sleeping in that room. We bought tickets and put her on a bus home early Saturday morning. After breakfast, the three girls gave me a necklace made from three odd-shaped granite chips wrapped with copper wire and hung from a leather thong. They had wrapped the rocks in art class, then put them together on one piece of leather. I don't wear jewelry, but I wore that necklace.

HOME AGAIN

Saturday evening back at the Trevor goat farm, three very happy but exhausted girls put their goats away for the night and went to bed shortly after dark.

Not long after dark, Billie Cloud showed up with Jimmy and Caryn. Tired as I was, I was very happy to see the youngsters. Jimmy made a bee line to the pens to see Gus, who ran to the fence from the other side to greet him.

After seeing Bianca off to school on Monday morning, I loaded Jimmy, Caryn and Lucy in the pickup to make another trip to Lometa. Jimmy picked out a billy that was a son of Big Red. He was just as red as his father and although he wasn't yet as large as his father, he showed some of the same temperament. Jimmy wanted to keep the goat in the cab on the way home. Since he couldn't, he sat in the middle looking in the rear-view mirror. I had to adjust the mirror so he could watch the goat lying in the bed of the truck. When we arrived back at the farm, I had only to untie the goat. Jimmy, "Little Red," Gus, Lucy, and Brutus were together the rest of the day. It was two weeks before Billie came to pick the kids up. A laughing Caryn took her first wobbly steps from me to Bianca's open arms two days before Billie showed up. Bianca took her around and let her walk every chance she could, and Caryn loved showing off her new skill.

A NEW VISITOR

The cold and rainy January fourth of the new-year brought another challenge to the Trevor household. Around three in the morning, Bianca was awakened by knocking at the kitchen door. She woke me up to see who it was.

When I opened the door, a cold, shivering, and miserable Esther Rockingham stood outside in the rain. "I didn't know where else to go," was all she said as she stood outside. I grabbed her by the shoulders and pulled her inside. She was soaked, shivering, and began coughing uncontrollably. I sent her and Bianca to Bianca's room to get Esther into some dry clothes. Esther was considerably larger than Bianca, so I got a clean pair of jeans and a shirt from my closet for her. "I'm sorry to be a bother, but I just can't be alone anymore." She said between coughing spells. "Can I stay with you for a while? Bianca told me how you helped her. Would you help me?"

"Yes, child. I will help. I don't know what I can do, but I will do something. But first," speaking to Bianca as Esther had another coughing spasm, "Take her to your bathroom, get her into a hot bath, hot as she can stand it. I'll fix some hot soup and bring it up."

When I took the soup into Bianca's room, I also took a pair of soft pajamas and a robe. "I'm sorry, Esther, I don't have anything better than these…"

"Mister Trevor, I have been sleeping in bus stations and outside under bridges before I made up my mind to come here. These are wonderful." She hardly got the words out before another coughing spell caught up with her.

"You are welcome here," I began. "Tomorrow first thing we will get you to Dr. Pick to see about that cough. While you are there, I will call Ms. Gomez to see what we have to do with you under the law. Then, if you are able, we will go get you some proper clothes."

The next morning, while sitting in Dr. Pick's living room, I called Stephanie to get her help. Stephanie arranged with CPS for Esther to stay at the Trevor goat ranch for the time being. She continued to work on Esther's case while I tried to make her feel at home.

Esther didn't take to the goats or any of the other animals at first. She did not help with chores and walked inside whenever invited to work with the girls training their goats. I thought the problem might be that she just did not feel good. She drug around for a couple of days while the medicine Dr. Pick prescribed did its thing.

All weekend, I watched a morose Esther walking around as if in strange country, Monday morning, after getting permission from Stephanie, I got Esther registered in school and took off for Lometa. Before the girls arrived home from school, I unloaded a well-muscled and beautifully marked Boer billy kid into the goat-run. When the girls got home that afternoon,

I gave them their snacks and shooed them out to train their goats. Esther joined them reluctantly. I joined them for the first few minutes. Bianca, Marianna, and Jasmine seemed to know what the new kid was for. They ignored him even though he bleated for their attention.

Esther finally noticed the new billy. "Wow! Look at that little goat. I haven't ever seen him. He is beautiful. Look at his muscles and his color. Look at how he holds his head up."

"Yes, he is a good looking goat, but he is untrained. I guess I'll have to take him back tomorrow. The girls who want to train goats have too much to do already." Esther did not take the bait. She just leaned on the fence for a while looking at the goat and watching the girls put theirs through their paces. I carried Caryn and took Jimmy to walk the fence looking for goats to rescue. Occasionally, I would allow Caryn to walk a ways, but she soon held her hands up to be carried. An hour later, we returned to see Esther taking handfuls of alfalfa hay to the new billy. When she saw me walking back, she dropped her hay and walked back to the house. At supper, the girls were very animated and giggly except for the pensive Esther. After supper dishes were cleared and washed and I had put Caryn and Jimmy to bed, Esther found me in the hallway alone.

"Can I talk to you?" she said with eyes downcast.

"Sure hon, what is on your mind?"

"I don't know how to train a goat."

"The main thing in training a goat is to love it."

"Well, I can do that."

"I know you can. Why are you asking?"

"Would you let me train the new baby goat? I don't know how long I can stay, but it seems shameful for the best looking goat to not be trained."

"Sure does; okay, you can begin tomorrow. I think that would be a grand idea. Have you picked out a name?"

"Could I call him Eloy?"

"Sure, but why Eloy"

"My mother's name was Elaine and my father's name was…is Roy. So you see, if I name him Eloy, he would be named after the two most important people to me." There was a practiced no show of emotion in her voice, but a tear slowly made its way down the left side of her face.

"I think that is a fine idea," was all I answered. Esther turned to walk back to the kitchen. I started to call out to her, but didn't know what to say. Sometimes when a person doesn't know what to say, nothing is the best thing to say.

The next afternoon, there were four girls tending goats. Esther took on her share of the chores without a word. The other three girls accepted the help without a word. It was as if the world was back where it should have been all along.

TURN AROUND

The rest of that school year went well as it could considering the hurdles that the history of both Bianca and Esther caused. Esther oscillated between joy and sorrow almost on a daily basis. She had many difficulties at school due to teasing from classmates and her own tendency to be defensive and lash out. The worst problem produced a week's stay in the alternative school for fighting a girl that called her a "social reject." I had no experience in this kind of behavior, but I supported Esther and Bianca through all their situations. By support, I mean they had to solve their own problems as much as possible, and I never berated them for mistakes. When consequences were prescribed, I made sure they were served. Esther was very apologetic each time she got into trouble, but the frequency of problems increased as the year progressed. Stephanie was the one to point out that although frequency increased, the severity of problems were decreasing and her grades were still good. Esther was coming around slowly. Bianca's primary problem had to do with academics. That battle was fought daily in homework and reading sessions after the evening meal.

Stephanie Gomez was becoming more and more a part of the family picture. I continued to regularly ask her out, and she often joined Bianca,

Esther, and me for church and Sunday lunch. At least once per week, she visited the ranch specifically to check on Esther and get a feel for her progress in school and in her acceptance of her new situation. Unknown to Esther or me, Stephanie was searching in her network for a black cowboy named Roy.

ESTHER'S RESCUE

Although they made good grades, reading was a problem for both girls. Bianca made excellent grades in reading class, but like her teacher indicated, and as even I could see, she had problems with the English language vocabulary and reading fluency. She could read most passages, but very slowly. She struggled so hard to read the words, that by the time she finished reading most paragraphs, she had forgotten what it was about. Her comprehension scores were very low. Throughout the year, she read with me after the evening meal. Gradually her fluency and her comprehension were improving. Esther had her problems with both fluency and comprehension, but she was willing to work hard and progressed quickly under my tutorage. The most impressive statistic for Bianca was that although she had considerable problems with the English language and reading, she worked so hard for the teachers that she made honor-roll every grading period.

Bianca's math grades and scores on benchmark tests were better than average. She worked daily on the lessons prescribed by her teachers and her teacher said she progressed very well. Esther seemed to be mystified by mathematics and my explanations did not help. Eventually, the team learned to give the lessons troubling Esther to Bianca, who would look at the concepts and be able to teach them to Esther. I felt a little useless except that occasionally Bianca would need me to explain one of the fifth-grade concepts to her so she could teach it to Esther.

Altogether, the girls were progressing well with their schooling, their social relationships, and training their goats. They were developing a good rhythm until Stephanie's call.

STEPHANIE'S DISCOVERY

One evening after all the chores were done and Lizbet had served dinner, and all four girls were busy doing their homework, I was the only one available to answer the phone. In a very serious tone, Stephanie asked to speak to Esther. Before I could hand the phone to Esther, Stephanie changed the request to "May I come out to talk with her?" Of course I agreed, but a foreboding tone in Stephanie's voice made me ask what it was about. "I found her father, but he refuses to come see her."

"OK, come on out." I could not decide whether to tell Esther anything or not. I decided not.

Nearly thirty minutes passed before she arrived. Ten more minutes passed in greetings and Stephanie making herself ready to talk to Esther. Finally they sat alone in the kitchen. Stephanie took Esther's hands in hers looked her in the eyes and began. "Esther, honey, I found your father."

Before she could finish, Esther jumped up and squealed and asked many questions in a rush, "You found him? You found him? Where is he? When is he coming? Is he with you?" All that excitement turned into disappointment when she stopped to look into Stephanie's eyes. Now downcast, she sat down crying, "I knew it! He doesn't love me either! He doesn't want me."

Stephanie let her cry for a moment, then began again, "Sweetheart, I don't think it is fair to say he doesn't love you or want you. Remember, he didn't even know you existed until today. He has a lot of catching up to do. He has to get used to the idea of having a dead wife and a nearly grown daughter."

"He didn't care enough about Mom to come home!" Esther wailed.

"Sweetheart, he did not know about you or your mother. He didn't want your mother to know about him either. You see, he left her to find a better place for them. He worked hard at whatever job he could find, but he struggled just to support himself. He went back to bronc riding to try to win some quick money for a stake, but on his second ride, he landed on his shoulder and broke it so that he was too crippled up to ride again and saddled with a huge hospital bill. In desperation, he joined a bad group and was with them when they held up a small bank. A teller was killed; not by Roy, he didn't even have a weapon, but he was with them. Until about a month ago, he was in prison. He wants to see you, but he is ashamed for you to see him."

"But he is my father. I will love him just because he is my father. Can I talk to him? Can I see if I can make him understand that he is all I have?"

"Let's give him a little time. He is working at a construction job now and earning a living. It is hard work, but he is earning his dignity back. He is living in Arizona and has to stay close to his parole officer for a few more weeks. Let's give him that few weeks to help him feel his dignity grow, and let him get used to the idea that he is a father, then you and I will call him. Meanwhile, why don't you sit down and write him a letter, put a picture…no, put a lot of pictures of you with it and we will send it to him to introduce you. What do you think?"

Esther had stopped crying, but started again. "My poor, poor papa. I want to go see him. I know you mean well, but I want to see him. I know if he sees me, he will love me. Can you do that? Can you get me to him? I can hitch rides to get to Arizona. I will too! I will get to him and let him look me in the eyes and tell me he doesn't want me. I have to do that!"

"Esther, I believe you could do just that. If you insist on going soon, let me work on getting you safe transportation instead of hitching rides. Will you give me a week to try to get it arranged?"

Esther had stopped crying again. "You know, as much as I want a father, I was very angry with him for leaving us. I was feeling sorry for myself. Now that I know more, I feel sorry for him. I feel sorry for my mother. But I don't feel sorry for me anymore. I just have to see him and see if he will be the father I have thought he would be. I always dreamed he would be a happy man, always smiling, always loving me, always loving my mother. It won't be that easy. I will have to teach him to love me. I will have to take care of him until he does. OK, Ms. Stephanie, one week. I will write that letter tonight, and I will get lots of pictures; Mr. Trevor will help me?" She looked at me and got a nod of assent. "Come back to-morrow, please so I can give you lots of things to send to my father, Roy."

After Esther went to her room, I sat down with Stephanie. "You know she could run away and find him. You know also, that she will take off if this is dragged out past that week."

"Yes, I know. She is a strong girl. She doesn't know the dangers that wait for her between here and Arizona hitching rides."

"Don't forget," I reminded, "she has been on her own for a long time. She is fully aware of the dangers even if she has been able to avoid the worst of them. She is willing to risk them and determined to see her father to make him choose between taking care of her and feeling sorry for himself. What if I talk to Bianca and we kick in plane tickets for you and her to go to Arizona after he has had a chance to digest her letter?"

Stephanie nodded, "This plan is not usual. I asked for a week really to stall for time. I don't have a solution in my legal provisions, but I have plenty of vacation time that I must use soon. I could kick in a couple of days, or a week to take her to Arizona and see if this can work."

"Done!" was all I said before I kissed Stephanie goodbye. It wasn't a peck on the cheek either. It was a full, on the lips, bend her over backwards sloppy, 'I love you,' kind of kiss. I think Stephanie smiled all the way to her apartment, and not just because she had a plan for Esther.

***

Dear Father Roy,

I know you know about me now, and I hope someday you can learn to love me. I have love you all my life. But I dint know you. I have a pichure of you in your big white hat with my momma. She's dead now and all I have is you. In the pichure you have the bigges purties wide smile. I know a man with that smile got to be a good man full of love and fun.

I'm live with Mr. Trevor and Bianca and Lizbeth now, but while you are out there, this is not home. You are my home. I feel safer just knoing you are my daddy and are out there to help look after me. I'm near fourteen now. Lizbet is Biancas great grandma. I need my daddy. I need him to love me. I need to show him I love him. It won't be easy, but we can make it work out.

I put some pichures in with this letter to show you who I am so you know me when I get there. I'm comin to see you so we can make plans for our fuchur. One is just me. I smiled in the pichure for you so you culd see I can be happy. One is me and my goat. I'm training him for a stok show nex fall. I hope we can go together. One is me and Bianca, and Marianna, and Jasmine, and Mr. Trevor, and Caryn, and Jimmy. See the hole in the pichure behind me where nobody is? That is the place for you. Mr. Trevor said he would help find you a job here. Ms. Stephanie isn't in the pichure, she took it. You will like her. I think she is gonna marry Mr. Trevor. One pichure is me workin in the kidden pen. Mr. Trevor says that is the most important pen in the farm. I'm the one with the wheelbar.

I will see you soon. Ms. Stephanie is gonna take me to see you nex week. I can't wait!! I am so excite.
Your loving daughter,
Esther Rockingham

Stephanie was as good as her word. She was at the farm when the girls got off the bus from school. I had made it to the one hour photo that morning to develop pictures. Esther brought the letter to me for some help with making it better. I read it, but I told her I would not change a thing. The only things I could do would make it not as good. I said that letter would warm the heart of any father. Esther smiled and handed it off to Stephanie along with a stack of pictures to mail. Stephanie overnighted the letter.

***

The next Thursday, Stephanie and Esther got on a Delta Flight to Tempe, Arizona. Roy Rockingham met them at the airport with a bouquet of flowers for his daughter. He looked much older and his smile was not as wide and confident as in Esther's picture, but she knew him from across the terminal and ran to his arms crying, "Daddy, Daddy, I'm here, I'm here."

There was a considerable amount of paperwork to be done, but Roy Rockingham began the process of completing all the steps necessary to have his case transferred to Judge Peterson's court. Once he met Esther, there was only the questions of how he could get things done, not what he wanted to do. I talked to Mr. Talbert at the feed store. Mr. Talbert was constantly complaining that he could not get good help. He agreed to a one-month trial for Mr. Rockingham at minimum wages. At the end of the month, Roy would either get a pink slip or a raise. At the end of that first month, the raise was enough that Roy found a place for him and Esther to live and bought an old Ford truck. Roy was able to hire out his truck to deliver small loads of feed in order to earn a little more money. Esther continued to train her billy on the same schedule as the other three girls. Roy had found a house and ten acres to rent on the way from the Trevor farm to Marianna's house, so Roy took his turn picking up girls at the end of the day.

Esther thrived in his care. Her problems at school disappeared and she progressed nicely.

35

Passing Tests

*B*ianca didn't sleep well the night before the state reading test. She got up anxious and could hardly eat breakfast. I assured her that no matter the outcome, I was proud of her progress and if there was more we needed to do, we would just work our way through it. She said she wasn't worried, but I could see she was. She came in that afternoon obviously discouraged. I took her, the girls and Lizbet for ice cream trying to console her. "What is done, is done. I'm sure you did your best and that is all I can ask."

Nearly a month passed before the scores came in. Bianca was disappointed that she did not get commended. Commended would have been a score of two thousand, four hundred. She scored two thousand, three hundred twenty nine. I took her to see Judge Peterson so she could show him the results. The judge told her how proud of her he was and how she was growing up to be such a fine young lady. Bianca seemed to perk up a little from her disappointment when I invited the judge to eat the celebration lunch with us and he accepted. When we got to Louie's Steak House, Ms. Gomez, Jasmine, Esther, Roy, and Marianna were all there to help celebrate their victory over the reading test. They had decorated a table to honor all four girls' passing the tests. Louie served the girls himself. We had a great time and all the girls left the restaurant feeling like stars.

THE QUESTION

One day in mid-July as we were feeding goats, Bianca asked me if she could talk with me. "Of course, Sweetheart. What is it?"

"Later, after supper."

All through soup, sandwiches, and iced tea, I was worried. I thought of boy questions, girl questions, sickness, her family questions, and a myriad of other things that might be troubling her.

Seated on the couch, I asked, "Okay, Mija, what is troubling you?"

"Papa, remember you told me I could talk to you about anything?"

"Yes, and you can. Some things I don't know, but what I can answer I will," I was still apprehensive about the question.

"Why haven't you asked Ms. Gomez to marry you?"

I exhaled loudly. "Wow! Is that all? I mean, is that what is bothering you?"

"Yes, and that is not an answer. You said you had to figure out if she could fit in our family, right?"

"Yes."

"Well, does she?"

"I think…well…I think so, I mean…what do you think?"

"I think she should be getting tired of waiting for you to ask her to marry you. There are a lot of men that look at her...in that way. Haven't you noticed?"

"Well, yes, but...well, what if she doesn't..."

"Papa, you still don't have a clue when it comes to women! How can you be so dense and stubborn. I guess this is the reason God gave you to me. I have to teach you about women! Can't you see she is just waiting for you to ask? Honestly, Papa, I can see that you love her and she loves you. Anybody can see that! But if you don't quit stringing her along... Papa, I love you, but sometimes you drive me crazy!! Just ask her! If she doesn't want to marry you, then at least you'll know. If she does, well, fish or cut bait! Isn't that what you tell me when I'm afraid to do something?" Softly, she continued, "Papa, just ask her. If you don't ask, the answer is 'no.'"

Bianca stood watching me pace the kitchen. I stopped and looked at her watching me, "What? You mean now?"

Shrugging her shoulders, "Yes, Papa, now! This seems like a good time."

I paced the living room floor a couple more times, "How old are you again? You *are* right, you know," I said, almost to myself. "Sometimes when I am around her, I look at her face and...well, I can't breathe she is so beautiful. Then I think, 'What would such a beautiful woman want with me?' Do you think I will ever get over that?" Without a pause, I continued. "Actually, I hope not. It feels good all the way up and down my spine even if I *am* choking." I picked up the phone, dialed two numbers and hung up the receiver.

"Papa! Call her. Ask her out. Then when you are alone, and you can breathe again, ask her. What are you afraid of?"

"Her. No...of being rejected...Bianca, I'm nervous!"

"Of course you are! I imagine you are scared out of your mind," she said, almost pleading, "Work your way through it! You came to my house and faced four men with pistols loaded with only birdshot! You were very brave that night. This cannot be more scary than that! Call her!"

"When I went to your house for you, well, that was different. It was for you. I wasn't scared because…wait…Bianca, I *was* scared. I was terrified, but that was still different."

Bianca looked at me with a big smile, "You were afraid?"

"Yes, sweetheart, I was very afraid."

She grabbed me around the waist and looked up into my face. "You were afraid, but you came for me anyway?" I nodded. "Well, Papa, this is the same thing. If you don't ask her, someone else will. Papa, there was no one else I wanted to come after me. Ms. Gomez doesn't want anyone else coming after her either, but in her case, others are coming."

Finally, I called and made a date for a walk in the park and a talk.

Later that night, sitting on a park bench by the river, not far from the place she first fell in the water and kissed me, we talked about many mundane things like the weather, the kid crop, Gus, and her job. Trembling, I stood and kept my hand on Stephanie's shoulder signaling her to stay seated. I then got down on one knee. She seemed genuinely surprised. "Stephanie, would you m…I mean, Bianca and I have talked it over and we…well, we think you would fit. What I mean is…That is, I want… uh…we, no, I…Oh heck! Will you marry me?"

"Heck yeah!"

"You will! I mean…you don't want to think it o…okay, wait." Still kneeling, I stood and pulled the ring I bought nearly a year earlier out of my left front jeans pocket, then kneeled again. "When?" I asked as the ring slipped easily on her finger.

"Well," she said, "Oh, Castor, it's beautiful! Oh, yeah, the date. Bianca and I...I mean how about August, the first Saturday."

Stephanie grabbed me as I stood and kissed me hard again and again. "Yes, my love. I will marry you. I had just about given up."

When I came up for air, I grinned and chided, "You and Bianca already talked?! That sneaky, manipulative, pushy little broad! Bianca was right. Sometimes I don't have a clue. And now I wonder what I have gotten myself into."

Stephanie kissed me again and cooed, "Go with it Castor, you will enjoy it. It will be hard, but you will love it."

"Stephanie, I have a concern," I was suddenly very frightened and serious. Stephanie's smile faded as she seemed to anticipate the worst. "I was fooled once. I was married before and it ended badly. We were happy before we married, then after a short time and two children, there was no more happiness, only tolerance. I don't want that again. If we marry, we must promise to work at loving each other through all the problems that we will face. And, we must live up to that promise. Silence between partners breeds contempt."

Stephanie took my face in her hands, "Castor Trevor, though I haven't married, I too have had other loves that didn't last. I have been hurt and I'm sure I have hurt others. I promise I will not hurt you because of a fading love. I first fell in love with you because of your dedication to Bianca. I loved you because you put yourself in danger, and went to jail for her and rescued her from a very bad future. Facing rifles and pistols with birdshot!! For heaven's sake, what were you thinking? And you spent a month in jail for her! You don't get more romantic than that! I have found myself wishing I had some trauma you could come rescue *me* from. When I got to know you, I found a man who I can trust and who excites me at the same time, but also a man who has a difficult time trusting others. I have waited a long time for you to make up your mind; I have waited long after I made up *my* mind. I know it is hard, but *you* must trust. It is a choice, Castor. If you find you can trust me, we will have a great life. If you don't, we better call it off quickly, because we won't make it. You have my trust, but I must have yours also. So far as the 'silent treatments,' well, I will have to work on that."

***

Victor Castor Trevor and Stephanie Gomez Alaniz were married at ten am on the morning of the first Saturday in August. Stephanie's sister, Esther was the maid of honor. Bianca, Marianna, Jasmine, and Esther Rockingham were bride's maids in jeans, boots, matching western blouses and hats. Judge Peterson performed the ceremony wearing a big western hat and a brown suit. Jake Trevor stood as best man, Roy Rockingham stood with Castor, Caryn delighted everyone as flower girl, and Jimmy Cloud was ring-bearer. And just to make things interesting, Stephanie's brother gave her away while Ashley gave her father away.

The wedding was attended by several of Bianca's distant family. Castor was especially glad to see Omar Buentello and Lizbet, who cried all through the service, in the audience. The old man seemed much older than the last time Castor spoke with him. Castor thought, "Soon, I will have to find someone else to feed the stock when I leave the place for a day or more." Billie Cloud didn't attend the wedding. She went on a drinking binge that lasted several days.

***

Castor took Bianca to Omar Buentello's funeral two weeks later. He was apprehensive that her mother and father might show up, but they didn't. Many of her relatives came to shake his hand or pat him on the back and some kept their distance. Bianca seemed apprehensive also. She clung to Castor's arm through the ordeal. Mrs. Buentello had plans to return to Mexico to live out her days on the family ranch in San Louis Potosi. She hugged Bianca and spoke many endearing words to her in Spanish. Castor did not understand most of what she said and nearly nothing of what she told him, as she held to his arms and cried. Stephanie translated later. Lizbet left for Mexico with one of her grandsons immediately after Omar's funeral.

***

Prices were up that year when I sold the kid crop. I banked more than usual after paying expenses and began looking for investments.

The property Bianca's family had lived on sold for nine thousand dollars per acre in November. Bianca now had a substantial college fund, and my house was paid down so far that I refinanced for shorter time at a much smaller payment.

The adoption finally came through in early December. Bianca was now Bianca Alondra Gonzalez Trevor.

I bought five quarter horses complete with tack, four mares and one stud. Marianna became quite a rider, and the other girls enjoyed the outings, but none but Marianna considered rodeo. She set up a barrel-racing course in the back pasture and began practicing hard almost every day.

36

The Family Grows

December tenth of Bianca's fourteenth year, Loren Alaniz Trevor was born to Stephanie and I. We had a huge celebration when we brought her home. Jake and his family joined Ashley and her husband to throw a party inviting everyone who would listen. Most of Stephanie's family showed up at the party or later for a week of almost continuous visitors. Dr. Pick announced her retirement after the birth. She crowed about delivering me and all my children.

Bianca immediately took over as caregiver whenever she was around. Volleyball, basketball, and track kept her busy after school and some weekends, but Loren was very partial to her big sister. When she was old enough to be away from Stephanie, Bianca took Loren to the movies and to her friend's houses when she could. Often, she would take Loren, and Caryn down to the kidding pens to watch her, Jimmy, and the girls train show animals.

In February of Bianca's eighth-grade year, Billie Cloud came for a visit. Jimmy was seven and Caryn four. Billie was moving to Wyoming to marry a rodeo cowboy. She said she couldn't take the kids because the man she was marrying didn't like children. She asked me to take Jimmy and Caryn on a permanent basis. She promised to visit, but not interfere. She also promised to send money to help with expenses. I nodded acceptance, but I knew neither the money nor the visits would happen.

Billie and I talked to Stephanie and Bianca about taking Jimmy and Caryn permanently. They both surprised me by being excited about it. Stephanie agreed only if Billie would approve adoption so the children could not be taken back. Billie readily agreed. That adoption took only six months. Their records were sealed and they were issued new birth certificates. Now Stephanie and I were responsible for four children, six if you counted Marianna and Jasmine.

I bought six Boer nannys and two billys. We were set for the next few years to buy and sell registered Boer's for show along with a few horses and the mainstay of my farm, the Spanish goats. I fenced off forty acres and piped water to raise a few cattle. I chose registered Black Angus because of the ready market for Angus beef.

Caryn quickly began calling me 'daddy' and Stephanie, 'mom' and did her best to not leave her new daddy's side. Loren joined us by insisting I take her with me wherever I went long before she could walk. Jimmy quickly adopted Stephanie as 'mom,' but continued to call me, 'Trevor' like his mother had since he was born.

Billie sent a Christmas card each year with pictures. She usually remembered to send a little money at birthday time. She never came back to see Jimmy or Caryn. When she was nineteen, Caryn looked her up. By then, Billie's husband was dead; a bull had stepped in his chest driving a rib through his heart, and Billie was living alone, working as a secretary to a trucking company. Billie welcomed her like an old friend. From then, they visited regularly, often meeting in Denver, Colorado. Jimmy never went to see his mother although he did call her occasionally.

MARIANNA

On a Wednesday, in March of their ninth-grade year, Marianna ran away from home. Though she traveled in a remarkably straight line, it took her several hours running across farm and ranch land to get where she wanted to go. She ran through fields of young corn and sorghum plants and woods sprouting new buds and leaves. The woods were scary places, full of skunks, foxes, and many other hungry animals recently awakened from winter hibernation, but she was so angry and hurt, she paid them no mind. Finally she reached her destination, the Trevor farm.

She cut through the woods bordering the farm and came up through the kidding pen. I had just completed repairs on the float that controlled the water level in one trough in the kidding pen and was about to return to the house through the herd of kidding nannies when Marianna appeared suddenly and seemingly from nowhere. She ran to me scattering goats, crying, and hysterical. At first, since I had no idea what the problem could be, all I could do was sit and hold her while she sobbed and tried to speak. I sat on the big rock in the middle of the kidding pen and took her in my arms. She laid her head against my cheek, but did not speak, "Just get through your crying, sweetheart. You are safe. We can talk later." While she shed tears on my shirt, I stroked her hair like I did for Bianca when she was upset, and Ashley before her.

About ten minutes later, she was breathing regularly and began to speak. She told me her step-father had taken too much of a liking to her and when she got home from school, he tried to rape her. She seemed to be feeling better, so I suggested we go to the house and get her some food. "You know I have to call CPS?" It was more of a warning than a question.

"Yeah, I know," she sobbed. "Mr. Trevor, do you think they will let me stay with you?"

I thought for a short moment before answering, "I don't see why not. I am a trained foster parent, certified by the State of Texas, and Stephanie is a State Certified social worker. How could you be in better hands?"

She smiled through the second wave of tears. "Then if you will let me, I want to stay here. This is really the only place where I really feel safe."

"Well, let's go check with the expert. Stephanie has much more experience in this kind of situation than I have. She will know how to make it work." We walked slowly toward the kitchen. Marianna seemed to need to think and gather herself for the next phase of this battle. A couple of times, she stopped and it seemed she was about to speak, but was very hesitant to continue. It seemed to me that she had something on her mind she was afraid to say for fear of a rejection. "Marianna, you have always been straight with me. I admire that about you. When you have something to say, you usually just come out with it. It seems like you want to ask me something important. Spit it out."

"Okay, here goes," she breathed deeply, "Mr. Trevor, I don't mean I want to stay just tonight. I want to come live with your family." She fell to her knees and took on a begging posture; I was astonished, and uncomfortable. "I wouldn't be much trouble. I would be willing to sleep in the barn if you want. I will work hard to not be a big expense and I will work and give you all the money I earn."

I reeled from the rapid-fire list. I could see she had thought about this more than just today. *Things must be really bad, have been bad,* I thought. I knew I was at another decision point that would dictate some of the rest of my life, but this decision needed no time for worry and weighing. "I'll tell you what. First stand up. I am just a man, so never get on your knees to me. You never have to beg from me." I said as calmly as I could while hugging her close to my chest, "let us go talk this over with the rest of the family. And…just so you know, you have my vote."

Stephanie stepped into her role of social worker after feeding the sad girl a plate of dinner leftovers, and soon the story came spilling out. Marianna had been living with her aunt for the past couple of years. Her mother was very ill under a Doctor's care in Mexico. Marianna had not seen her for at least two years. Her father had left for South Carolina three years ago taking her younger brother with him. She had not heard from him except two times in that three years. Both times, he told her he was on his way to get her, but he never showed up. Her aunt had gone through a very emotional divorce, and now was remarried, but newly separated. The man who tried to rape her was actually a step-uncle. Bianca came into the kitchen shortly after the questions started and sat down beside Marianna holding her friend's hand.

Bianca told of her experience with the step-uncle. "He's just all over you," she said with disgust in her voice. He's old and dirty. The looks he gives you makes you want to run. He's scary. He seems to think that the girls love him, even when they take his hands off them and push him away. I'm glad Marianna finally got away from him. Papa, don't make her go back."

When the CPS agents arrived, they listened intently to her story, taking copious notes, and considered her request to stay with the Trevors. Shortly, Ms. Davis and Ms. Larue made a couple of calls. Looking at Stephanie and me, they asked if we were okay with Marianna staying with us for a few days. "Absolutely," I answered and Stephanie nodded. Before they left, they told Marianna that they would be questioning her step-uncle.

"I don't think you will find him," she answered, "he will be halfway to the border before you get to my aunt's house."

Ms. Larue smiled, "We have a number of questions for your aunt also." They left, both talking on their cell-phones with someone.

My mind went back to former encounters and I thought, *Finally, a couple of CPS workers that make sense and want to serve the kids!*

Stephanie and I called for everyone to come to the table in the kitchen. Loren and Caryn had to be gotten out of bed. They both came in sleepily and sat in my lap. Jimmy had been standing just outside the door, quietly listening. Before the talking began, he slipped into Marianna's lap. That boy's instincts amazed me. Bianca held tight to Marianna's hand as if the next decision would be a close one. Jimmy put his arms around Marianna and laid his head on her chest. Stephanie opened the discussion by telling the younger children that Marianna would be staying with them for a few days. No one asked why. Instead they seemed to be waiting for the difficult decision. "She may, I want to emphasize, *may,* be staying with us for a long time. Loren and Caryn looked at each other as if to ask, "For this, you woke us up." Stephanie continued, "Marianna has asked to stay with us permanently."

Caryn smiled, "You mean like to be fambly?"

"Yes, sweetheart, to be family."

That got a reaction from the two little ones. They both jumped down from my lap and ran to Marianna, hugged her then danced around the room squealing, then hugged her again. Soon, their antics had everyone laughing.

Stephanie grabbed Marianna and hugged her hard to her breast, "I guess it is unanimous!" she exclaimed. "We have thought of you as family for as long as I have known you anyway. And, by the way, family doesn't sleep in the barn, and they don't owe anyone for a place at the table. Family belongs. You belong. You already have a bed in Bianca's room. If you two think you can get along, you can share that bedroom."

Bianca smiled and began ushering Marianna out of the room, "Don't worry mom, I'll take care of her tonight, but we may need to get some things from the store tomorrow." Stephanie nodded understanding and approval.

Several visits later, Ms. Davis and Ms. Larue told Stephanie and I that the aunt would not give up the man, who tried to assault Marianna and now could not be found. In addition, their contacts in South Carolina had told them Marianna's father was living with a woman who would not support her going to live with them. From the condition of the house, the attitude of the woman, and the delinquent habits of her brother, they didn't recommend pursuing the idea of placing Marianna with the father. Soon, Marianna was officially also a member of the family. Stephanie and I were appointed permanent guardians by the court. We immediately initiated adoption proceedings.

Jasmine spent so much time at the Trevor farm, she was considered a member of the family also. She expressed some jealousy that Bianca and Marianna were able to be together much more than she could be with them now. I talked with her telling her she was the luckiest of all because she had loving parents and brothers and sisters in two families. I tried to make it clear that if she had had a bad home life, I would be proud to bring her into the family officially. She finally agreed that she was very lucky. "My father still won't brush my hair, though," giving me a sideways glance and grin and a huge smile.

37

Jimmy's Questions

Jimmy and I with occasional help from the two older girls, built a tack room of rock gathered from around the farm. The rocks were mostly odd-shaped, four-to-six-inch thick limestone. While the building was going up, Jimmy showed quite an aptitude for digging through the pile and finding rocks that fit together closely for small mortar joints. He seemed to know instinctively that small joints made for a stronger wall. He also got quite good at mixing the mortar to exactly the right consistency to support the joints until they could dry. He was not yet strong enough to place the rocks, but I let him hand me rocks and direct their placement. The foundation took a week of preparation, the walls, windows and doors another two weeks, and the roof about four days. Jimmy pushed me hard because he wanted it finished. The completed building was impressive with wooden doors, shutters, rock walls and a sheet-iron roof.

After the tack/feed building was finished, I took Jimmy on a trip to the Paul Whitehead ranch, a ten thousand acre spread just outside Kerrville, to buy three more quarter-horse mares for breeding and riding. While there, we picked up a four-horse trailer real cheap, and Mr. Whitehead gave me a young paint mare for the little girls. On the way there and back, Jimmy talked more than he had in all the time I had known him. He asked question on top of question about whatever came to mind. After a while, I began to feel Jimmy wanted to ask a special question, but he was afraid to know the answer. Taking a stab, I asked, "Jimmy do you want to know about your dad?"

Jimmy looked frightened at first, then he said, "Yes, Trevor, I think I was going to ask, but I am a little scared."

"What are you afraid of?" I asked, genuinely puzzled.

"I don't know. Maybe since nobody talks about him, maybe he was a really bad man. If he was, maybe I'll be a bad man too."

I had to smile, "Jimmy, I knew your dad very well. He was not a bad man. He was my friend. Your dad was a very good man, in fact, in my mind, he was a hero. I am sorry I haven't told you about him before. He was very good with animals like you are. Not quite as natural as you, I think, but he loved animals and he was the best horse trainer I ever knew. I have a picture of him that survived the fires. When we get home, I'll show it to you and tell you more."

When we got to the Trevor farm and had taken care of the new horses, we went to the office. I pulled out a picture album that had partially made it through the fires. With Jimmy anxiously watching over my shoulder, I thumbed through to the page I was looking for. "There he is, Jimmy," I said pointing to a 5X7 black and white of a young dark-headed, dark skinned man on horseback leaning on his saddle horn with his right forearm. His hat was in his right hand and he was looking intently at and laughing with a tall dark-headed woman who was a younger version of Billie Cloud. Writing at the bottom of the picture read, Jimmy and Billie Cloud. "That is your mom he is laughing with. This picture was taken years ago when I lived in a different place. Your dad and mom both worked for me. He broke horses, but he refused to break their spirits. He had a way with them. They seemed to want to please him, like they were close friends. I never saw a horse buck when he got on. Your dad was quite a man."

Jimmy took the picture out of the album and looked closely at his parents. "Can I have this picture?"

"Sure, Jimmy. I'll go to Wal Mart tomorrow and make a copy. I'll get a frame so you can have it behind glass. It'll last longer that way."

"Trevor, what happened to him? My mom would never tell me about him."

"Jimmy, your dad was a very brave, and good man. He was the kind of man you could depend on in a pinch. The worse the problem, the harder he would fight. The worse trouble a friend was in, the more he would help. One day, there was a fire at Jessup's barn across the highway from my place. Mr. Jessup had a lot of horses stabled in that barn, fourteen I think. A few of those horses, your father had trained from yearling colts to good riding and herding stock. Your dad saw the smoke first and drove his truck over to Mr. Jessup's barn. Right away he started getting horses out even though the barn was fully on fire and Jimmy was alone. Your mom saw him drive away and followed shortly after. He was too late to save them all; he knew some would die in the fire, but he was determined to get all he could out. He led two mares and a stallion out. All three had severe burns and were panicked. They were screaming and pawing with pain and fear. There were more horses trapped, tied or in stalls, and screaming. Your dad, being who he was and loving those horses, well, he had to go back for them. Your mother and Mr. Jessup begged him to not go back in, but he just couldn't stand knowing the pain those horses were in. The horses in the fire were screaming for help. He went back into the fire. Shortly, five more horses came running out, but your dad was still in the barn when it collapsed a few moments later. He didn't have a chance. He died in that fire. The coroner said one of the horses had kicked him in the head and crushed his skull. Part of your mom died in that fire also, she was never the same, her spirit changed. She was pregnant with you when your dad died. You were born seven months after that fire. That picture was taken about two weeks before the fire. Your mother had just told your dad that she was going to have you. That big smile on your dad's face was put there by the news that you were going to be born. Your mother told him no matter whether you were a boy or girl, she was going to name you Jimmy, after him." By the time I got all the story out, Jimmy was choking on the words and crying.

"You are right, he was a brave man," was all Jimmy could get out through his sobs.

"Yes, he was, and if he could know you, I know he would be very proud of the kind of young man you have become."

Jimmy hung the picture of his dad and mom over his bed so that he could see it last thing before he went to sleep at night and first thing when he woke in the morning.

38

Increasing Business

Bianca, Marianna, Esther, and Jasmine all showed goats each year after that first attempt. Each succeeding year they took turns winning, placing and showing. At my urging and with some help training her mare, Marianna, who was the steadiest in the saddle, started barrel racing. She quickly became well known on the weekend rodeo circuit and won some serious money for herself. Jimmy, with his ways with animals, coaxed a huge red sow and twelve piglets out of the woods into a make-shift pen and suddenly, Jimmy was in the hog business. We fenced off a piece of the kidding pen and the run for them and kept them well fed so they would stay put. From those piglets and a few more he coaxed out of the woods, at age nine, Jimmy began showing and selling winning mixed-breed hogs.

IN THE FEED STORE

I bought almost all of my feed from Sean Talbert's store. Since Sean took a chance on Roy, I bought little in the way of feed anywhere else. Sean was also a friend from high school. Shortly after Marianna came to live with the Trevor family, she accompanied me to pick up cattle cubes, salt licks, and the donkey feed with a little sorghum syrup mixed in that Gus was partial to. We were both dressed in jeans with wide belts, plaid shirts, boots and white, Palm-leaf hats. Marianna was a comely girl who looked older than her years. When we walked in, Sean was looking intently at a brochure advertising a feed-mixing machine that would allow a feed store to custom mix feeds and bag them right in the store. Feeds for mixing could be bought from local growers giving the growers bigger profits and providing substantial savings to the store. Sean shared some of his dream of having such a machine in conversation with us as he looked wistfully at the brochure. He was so caught up he had to tell us about it before we could make our order. I got excited for Sean. I could see that huge feed profits would be possible from such a system, and it would be of great benefit to local people. Everyone locally would win. Marianna mentioned that after he got it going, he could even use the same trucking firms that delivered feed to them to export feed to other areas, cutting his delivery costs. Looking at the cost, and after some quick figuring, I told Sean that I figured the store could have the machinery paid for in just over a year and then be making double the profits of buying and selling national brands, while paying local growers premium prices for the raw feeds and underselling the national brands with better feeds. There was even a machine attachment that allowed making cubes of various sizes.

Sean was drooling over the brochure such that I asked him why he didn't buy the machine. Sean answered that he would, but his credit was not good enough to get a loan that big. "Besides, I'm upside down on this building as it is." Marianna asked if he would be willing to sell part of the business to buy the machine. I backed up a step, surprised at Marianna's question and a little scared about where it might lead. Sean thought for a minute and said he would consider selling some of the business for a chance at that system. I was surprised at the attention and insight displayed by this young girl I thought I knew.

She looked at me with a question in her eyes. Then she asked the question out loud, "What do you think? Would this be a good investment?" I thought for a short minute then gave her a nod, meaning I would back her.

About that time, Gene Hoursch walked up behind Marianna. He was dressed in broken down boots, ragged and dirty jeans, and a ragged green, plaid, long-tailed shirt that he let hang out almost to his knees. He was an XXL across the shoulders, but not in length. Gene had been sitting with a couple of other hanger-ons playing checkers and spitting tobacco juice on the floor when Marianna and I walked in. Gene was two inches shorter than my five-eight, and seventy pounds heavier than my hundred fifty. He spoke as he walked toward us interrupting the discussion. "Got yourself a pretty good set-up, I hear, Injin boy."

Past experiences going all the way back to junior high school told me that I was not going to like what Gene was up to. "I'm doing alright, Gene, thank you. Please, let us continue our conversation with Sean."

Gene was the campus bully from seventh grade on. He got his growth and size early which made him larger and heavier than most all the other boys. From seventh grade, I was his favorite target. I got my growth much later and never achieved the size of Gene Hoursch. I endured being called "Skinny Injin, Redskin, and Red Pencil Neck," among the names that did not have curse words. Gene was fond of walking up behind me and slapping me on the back of the head, and on the odd occasion knocking me to the ground scattering my books and papers before laughing and calling me a coward Indian. Several times I got fed up and fought back, but Gene had the advantage. Even though I got a few good licks in, drew blood more than once, I went home often with a bruise we called a mouse on my cheek, a bloody nose, or black eyes.

Gene continued, looking at Marianna but talking to me and ignoring my request to leave us alone, "Yeah, you got that purty, brown-skinned wife, and two brown-skinned concubines. This one looks ripe for the plucking."

I looked at Gene almost pleading, "Gene, for heaven's sake, she's only thirteen."

With his tobacco-stained smile, Gene continued, "She's old enough. She looks good to me in those tight jeans. How about it honey?" Marianna

showed some fear, but I could see a deep-seated anger taking over her being. It showed in her face. I figured I was in for another school-yard type
brawl. One thing I knew, Gene did not know me since the marines. I still
had a few skills and was willing to use them. If I had to fight, I would
not quit until I won or died. Still, discretion is the better part of honor. I
decided to leave and come back later.

"Leave her alone Gene, she's just a kid. Come on hon. Let's go." Over
my shoulder, I spoke to Sean, "We'll come back later, Sean, when the air
is better in here." I took Marianna by the right elbow and started toward
the door.

"She's a Mescan kid," Gene responded, "Nobody will care."

Used to taking advantage of those weaker than him, or on the social
rung that made them afraid to try to get assistance from those in authority,
Gene hijacked and took money from men he knew to be in the country illegally, and hit on their wives and daughters. They did not dare fight back
too hard for fear of attracting the authorities. Although in reality he was a
cruel toad, he had convinced himself he was stronger, smarter, and more attractive than the Hispanic males and that he was irresistible to the females.
Ancient history all the way from grade school gave him the feeling he still
could push me around. He was not accounting for my stint in the Marines,
or that Marianna was not in the country illegally.

Gene grabbed Marianna's left arm as I led her past him and swung her
around to face him. He was ready for her to resist and fight to get away,
which she did at first. He prepared to jerk her around, planting his feet
shoulder width and knees slightly bent. She suddenly stopped struggling,
swung around as light as if she were dancing, faced him straight on, took
a short step toward him with her left leg, and kicked with her right foot.
She planted the square toe of her right boot hard between his legs. "I care,
you overgrown frog. Rana pendejo!" she spat at him as he groaned and
grabbed his groin.

Gene was built in almost a square, nearly as wide as tall. The man
was very powerful in his arms and shoulders, used to lifting and throwing
hundred-pound bags of feed and hundred sixty pound hay bales. People he
picked on seldom fought back, especially the women. For a few pregnant

moments, the room was silent. For those few moments, Gene stood still with his eyes bugged and rolling back in his head, his mouth moved but no sound came out, his hands automatically grabbed his crotch. Like a big, tall tree leans slowly then falls gaining speed until it hits the ground, Gene leaned to his right without changing his posture, then fell, rolling into a ball on the way down. The pier and beam building shook when he hit the floor. It was several seconds before he could make another sound and then it was only another groan. Marianna had surprised him and connected like no man likes to consider being kicked. It would be a while before he would be able to walk straight, much less recover enough to drive himself home. I thought he would always consider carefully before making such a move again.

With Gene on the floor, Marianna's face changed from anger to grinning at me. "We were talking business before this pendejo (stupid one) interrupted," she said, "How about we talk it out all the way? I'm interested." I nodded, still wide-eyed and speechless. She stepped over Gene's head as she walked back to the counter. Gene flinched, jerking his left arm over his head, warding off an expected kick. He expected it because, after all, he would have kicked anyone he got down on the ground.

I looked at her in wonder and spoke in a whisper, "Karate Classes?"

She shook her head and smiled a knowing smile, "Mean step-dad, and maybe a little PMS."

I couldn't help a smile laced with wonder, "Well, I guess that is one conversation we don't have to have. I was dreading that anyway."

Fifteen minutes later, Marianna and I had agreed to buy twenty percent of the feed store in the form of the new mixing machinery and a generous stake for buying local feed to mix, printed sacks, and some spots on the radio to advertise to local farmers and ranchers. Sean went to Don Stence the next day and had the papers drawn up. When we left the feed store that afternoon, neither Marianna nor I looked again at Gene who had just then made it to a sitting position on the floor where he had fallen. We walked by ignoring the man who could not yet speak.

"Do you treat all the guys that way that show an interest in you?"

"If they put a hand on me, pretty much." We had a good laugh over ice-cream. "And, by the way Mr. Trevor, I'm nearly fifteen."

I grinned, "I'll make a note. We may want to talk about some other options for you to use in defending yourself. You keep this up and I will never get your married off." I never again looked at Marianna as a little girl, nor treated her as one. Several times over the next few weeks, I burst out laughing at the recollection of Gene's face just before he fell. I always said the same thing to myself as I shook my head in wonder and laughed until tears flowed, "Felled by a fourteen-year old girl! Couldn't have been better and man, I'm glad I saw it."

MARIANNA'S CRISIS

One afternoon, soon after the feed store incident, while Bianca, Jasmine, Jimmy, Caryn, Loren, and I were all at the barn or kidding pen taking care of chores and training, Stephanie came in from work and found Marianna crying on her bed. When Stephanie walked in, Marianna tried to hide that she had been crying, but Stephanie would have nothing but the truth. Marianna produced a letter from under her pillow that had been given her at school by a neighbor of her aunt. It was in Spanish from her mother. The envelope had been addressed to Marianna's aunt, but the letter was for her. It had been dictated to a friend and mailed over a month before. Stephanie translated it as she read it out loud:

My dearest darling Marianna,

I haven't seen you for a long time. I know you have grown and I'm sure Tia Elena is taking good care of you. I hope with all sincerity that you are doing well in school and not neglecting any little part of it. By now, you are a beautiful young lady with your father's black-as-night wavy hair, and your natural dark complexion. Remember what I told you about the boys. There will be time enough for them after schooling. I'm sure they must be after you like flies after a piece of ripe fruit.

I wrote to tell you how much I love you and how much I miss you. Marianna, I want only the best for you. I want you to have a good life, but mija, it is up to you. I have some small pieces of advice for you to consider:

Always be honest.

Never talk about someone behind their back.

When you make a mistake, say you are sorry and mean it.

When you make a mess, clean it up quickly.

Be ready to forgive every chance you get.

When you look for a job, do something meaningful, not just something profitable.

Never go out to hurt someone, even when they have hurt you first.

Look for someone who has it worse than you, and help them.

Treat all others with respect.

Defend yourself when you have to, then with all your might.

I'm sure there are more things I should tell you, but I'll leave it with just this: Read about Jesus and His teachings, and follow Him.

My darling daughter, this will probably be my last letter to you. The doctor's are telling me I won't see summer. This illness has made me very sick and I am in great pain. I will rest well knowing you are taken care of. Please write me soon.

I love you,

Mama

Stephanie looked at the letter. The sending address was clearly written on the outside. Marianna was sitting on the edge of the bed with a stoic face, but tears flowed freely. "How long has it been since you saw your mother, Marianna?"

The youngster looked up with pleading in her eyes, "It has been over three years. The summer before fifth grade was when she left me with Tia Elena. She was getting sick and went to Mexico to get well."

Stephanie was thinking and asking at the same time, "Have you ever been to the place she is living now, in...Pueblo Santia?"

Marianna stopped crying hoping she knew where this question was leading, "No, I have never been to Mexico. I was born in McAllen, Texas and we moved here when I was a baby." Tears were now running down both sides of Marianna' *and* Stephanie's faces,

"Sweetheart, do you want to go to see your mother?"

Marianna thought for a moment before answering, "Yes. Yes, I would like to see her once more, but I can't ask you or…"

"My sweet, you can ask. Perhaps you shouldn't have to ask. We'll talk to Castor after supper. You and I can both speak the language, and we can read a map. What could be so difficult?"

After supper, Stephanie and Marianna sat down with me. I had taken care of Marianna's chores and was wondering why she hadn't even come out to train her goat. Stephanie read the letter, translating into English for me.

At the end of the letter, I looked at Marianna and asked, "Marianna, I am ashamed that we haven't thought about taking you to see your mother before now. Do you think you can miss a week of school to go see your mother?"

"I'll do whatever they ask to make up work," she volunteered.

"Okay," I said, "tomorrow I will go to school with you to talk to whoever we must to make arrangements. Stephanie, can we be ready to go by the next day?"

"I don't know," she answered. "While you are at school, I will contact the Mexican Consulate to see if we can get a special visa or passport of some kind. If it works, we might be able to leave tomorrow afternoon."

"What about the other children," I asked. "It would be great if we could take everyone, but we can't be sure there would be accommodations in the small village for seven people and the little ones would require shots and would slow us down." Stephanie made a call to her sister and soon had someone to stay with Jimmy, Caryn, and Loren. Bianca would stay with Jasmine and the two girls would make sure all the animals were fed while we were away.

Stephanie found a sympathetic ear at the Mexican Consulate. By noon, she had emergency visas for all three of us to travel to the small village and back. I was not so lucky. After explaining the situation to the assistant principal, she informed me that the next week was state testing week and that Marianna could not miss school. "You don't understand," I said, "she *will* be missing school. That is not negotiable. We just wanted to do it as legally as possible so she could still be in good stead in her classes. What can we do?" The lady was young and had no ring on her finger, so I guessed she was not married and probably did not have children.

"What you can do, is postpone the trip until after the testing so Marianna can go to the next grade," the young lady stated flatly.

Sometimes a man just has to do the right thing. Others may not agree or understand or they may not agree because they don't under-stand, but if he does the right thing, he can be at peace with himself. It was obvious I was not going to make this person understand or agree that taking this girl to see her mother was the right thing to do. I stood, thanked the lady kindly, took Marianna by the arm and led her out into the outer office where I paused to call Stephanie. "Get home and finish packing," she told me. "When I get home from the consulate, we will have all the paperwork we need to get across the border, negotiate our way, and get back."

I took the time to have Bianca called to the office before we left. "Sweetheart, it looks like we will be traveling before you get out of school. Your aunt Esther will be staying at the house for a few days until we get back. I know you are planning to stay with Jasmine for the time we are gone, but do you think her mother would allow her to stay with you? I would feel much better if you were at the house for Caryn and Loren. Your Aunt Esther doesn't have any children and may not know what to do if one of them gets sick or lonely. Would you mind?"

Bianca smiled a knowing smile, "I'm way ahead of you, Papa. I've already talked to Jasmine and she talked to her mother. We are all set. I got to feeling a little selfish after asking to stay away while you and Mom are gone, so I set it up to be at home and have Jasmine there to help."

I hugged her and kissed her on the cheek, "I knew I could depend on you, I just didn't know how much. I guess that is why I picked you."

Bianca smiled, "I picked you, you silly man. Then God gave you to me." Bianca and Marianna hugged and said their good-byes, then Marianna and I left hurriedly for the Trevor farm.

TRIP TO PUEBLO SANTIA

By one thirty we were an hour into the trip to Mexico, and had stopped to eat lunch at Taco Cabana in San Antonio on IH 35. By six, we were checked into La Posada, a hotel in McAllen, Texas. The plan was to get a good night's sleep and cross the border early the next morning. It was Friday. With any luck, we figured we could be in Pueblo Santia around four in the afternoon on Sunday.

The hotel did not allow more than two per room, so I rented two adjoining rooms. Stephanie and I slept with the door open. When I woke up at three am for a nature call, I stumbled over Marianna asleep in a blanket on the floor beside our bed. She remained asleep but grumbled something incoherent. When I awoke to the alarm at six, she was back in her room packing.

We had checked out and breakfasted on tacos by seven, and were thirty miles into Mexico by eight. Stephanie had gotten us across the border and quickly through the inevitable checkpoint. She knew that there was a ban on anything electronic being transported into Mexico. The consulate had been very clear about not taking computers or such on the trip. Before making it home for the final packing, she went to Wal Mart and bought several hand-held electronic games. Whatever is forbidden at the border immediately becomes illegal tender and much desired. At the checkpoint, two guards began going through all our luggage while a third watched holding an automatic assault rifle. Guessing the one watching to be the one in charge, Stephanie approached him and asked him if she could show him something. She took one of the games and huddled with the chief guard. She said she had noticed his wedding ring and guessed he had a son or daughter who would enjoy the game.

"Senora, this is electronics," he said, "It is contraband. And I have a son *and* a daughter."

"Oh no, this is just a game that uses electricity. Electronics would have to do with computers. And I happen to have another different game here." She pulled a second from her pocket. "Oh, and I guess I won't have a need for these extra batteries. Why don't you take them for the games?" In less than ten minutes we were on our way. Stephanie had four more games to use as needed.

Marianna rode in the seat immediately behind Stephanie looking wide-eyed at the poverty and desolation she saw surrounding the opulence of a few ranch houses.

We arrived in Pueblo Santia a little after noon on Sunday stirring up a dust cloud behind us on the dirt road. As we drove into the dusty little village, we had to stop and wait for a funeral procession following a pine casket carried on the shoulders of six village men. Without a word, Marianna jumped out of the truck and ran to the procession. I started to go after her, but Stephanie put her hand on my arm stopping me. Marianna stopped a weeping lady at the end of the procession and talked to her briefly. She then returned to the truck and got in the back seat. Her face was set and she stared after the casket.

"Let's follow the line of mourners. In the casket..." She said. "The lady to be buried is my mother. I want to say good-bye." She was calm, but tears ran freely down her cheeks giving away the sadness in her soul. We got out of the truck and walked behind the slow procession, then joined the mourners in the cemetery.

Marianna stayed behind kneeling beside the open grave after everyone else had gone. Stephanie and I gave her the solitude she seemed to be wanting. We waited in the truck watching her weep and talk to her mother. The men assigned the task of filling the hole sat a respectful distance away and waited patiently. After a long time spent on her knees beside the grave of the mother she loved but had not seen in a long time, Marianna slowly rose to her feet and quietly got in the back seat of the truck. She seemed at peace. She was through weeping for her mother.

"The lady I talked with said she had a few things to give me from my mother. Can we get them and then go back now? This is not home."

The grieving but stoic Marianna said little more until we turned into the gate to the Trevor farm three days later. *"This* is home. You two dear people, Bianca, and the little ones, are my home," she said flatly as we rumbled over the cattle guard into the yard. "Thank you for taking me to see my mother. I don't know why, but that was important. I still feel a little sad still, but good too. She is not hurting."

39

Turning Fifty-Five

On my fifty-fifth birthday, I was happily married with five children ranging from two to sixteen and counting Jasmine, one fifteen-year old that stayed around so much she might as well have been mine. We had an explosion of grandkids after the trials with Jason. Between Ashley and Jake, we now had four healthy and happy grandsons and a granddaugter. Ashley brought a gaudy cake she baked for the party. She very generously place "50" on the cake instead of "55." She and Everitt came with their boy, Everitt Jr., two years old and Carroll, just walking. Jake and Martha brought their three, Jason, four, Richard Castor, two and Davis also just walking. All the grandchildren brought a twinkle to grandpa's eyes thinking about the future fun I would have playing with them and watching them grow. That night, the house was full of happy noise as kids romped and grown-ups laughed and told stories. We got up a game of forty-two, then played a round of spades. By then, all the grandsons and Caryn and Loren took over the game table. I got out two more sets of dominoes for them to build and crash. At bedtime, cots and pallets were set up in the study, hallway, and in the living room to accommodate all. After all the kids were bedded down, I walked through the house just to marvel at all this family. Bianca's room was at the end of the tour. Bianca was up, but the other four were asleep. Jasmine had come to join the fun. Caryn and Loren were sound asleep on a pallet next to the wall.

"What are you doing Papa? Why are you still up?" she asked, brushing her hair for the night.

"Come with me for a minute, will you?" Bianca looked puzzled but she got up, placed the brush quietly on her dresser, then joined me, "Where are we going?"

"You'll see."

We walked from room to room looking in on sleeping people. "Aren't they beautiful?" I asked as we came to Jimmy and Caryn's room that held Jimmy and three grandsons that night."

"Yes, Papa, they are. But what are we doing?"

"We are just admiring. You know…none of this," waving my hand around, "would be happening if you hadn't rescued me; this house would not exist and these people would all be somewhere else. Well, maybe I would have Jimmy and Caryn, but I wouldn't be prepared for them."

"Papa, the way I remember it, you came to my house and rescued me."

"Sweetheart, when you came to help me early that first Saturday morning and ran away thinking I was going to whip you with that rope," I began to explain, "I was doomed to die a lonely old man full of sorrows and bitterness, ignoring the people who loved me most. You jarred me out of that self-pity and eventually into this total wonder of a life with all these people I love so very much. None of this change was comfortable, and some of it was downright painful, but I can't thank you or reward you enough for helping me climb out of my dark pit and into this light. Why, my beautiful child," I continued, holding her face in my hands, "you even pushed me kicking and screaming, into asking Stephanie to marry me! I really didn't know how much I needed a companion, but somehow you knew, and you wouldn't let me settle for less than her. You are an amazing blessing to me. I feel so rich and highly favored. I feel like I have been saved from an awful fate and given a great life. You did this. OK, perhaps you were helped a little also, but it seems I have done so little to gain so much."

At sixteen Bianca had grown to almost five-foot four and one hundred twenty pounds of strong, athletic, and beautiful girl. She hugged her 'Papa' with her almost-black eyes shining in the dim light of the hallway. Her sun-darkened face was framed by her shiny, freshly brushed, thick, raven hair. I reflected that I had not seen a more beautiful girl since Ashley was that age. She laid her head on my chest and wept softly, "I guess we rescued each other," she whispered. "What an unlikely pair we made! A self-pitying, broken, but good man, and a scared little abused eleven-year old girl. But, that is God's way. He takes the most unlikely and performs great miracles. You taught me that from the Bible. I know He loves me very much. I know this because He gave you to me to be my Papa. You are my present from God." Holding to each other's waist walking side by side with her head leaning on my shoulder, we walked her back to her room. Marianna was awake.

"I heard you talking," she said. "I broke into your little perfect world also and also caused you trouble. I too think you are a gift from God and I think it's time. I've been thinking that I should be calling you 'Papa' too. 'Mr. Trevor' seems so formal. Is that okay?"

Before I could answer, Bianca said, "That's okay."

I shrugged and said, "What she said. Marianna, I am honored. I don't think of you in any other way than my beautiful, perhaps a little headstrong, daughter. The title, 'Papa' is the best present I could get for my birthday." A short group hug followed. Both girls demanded I brush their hair one more time, which I gladly consented to doing. Before I finished, Jasmine woke up and demanded her turn. As I walked away down the hall, I heard Bianca whisper to Marianna, "Now, I guess it is official. We are sisters."

Jasmine chimed in, "Can I get in on this too?" Bianca and Marianna answered in unison that all she had to do was get permission to call Mr. Trevor 'Papa.'

"Oh, I started that a long time ago. Haven't you noticed? What took you so long? After all, he has treated us as good as Bianca since we were in fourth grade." When I finally made it back to mine and Stephanie's room, she met me inside the door handing me two hairbrushes. "I want some of that attention also," she said pouting a little.

"My dear, you will be attentioned out before I get through with you."

"Shhhh!" she giggled, "we have guests all over the place." I assured her I could be very attentive without making noise.

Through the tender moments, no one at the house heard Gus bray then squeal in pain before trampling something into the dirt at the kidding pen.

40

Gus and Little Red

The morning of fifty-five years and one day, I got up earlier than usual. Something nagged at the edges of my mind and the sharp pain in my chest bothered me. I couldn't identify what the nagging thing was, but it had to do with the kidding pens, and maybe a dream. Stephanie fixed coffee as I dressed for chores and kissed me good-bye in case I didn't get back before she left for work.

Hackles rose on my neck as I approached the kidding pens. Gus was standing at the back of the pen with his muzzle buried in a bit of dried grass, but he was not grazing, just standing looking dolefully around, much like I had first seen him at James Burrus' ranch. Several nannies were milling about as if everything was right with the world, but still something was wrong. Halfway to the pens, I spotted a crushed white palm-leaf western hat leaning against the boulder in the middle of the pen. A newborn kid was chewing on the brim. Wondering what had happened, I spotted the pet goat first. Little Red was lying very still and stiff in a pool of blood. I was climbing the fence and almost in the pen before I saw the man.

He was lying prone, face up partially hidden by the grass growing next to the fence. The man's eyes were open and there was no movement. I knew long before I got to the man dressed in jeans and a bloody green and white plaid shirt, that he was dead. I also knew who the dead man was, and could easily piece together what had happened.

Since it was Monday, the girls and Jimmy would be up soon to do their chores and get ready for school. They didn't have to catch the bus since Bianca now had her own pickup. Actually, it was my old red pickup, the one I bought while in jail, but I had given it to her when she passed her driver's test. I ran back to the house and had a whispered conversation with Stephanie who had started on a big taco breakfast for all the school kids. I called the sheriff's office to report a death, then moved Stephanie's suburban to the front of the house and the old pickup to the kidding pen parking it between the body and the house.

Warned by me, after they were fed Stephanie rushed the kids out the front into the suburban. She told Bianca that I needed her truck and that she had to deliver Jimmy and Caryn to the elementary school before the three girls could go to the high school. When they asked about their jobs, Stephanie told them I would handle the feeding chores. Unseen by the children, was the coroners vehicle and the black and white that had arrived at the kidding pen.

"You know Mr. Trevor, that mule will have to be put down," the coroner announced after he pronounced the man dead.

"Gus? Why? He was just protecting us," I began my argument. "That man threatened to kill me five years ago. He even made an attempt. You want to see the scars? Gus stopped him back then; broke his arm. It appears he stopped him again. Who do you think killed that goat? By the way, he is a donkey, not a mule."

The coroner shook his head, "It makes no difference. Any animal that kills a human has to be put down. It's the law. I can get the deputy to do it for you, if you want."

I looked at Gus who for the first time since I bought him, had allowed two strangers into his pen without challenging them. It was that realization that prompted me to look closer at the old donkey. I noticed a definite wobble in his step, especially on the right side, the side away from our sight. "Wait a moment," I said to the two officials as I walked toward Gus talking to him quietly. Gus kept his head down while I approached. This was not normal. Usually, Gus would be standing as tall as he could with ears forward to listen, or ears back to signal attack. I steadily talked softly to Gus as I approached, and looked for other clues. Gus kept his head down, but turned to face me. That is when I saw the knife sticking out of his ribs and pink blood-bubbles running down his side. Gus coughed up a dark-red glob, which I took to be a mass of coagulated blood. When I got to him, the old donkey gave up and after taking a trembling step, fell on his left side. He tried to bray, but could only gurgle. Gus was choking on his own blood. He was dying, and there was only one thing I could do to help him.

I walked quickly to the house and brought out my .270 deer rifle. "I'm sorry, old friend. You are hurt too badly to heal, and you are suffering too much for me to stand." One shot and it was over. Gus jerked, trembled, then relaxed and lay still. I had to stand over my old friend for a few moments and wipe my eyes before I could face the two men watching. I walked over to Gus' side and pulled the ten inch blade out of the old warrior's lung. "This," I said handing the knife to the coroner, "was intended for me and mine. That kid goat and that old donkey probably saved the lives of several of my family. He would have come into my house and killed any and all. My sixteen-year old daughter and I would have been his primary targets."

The trampled body of Tio Flaco was bagged and loaded into the old ambulance to be transported to the county morgue. When he turned the body over to help determine how the man died, the coroner found a silver plated revolver with a pearl handle under the body. He noted old and deep scars on the man's back.

Probably from childhood. Might explain a lot, I thought absently.

I went back to the house to tell Stephanie all I knew and suspected of the events. She listened in silence nodding her understanding, then called one of her brothers. For the next two weeks, the Trevor house and grounds had friendly eyes watching for intruders. Nothing more came from Tio Flaco's associates.

Jake, Martha, Ashley, and Everitt were informed in a group. Jake and Everitt offered to help me bury Little Red and Gus, but I thought it more respectful if I did it myself. I decided to bury Gus in the shade of a spreading oak growing out of a rocky knoll. The tree was the one that the old donkey liked to stand under while watching for strangers. Loren rode in my lap on the tractor as I dug the hole in the rocky ground, pulled the body in, and covered it. The nagging pain returned to my chest when I buried Little Red under the same shade on another side of the tree.

I returned to the house around ten thirty, still feeling very sad for my two hero animals. Stephanie had prepared a crock-pot lunch before she drove away for her work in town. Jake and Ashley were packed to leave immediately after lunch. I spent the remainder of the morning being papa and grandpa. I lead all the kids down to the horse corral and took each for several rides on the gentlest quarter-horse mare and the little paint, then at Loren's insistence, took them all on a long ride on the tractor. At Caryn's insistence, we played Ring around the Roses, hide and seek, crack the whip, and finally, with my two youngest grandsons in my lap, we played twenty questions. I was amazed at how healing it was for me to play with my children at their level. It was healing for me and relationship building for all of us. Jake, Ashley, and their spouses took a long walk around the place deepening their relationships also.

Noon came too quickly and soon all had eaten and finished packing their cars for trips home. After the rest of the children were gone, I took Caryn to school, and Loren had her favorite playmate all to herself. I was happy to fill that role, especially on that day. We saddled a big mare and went for a ride checking fences, came back for a nap, then fed animals. Loren chattered about almost everything, and asked, "Why?" many times, but I was deep in thought about how thankful I should be for all I now had and the life I was privileged to live.

I took all the older children for a walk that evening to tell them about the night and day's events. Bianca flinched a little when I told her Tio Flaco was dead, but she wept for the old donkey and the little red goat. "They were real heroes, weren't they Papa?"

"Yes Mija, they were. They probably saved your life and possibly the lives of others of our family. I can deal with losing even two such fine animals, but losing you or any of my family would rip my heart out." I noticed at that moment that the pain in my chest was finally gone.

Jimmy ran into the woods to grieve and so the rest of us would not see him cry.

THE DONKEY BUSINESS

Daylight Saturday found me, the three inseparable girls, and the three younger children on our way to James Burrus place in Mullin once again. We were pulling the horse-trailer with the Suburban to see if we could find another cantankerous donkey to patrol the Trevor farm.

Mr. James Burrus was both saddened by the news of Gus' death and proud of the old donkey's actions. "He turned out to be a good soldier," was his final comment on that subject. As a decorated veteran of World War II, Mr. Burrus had a good feel for what he said.

"Mr. Burrus, do you have another donkey like Gus?" Bianca asked hopefully.

"Well," the old man said as he pushed his hat back and scratched his head through a thick thatch of course gray hair, "I have one o' Gus' grandsons. His name is Buck. He's a three-year old that can't nobody ride and he's git'en the temperment of his granddaddy. He already bit two of the best mule skinners I know. You can have him cheap for three hunert dollars. That's him pacing the fence over there wanting to come check you over." Bianca spotted the younger version of Gus and smiled, then nodded to me. I made the deal for two hundred seventy-five dollars, then asked about purchasing a yearling female, one not kin to Gus. Marianna got the task of picking one from a group of six. I noted that she chose a well-muscled and gentle one.

Soon, we were on our way with the beginnings of a donkey business. On the way, we stopped and picked up another young red billy goat descended from Old Red. Gus, the man, expressed his pride in the Little Red. He would not take money for the replacement. When we unloaded the animals, Buck trotted straight to the oak under which Gus was buried. He brayed several times announcing his presence and challenging all comers. The girls and I were amazed at the similarity between Buck and his grandfather, in looks and audacity. Before nightfall, Jimmy was riding Buck with Lucy and Brutus following along. New Red hung back but followed at a distance. Marianna named the new female donkey, Fatima, after her mother.

The next October, Roy and Esther moved to New Mexico where Roy opened his own feed store featuring among the many brands, Talbert's Mixed Feeds. At the stock show, Jimmy showed Nicker, the Grand Champion Angus Bull. He cried all the way home after selling him to Arby's for breeding stock. That one sale, however, would pay for his first two years in college. The girls did well also and sold at higher bids than they had ever gotten before.

41

More Business

On a family outing to Louie's Steak House shortly after the stock show, Louie confided that he would shortly close the doors to the restaurant for good. When I questioned him, Louie sat down at our table and whispered reluctantly and sadly, that he was close to bankruptcy. The cost of help and meat added to the mortgage, left him with little to live on. I suggested we visit with Don Stence and try to figure a way to keep his business open. I believed that a good man like Louie deserved every chance to be successful.

With Stephanie's and my blessing and Don's help, the three girls and Jimmy used some of their livestock show and rodeo winnings to stake Louie again, buy a small slaughter house, and arrange for Louie to serve Angus beef grown on the Trevor farm. The way they figured it, I could sell my registered beef to the restaurant for more than I could get at market and still significantly decrease the meat bill for the restaurant. With the slaughterhouse operating as part of the chain, we could take the beef every step of the way from the range to the table at Louie's. The slaughterhouse would focus on turning a small profit from outside services while doing all the butcher-work for Louie's restaurant. The result was that Louie got high quality, fresh, range beef for much less than he had been paying for pen fed. In addition, the girls and Jimmy would trade off operating the cash register or waiting tables at no pay. In return, the kids would own twenty-five percent of the restaurant and a share of profits. They found that Louie could actually reduce prices, attract more business, and have a larger profit margin. Louie was happy to give up part-ownership in order to save the business and be able to support his family along with a night off occasionally. In addition, Louie hired Stephanie's younger brother, Roman, who was a great hand at barbeque, and added cabrito and boracho beans to the menu. Soon, he was attracting a steady clientele who would never think of buying a steak, and I had another good market for some of my goats.

Between the farm, feed store, slaughter house, and the restaurant, the kids learned much about business and earned money, which they banked against the cost of college. I had never before been so successful as a businessman. More importantly, I felt successful as a man and as a father.

42

Family Affairs and Growth

Bianca was barely seventeen the fall when Antonio began hanging around the Trevor place. At first I could not tell for sure which of Bianca or Marianna held his interest. In either case, I was willing to tolerate the boy, but I didn't like it. It soon became apparent that Bianca was the target of Antonio's attention. It was also apparent to me that the boy had no clue as to how to woo a girl. He just came over and hung around. I began putting him to work. I told him he needed, "to get your mind off the girls and help pay for the groceries you eat."

One night as the girls were settling in, I asked Bianca about Antonio. "Papa, isn't he just the cutest ever?" was the unwelcome response.

"No, Bianca, he isn't. He is a pain in the neck. I know he likes you, but he hangs around with me!"

Marianna began laughing out loud. "That's my fault, I guess. I told him if he wanted to get in good with Bianca, he had to be in good with you first."

"Wait a minute," I was somewhat amused and more than a little confused, "how did I become the gatekeeper to your love life?"

Bianca grinned, "Don't ask me, I didn't sic him on you. Ask the matchmaker over there."

Marianna laughed again and kept laughing as she tried to talk, "Well, every boy I don't want to deal with, I tell them they have to ask you first before I can go out with them." She was laughing so hard that she was shedding tears by now, "Until now, that has been enough to turn them away. They are afraid of you! But this one, this Antonio just keeps coming; he is soooo in looove."

Bianca threw a pillow at her knocking her against the wall. Marianna picked up the pillow and returned fire. She missed Bianca and hit me. Of course, I picked up the pillow and engaged. Soon the room was full of flying pillows and floating feathers.

When Stephanie appeared at the door with her hands on her hips, the fight suddenly stopped in response to the scowl on her face. "How dare you! You are throwing my pillows that I made slips for without regard to the things in this room that could be broken, I know it looks like fun, but just look at this room!!" Both girls looked around the room, suddenly serious. While she talked very sternly, Stephanie was gathering up pillows. She handed two pillows to me and kept three. "Who do you think will clean up this mess?"

Bianca spoke up, "I'll clean it up."

Stephanie looked at them both, "You bet you will; both of you will clean it up. When you leave in the morning, I want this room to look like a picture from Southern Living magazine!" The girls faces were showing the appropriate remorse even if their eyes were still dancing. "How dare you do all this damage without me!! Get 'em Castor!" The mock fight started again, this time lasting until all parties were exhausted from swinging and laughing. Stephanie threw her remaining pillow on Bianca's bed, recovered the one I was holding and threw it on top of the other, then grabbed me and dragged me out. "Man, that felt good!" she said. We shared a good giggle while walking quickly to our room before Bianca and Marianna could recover and reload.

Stephanie and I were in bed about to doze off after a trying day when the door flung open and in poured Bianca, Marianna, Jimmy, Caryn, and Loren all armed with pillows. The war was on once again. Stephanie finally called a halt by offering hot chocolate to anyone who would go to bed after they had some. All warring parties took up the treaty.

"Two things," I said to Bianca and Marianna as they drank the sweet chocolate. "Two things I want to say. College is still the aim. Play the field, okay, but don't lose the dream. The second thing is, why don't you, Bianca, let me take you and Antonio to the movies on Saturday?"

"Hey, what about me?" Marianna injected with a tone of a little feeling of being left out.

"Tell you what," I said, "why don't you get Jasmine to invite a date and join you. Mom and I will find a babysitter and we will make it a quadruple date. Oh, wait! Stephanie, would you like to have a romantic evening with me and three other couples on Saturday?"

"Sounds like fun," she smiled, "but there is one condition. The next Saturday, the two oldest girls in this house babysit, get Jasmine to join if they want, while I take you out on a one on one romantic date! Deal?" she asked looking mainly at the two oldest girls who smiled,

"Deal!"

I shrugged, "I win twice. Deal!"

That Friday night, the family attended the local high school football game in various capacities. Bianca helped at the game by running marker chains, Marianna played the clarinet and marched in the band, Jimmy somehow had landed the job of keeping footballs clean and ready to put in play, and Stephanie and I sat in the stands with Caryn and Loren. At the end of the game, Jimmy picked up a partially used stands horn normally used by zealous fans to emphasize their approval, or disapproval of a play or a call by the referee. He hid it in his jacket and held on to it.

ISIDRO

The next afternoon, Saturday, a truck-load of alfalfa hay that I had ordered two weeks before arrived unexpectedly. Antonio had come to 'help' before the expected date. Stephanie watched Caryn and Loren playing with Lucy in the yard as she prepared a cold cut tray for the baby-sitter and children to snack from while she and I took the three girls and their dates to the movies. Antonio, Bianca, and I tossed the sweet-smelling bales of alfalfa from the truck to the loft while Marianna and Jasmine stacked them inside. The driver leaned against the truck fender waiting for his truck to be emptied of its cargo so he could complete his trip for the day. Jimmy was busy feeding goats, walking his new show-steer, and running water for his hogs. Stephanie was the first to notice the thin boy walking into the yard from the cattle guard. She stopped her cleaning in the kitchen and silently watched him walk stiffly into the yard. Something about him seemed familiar, but she did not know him.

His tousled, filthy, black hair hung straight below his ears, seemingly not washed or combed for a long time. The boy was very thin and dressed in a ragged blue t-shirt and faded jeans with knees torn out. His shoes were canvas-top deck shoes...at least that is what they were at one time. There were so many holes in the shoes, several of his dirt-blackened toes protruded, the big ones beyond the worn soles. The boy and everything he wore seemed stiff with dirt and grime and weariness.

Stephanie came out the kitchen door and called for me. Bianca heard her and looked. There was no hesitation. She screamed and jumped on the cab of the truck, slid down the windshield and hit the ground running to grab the boy in a bear hug. He made no move to avoid her and fell to the ground in her full embrace. Bianca held him close crying, "Isidro! Isidro! Isidro! I didn't think I would ever see you again, but you are here. You came back!!"

By the time Bianca had recovered enough to sit up still holding the boy, Stephanie and I were standing over them and the other two girls were climbing out of the hay loft. Antonio hung back looking on curiously. All four family members stood silently around the two with looks of wonder and curiosity playing about our faces. Bianca finally looked up. In a clear, bright voice full of happiness and her eyes shining with tears, she declared, "It's my brother. It's Isidro. He has come home!"

Stephanie took over. "Isidro, you look hungry. Pareseque tiene usted hambre. Venga conmigo. Come with me. Let's get you some food, a bath, and clothes." Stephanie and Bianca walked Isidro inside the house while Marianna, Antonio, Jasmine, and I quickly finished unloading the truck. I paid the driver, then we walked inside to find Isidro hungrily eating a sandwich and drinking a tall glass of milk with Bianca's arm around his shoulders. Her smile was broad and bright. Her eyes were finally dry.

Stephanie sent the rest of us to the movies while she stayed behind to take care of Isidro and the little ones. Bianca wanted to stay, but Stephanie talked her into going to have a good time so she could get enough information to see what she must do for Isidro.

Saturday night went well. The three couples had a good time. They ate, laughed, went to the movie, laughed more, went for ice-cream, and laughed until they cried. It seemed everyone had such a tough week that they all had a case of the sillies. Bianca seemed especially happy because her brother was found. Antonio and the other two boys seemed a little confused at first, but they all went with the flow and eventually contributed to the fun.

When we got back to the Trevor farm, Isidro was in a talkative mood. His story came spilling out as if he had grown very tired of holding it in. He told of living well in Mexico until a few months back when his Tio Flaco had him brought to the gang headquarters with two of his friends. Without warning, the gang beat the boys unmercifully, Tio Flaco flogged them with a buggy whip, then told them they were members of the "Thirteen" as soon as they completed a few 'tasks.' "I did not want to do the mean things they told me I must do, so I ran away. I hid from them for almost a year before I decided to find mi hermana, Bianca. I never forgot how you protected me when I was little," he said to Bianca. "I don't know how I knew, but I knew exactly what direction I must go to find this farm. Somehow, I knew you would be here. I have been walking for a long time, about three weeks I think. I did get a ride for about fifty miles, but I walked the rest. I slept on the ground, ate bugs and things out of garbage cans at night and walked. I hid during the day to avoid the police, but I made it to where I knew I would be safe. I remember you too, Mr. Trevor. I remember you leaving good food for Bianca and me when I was little."

Bianca gave me a look I did not understand, then told Isidro he would never have to worry about Tio Flaco again. "I promise we are safe."

Jimmy gave Isidro his bed for the night and slept on the floor. Both slept well.

CHURCH DISTURBANCE,

The next day, Sunday morning at church, Isidro sat with Jimmy and Stephen Colins. He had a new haircut, a bath, some new clothes, and with a good night's sleep, he had lost most of his look of weariness. I marveled at the resilience of youth. The three boys were all of the age that it did not seem to them to be cool to sit with family. I had misgivings, but remembered my middle-school years and the strong desire for some independence. Never-the-less, because I also remembered the trouble a youngster can get into and cause, I warned them sternly to be good.

During the sermon, the most boring part for any youngster, Jimmy took the horn he had found Friday night, out of his pocket to show off. He handed it to Isidro who did not know what it was. Isidro looked it over and handed it to Stephen.

When Stephen pushed the button that released compressed gas and sounded the horn, the preacher was at a quiet, thoughtful section of his lesson. Every one of the two-hundred plus people in the building jumped reflexively and turned to find the source of the sudden interruption. The boys had no place to hide. All three slunk down in the pew leaving no doubt where the noise came from.

Quick on the uptake, the preacher made like he had planned the scare to wake people up, and worked it into the lesson. There were stern looks, giggles, smiles, and a few members tried to ignore that it had even happened. I wasn't buying the preacher's attempt to cover, and Stephanie was totally embarrassed. Her blush showed through her dark complexion and she couldn't look anyone but Jimmy in the eyes. The look he got would have melted stone in a snow storm. Immediately after the blast, I took Loren in my arms and Caryn by the hand, walked to the pew where the three boys were sitting, then slid into the pew between Jimmy and Isidro. Without saying anything, I took the horn from Stephen and put it in my jacket pocket. I then faced the preacher with a solemn look on my face that I hoped did not give away my amusement. Bianca and Marianna gave each other knowing looks and tried to help each other keep from giggling. Even though she saw the humor, Stephanie was too embarrassed to stay around and visit after the services.

When we got home, I got the full story from Jimmy. Since he took the blame, I believed his story. Isidro was still wondering exactly what had happened, and Jimmy was appropriately remorseful. I grounded him from contact with his animals and put him on KP until the next Saturday. For Jimmy, a sound beating would have sounded like a vast improvement on the deal, but he accepted his fate graciously and without comment. Bianca and Marianna stopped giggling when I divided Jimmy's chores between them and gave them the task of keeping Isidro busy also. The girls complained that their punishment was not fair. "Fairness has nothing to do with anything," I said. "Every act, good or bad, has consequences for the actor and all those close to the actor, so be careful that the consequences are favorable." That was the answer I gave to their questions of "Why me?" and their assertions of "This isn't fair." By Thursday, Jimmy was begging to be able to see his pets, but I would not give in. Saturday, he was up and at the pens long before dawn. Buck, and Lucy followed him closely everywhere he walked that day. He carried Brutus stroking the old cat that he usually ignored. I did not realize that the consequences would impact the animals too, but they did. The animals had missed him as much as he them. Freedom to Jimmy involved animals.

An old hand at this process by now, Stephanie had cut through the system so that Isidro was officially a member of the Trevor household in less than six months. Although we did not pursue adoption, there was never any doubt where he belonged. We celebrated at Dairy Queen with ice cream.

OLD ROOSTER

One cold, heavy, dreary, Thursday morning in October, I left the house early to begin the morning's feeding. I was greeted by a saddled sway-backed, brown and white paint mare standing on three legs outside the new tack room. Markings on her left withers looked like two hands with fingers spread joined at the wrist. The saddle cinched to her back showed many years of wear. The saddle-horn leather had long ago torn off leaving an oaken stub sticking up from the raggedly covered cantle. The wet seat of the saddle shined from years of being polished by a rider wearing jeans. The horse stood with her head down nickering softly at me as I approached slogging through the mud from the slow rain that had fallen for the past two days. "Hello, Two Hands," I whispered softly to her as I patted her neck. She nickered a sound of recognition and expectation of grain as I passed walking toward the feed shed. The only other sound not made by me was the constant drip of water from the tack room roof.

After looping a feedbag filled with oats and a handful of corn around her head, I left Two Hands munching and began the search for Two Hands' owner. Looking closely, I could see the tack room door had been opened and I could dimly hear a man's heavy breathing as I got closer. It was definitely the sound of heavy sleep, but not a snore. When I quietly pushed open the door, the strong smell of tobacco hit my nose like a hammer. My eyes were not used to the dark yet, so I could barely make out the image of a dark-brown, tall, thin, and well-worn older man sleeping on his stomach atop a bed of paper feed sacks. When my sight cleared, I could see makings and the crushed butt of a hand-rolled cigarette laying on a sack beside him. The old man had the long body and short legs common to the build of Cherokee men. Other tribes had laughingly attributed the peculiar build to the Cherokee distaste for walking. They say the Cherokee began losing his legs when he learned to ride horses. This man's long salt and pepper hair was gathered into a pony tail spread out behind his head like a horse's tail extends when at a full run. He was dressed completely in denim, shirt, jeans, and jacket with a wide, well worn, tooled leather western belt. His sharp-pointed riding boots had once been black, but were so scuffed up one could hardly tell. They were still on his feet. A little to the side laying on a feed bag, was his medicine bag still tied to his neck. A very worn and dirty black hat with a leather band sporting one owl tail-feather lay a foot in front of his face. I thought it looked like the man just fell on the sacks and went to sleep without trying to get up. I eased the door closed and walked through the winter's cold early morning mist back to the main house. My nose had twitched at a peculiar odor in the tack room. It wasn't just the stench of tobacco, or the odor of the leather of saddles I smelled. I associated the odor with sickness…bad sickness.

When I got back to the kitchen, I was met by the more pleasant smells of strong coffee, and good food cooking. Stephanie was busy stirring up a batch of egg, bacon, onion, potato, and cheese, and warming tortillas to make breakfast tacos the kids loved early before school. On one burner, a pot of hot chocolate simmered.

"Remember me telling you about Old Rooster?" I asked as I poured a cup of coffee.

Stephanie looked up, "Is he here?"

"Yes. Looks like he rode in during the night and collapsed in the tack room." I poured some cream and sugar in my cup of coffee. "He'll come rolling out when it is full daylight."

"What are you going to tell Jimmy?"

"That's not my place. Old Rooster will have to cross that bridge."

Stephanie stopped stirring and looked questioningly at me. "Jimmy has a right to know his grandfather."

"I have a feeling that Old Rooster is playing his last hand and has come to meet his grandson. Whether he tells him or not...well that's another story and his business, but I hope he does."

"You mean he is dying?"

"I don't know, but I have a hunch. He's awfully thin and I picked up an odor. Not a good one."

Around 7:15, the thin and severely wrinkled old man dressed in his stained and ragged denim with cigarette makings in his jacket pocket and a worn Skoal circle on his left rear jeans pocket, black hat complete with owl feather, and down-at-the heels boots walked into the kitchen unannounced.

"Who is this, Castor? Have you hired a maid?" The brown-stained smile and the twinkle in his eyes told of long wear, but good humor covering pain.

"Stephanie, meet Rooster. This is the dried up old coot I was telling you about."

"Welcome, Rooster...or should I call you Mr. Cloud?" Stephanie gave him a welcoming hug and kissed him on the left cheek.

"Sweatheart, anyone as pretty as you, fixing food that smells that good, and giving me a kiss to boot, can call me anything you want."

"Castor tells me that you are Jimmie's grandfather," ventured Stephanie with an unasked question still hanging in the air.

"Yes ma'am, I am. And to your other question, Yes, I plan to get to know my grandson...if you will allow me to hang around for a while and work for meals."

"Rooster, I owe you many meals from years ago. You are a welcome guest," I answered while pouring Rooster a cup and motioning him to a chair. "Still take your coffee black?"

"Yep. Black as my heart with a spoonful of sugar. But if you won't let me work, I won't stay."

"I guess I could use a good fence rider," I offered, "and someone to help the kids train their animals for show," I continued.

"Don't know if I want to work *that* hard," the old man grinned, "but I guess if you are going to be that way, I'll give it a go."

"Are you going to tell Jimmy who you are?" Stephanie's direct manner of leaving no questions took the old man back for a second.

"Yes, I have to. I am soon to join my ancestors, you see. It is time I passed on the family stories. Jimmy is the only grandson and it has been too long. But I have hope that I am not too late."

Rooster would not take a place in the house. He opted instead for a cot in the tack room. However, he was seldom late for a meal except close to the end.

Every day for the next two months, Rooster took Jimmy and Caryn with him riding fence, feeding, or whatever he was doing. He told Jimmy of his father and never indicated that Caryn didn't have the same father. He told of their family back many generations before the white man came to this land. He recounted the difficulties of the trail of tears in 1838 and 1839, when the Cherokee nation was driven out of South Carolina and Georgia to Oklahoma and Missouri. He told of the hard years after his family settled on the reservation in Oklahoma. He told of their ancestors who were farmers, horse thieves, policemen, chiefs, honorable men, liars and murderers. He told of the family trait, that of being able to live in peace with animals. He told of Jimmy's grandfather that lived through a winter in a cave of hibernating bears, of horse trainers and snake charmers. But mostly he talked of Jimmy Cloud, the boy's father and expressed hope that they both could be a good man and woman like their father and mother.

One morning, almost exactly two months after he arrived, I found Rooster lying peacefully on his cot in the tack room. The old man had died in the night with a satisfied smile on his face. His job was done and done well.

Rooster's funeral was held on Christmas day. Jimmy did not attend. Instead he went into the w   oods for a few days, after the manner of young Cherokee braves like Old Rooster had told him. He went to get a vision. He came back with a different walk. He came back proud. He knew his roots and his sign, and was pleased.

TURN AROUND

During the summers, Bianca, Jasmine, and Marianna took summer classes offered so they could get ahead in school. By the fall of their fourth year in high school, Bianca and Jasmine had made up their lost year, and Marianna was ahead so that she had only two courses to complete. They were seniors getting ready to graduate.

At the beginning of September, one night after supper, Bianca asked to talk to me and Stephanie about something serious. Just like all the times Bianca asked to talk later, I had all sorts of visions of terrible things she could be wanting to tell me. I was very worried that the subject would be about dropping out of school, pregnancy, trouble with the law, or any of an assortment of other possible catastrophes common to young women.

Bianca took my right hand between hers, "Papa, remember the money set aside for me to go to college?"

"Yes, sweetheart," I said running a whole new set of worries through my mind.

"I've been talking to the girls." 'The girls' was her shorthand for Marianna and Jasmine. "I want to use the money a little differently. With the money we have earned at the livestock shows, our business investments, and our animal sales, if we pool our money, live together, in an apartment through college and one of us works part-time each semester, we can all go to school on about half the amount of the money in the account. We could all get our majors at Texas A&M in College Station. If we do that, there would be enough money left to send Isidro, Jimmy, Caryn, and Loren to College when their times come. Mr. Stence has been very shrewd about investing, and the money is nearly doubled. It could double again before Jimmy starts college, and he has a good nest-egg of his own already. Would using the money that way meet with your approval?"

I breathed again. Stephanie gave me a "What were you so worried about?" look. She got up saying, "I think you two can handle this. I need to bathe Loren." Then she left after patting me on the arm and kissing my cheek. "See, aren't you proud?"

"When will I ever learn to trust the character of this girl?" I thought. *"Why do I bother to consider worst case things?"* Aloud, now holding Bianca's hands in mine, "Bianca, you have every reason to be self-centered and absorbed. The money is yours when you graduate from high school, so you are in control. Instead of looking to use the money for yourself, you have essentially proposed to take your friends with you, then instead of living a life of ease,

you want to turn the rest over to the family to give the younger ones a start. Do you have any idea how proud you make me?"

"Papa, I will never forget where I would be and what would have happened to me if you had not come for me. It would be selfish of me to not help out."

"Sweetheart, how could I counsel against my daughter demonstrating that she is a person of character. I really have no legal say in this decision, but I appreciate your bringing me in and of course I approve." Marianna, who had been listening just outside the kitchen door, gave out a silent 'yes-sss!' complete with a hand-pump. She would be the first in her family to finish high school, much less go to college, as would Jasmine and Bianca be the first in their families. Hopefully, none of them would be the last.

I had ignored the little twinges of pain in my chest for some time. Lately they had become more bothersome and painful, especially when I worked hard. Sometimes it got hard to breathe. I felt like it was my age catching up to me, but I decided I had to see the doctor about it, sometime soon.

43

Taking the Girls to College

This was a great day. Like all great days, it was laced with sadness. I took Bianca, Jasmine and Marianna to Texas A&M today. They were excited to move into their apartment on Glade Street, just off the campus. The stairs were a bit much for me. Luckily, two college boys from a first-floor apartment saw the girls and decided they must help. I'm certain the deciding factor was that Bianca, Jasmine, and Marianna are all beautiful girls. It was late in the day before we got them moved in and unpacked. I took the girls and the helpers to supper then ice cream. It was a good time. We laughed a lot and told many stories of the good and hard times we had.

I was very tired and felt a little queasy, so I decided to spend the night in a motel on the way home. I figured I could get an early start tomorrow and make it home before Stephanie left for work. I had a day planned with Loren. I wrote in my book, "We'll go riding then go for feed in town.

Of course we will stop for ice cream. I called Stephanie to let her know the girls were moved in, safe and ready to begin their college careers on Monday. We talked for a long time. I was feeling sad and Stephanie, as always, listened to me and sympathized. I knew I would miss the girls, especially Bianca, and I guess I just needed comforting. The triplets, as I have become accustomed to calling them, have become so independent lately that I seldom see them. I guess that is a good and natural thing. Maybe I won't miss them so much now that I have gotten used to them going their own ways. On the other hand, I will have so much more time now for Stephanie and the other children. Caryn is eight now and blossoming into quite a student. She looks more like her mother every day, showing her Indian heritage in her dark hair and fine features. Jimmy could care less for school at eleven, but he is doing a man's work around the farm and doing well enough that he will be able to get into a veterinarian school someday. Loren is almost five and the apple of my eye. I will be able to take her more places and enjoy her more this year before she starts school. Isidro is almost a man at fourteen. He has grown tall and strong. I worry about him sometimes. He seems to just cloud over some days and not say much. He seems angry and holds it all in, but he does pull his weight on the farm and does well in school. There is just something…My Stephanie has just about decided to retire from social work to spend more time at home. That will be great. Things are generally looking good for the future…I am so blessed. Its late. Going to bed so I can get an early start."

44

Bianca Takes Over

I wanted to tell Papa's story, but I after finding his diary, or "Book" as he called it, I used it almost exclusively to tell our story in his own words. I took out the dates, the occasional irrelevant entry, and a lot of the details that would tell too much. There are many things he left out, but I did not feel it was my place to add to his memories.

The maid found Papa in the motel room around eleven the next morning after the last journal entry. She said he looked like he was asleep still, but since it was check-out time, she tried to wake him but couldn't. Papa died in his sleep on a Thursday night at fifty-nine years and eleven months of age. He had a massive heart attack that the doctor said he could not have known was coming and that he had not suffered.

I was in standing in line Friday morning, to register for American History 101, when a messenger from the Academic Dean's office came to get me. When I got to the office, Jasmine and Marianna were already there.

They were holding each other up and crying bitterly. I immediately felt a dreadful mist come over me. I did not want to hear what they had to tell me. I almost turned and ran, because instinctively I knew what they were going to say. When Marianna saw me come in, she motioned me to her and Jasmine. While they held me, Jasmine told me, "Papa's gone." That's all she could say. The next few days were a blur and it took me some time to get into my studies at college, but I kept at it, telling myself that it's what Papa would have wanted.

Papa's funeral was on a very sad day. I don't recall much of what the preacher had to say. I just remember he had some very nice things to tell about Victor Castor Trevor. What struck me most was the people who came to pay their respects. Judge Peterson was there along with most of the members of the church Papa attended. Newly elected sheriff, Bill Wagoner attended; Dr. Pick sent flowers with a message that she simply could not face the funeral. Stephanie's family of course, was out in force and helped with everything. There was a curious group of three dark Hispanic men dressed in new jeans, white palm-leaf hats, western belts, pearl-buttoned shirts and black boots. The leader was a man I recognized from the night Papa rescued me from a beating at my parent's house. He had a stiff knee and walked with a pronounced limp. As he walked away from Papa's casket, he came over to me with his hat in his hand and patted my shoulder, then he handed Stephanie an envelope of money. "To pay for some of the damage," he said. Representative to the Senate, Randy Watkins, Don and Kay Stence, Louie from the restaurant, Mr. Talbert from the feed store, Gus from Lometa, and many Others, who admired Papa for his integrity and kindness, were present and obviously moved by the life of my Papa. One of his friends from school, a ragged stump of a man came in, and looked at Papa, then left crying. Marianne seemed surprised by him. Jimmy and Isidro served as pall bearers. As we were leaving after the funeral, the funeral director came to me with a small box. Marianna, Jasmine and I were together. He said, "Your mother said to give this to you girls. She said it belongs to all of you." In the box, we found the leather-thong necklace complete with three granite chips wrapped in copper wire, now corroded, that we gave him years before. We all marveled that he was still wearing it when he died. Stephanie told us later that he took it off only to bathe. Marianne said it best, "That is how much he loved us." We gave the necklace back to Stephanie and she treasures it.

After the funeral, it took us a few days to come out of the fog, but we resumed our lives just like we assumed Papa would have wanted us to do. We still miss him. But we all feel him watching over us and we feel comforted by his presence and the things he taught us directly and by his life.

I owe my good life to my Papa, the good man who came to rescue me from a life of misery, armed with only his love, courage and...birdshot!! Now that was a real man!"

Epilogue

So here I am, watching from where, I'm not sure. I don't know my location, but I can see everything that concerns my family. I can see, but none of the rest of the people I have run into here can see. It's like a window I can see out of, but no one else can even see the window. I watch my family closely, but I can't do anything except watch. They are on their own; except, well, they have each other and their faith. I guess that is all that can be asked.

I ran into my grandfather. More accurately, he came to see me. I started to say "He came to see me one day," but that is all we have here. It is always day. For me it is always a warm day with a cool breeze. I smile a lot. Grandpa welcomed me and seemed very happy to see me. You might be wondering if he asked forgiveness for the way he used to beat me. Well, it doesn't work that way here. You see when we get here, we are already forgiven, so we are past all that. The way I was treated back there wasn't right, but eventually, it made me a man better prepared to take care of the people God decided I needed to take care of. Grandpa doesn't look the same; he looks much younger and happier than when I saw him before. I guess I don't look the same either. But I knew him when I first saw him and was very glad to see him also. He brought dad to see me on his second visit. We had a great reunion.

Mom came to visit. She is as beautiful as I remembered. She sang a song to me I had not heard since I was little. It was about being a good little boy and growing to be a good man by listening and learning from mom and dad. I can't recall the words, but it made me cry to hear her sing it. That's another thing, here we cry without sadness, because it is always from joy. Hearing my mother sing that song brought me such great joy that I felt it all the way through my new body. That's one more thing great about this new place. I have no heart pain. I had gotten so used to it that I didn't notice it much. My new body is not built like the old one, this one is built to last.

I watch my family as they grow. I see things differently from here. I see them being helped and hurt, helping and hurting others. When I was down there, I tried to keep them from suffering. From here I can see the pain Bianca, Mariana, Jasmine, Ashley, Jake, Esther, Jimmy, Caryn, Isidro, and even Stephanie, Loren, and all the others must go through. But the pain seems to have a purpose. It is not for their hurt, it is to help them grow into better people. It seems I was right, growth hurts, but there is more to it. The pain helps people understand others and grow to be willing to help others through their pain. That is, of course, if they are allowing what they suffer to train them instead of allowing the pain to make them into bitter and mean people. It seems to be a choice. The choice is not whether to be free from pain. Pain comes to us from way back in history; it comes as a result of a disobedience, a disobedience that is repeated in every generation and brings on more pain. The choice for each person is whether to learn from the pain or not, and whether to cause others to have pain or to try to help them get through their pain.

I watched my funeral. It was nice. I guess Bianca seemed the most upset, but Stephanie seems to miss me the most. I know they will be fine. I don't like seeing them hurt, but I know they are strong and will all grow stronger from the sadness and pain they feel. Things will get better, or worse. It depends on how they use it. Caryn and Loren nor my grandsons, or Carroll seemed to understand. I guess that too is a blessing.

Rooster welcomed me here too. He seemed to be as surprised as I am that we came to the same place, at least we joked about it. He looks fine. He's not all wrinkled up and old and sick, but as young and healthy as he was when I first met him. He laughs a lot, just like when he was back there. I have seen no sign of Tio Flaco.

There is a lot happening to the family that you might want to know about. I don't know if I want to tell those stories or not. Maybe you will hear from me again, maybe not. Oh, Omar and Lizbet have both come to see and welcome me. What a fine looking man Omar was when he was younger! And Lizbet, well, she was…is,…a beauty. She looked a lot like Bianca. I haven't gotten used to time here, or rather that time isn't. Makes me wonder if it ever was, really. Bianca is almost through college and engaged to Antonio, who is also almost through college. I get the feeling that he would not have gone except he wanted to be close to Bianca. Smart boy. Marianna completed college early with a degree in business and started her own enterprise. She raises quarter horses and teaches horse-back riding and barrel racing. She bought Kermit Herring's place after he died. That's another thing. Marianna's mother came to welcome me. What a nice lady! I found myself wishing I had known her before. Jasmine left A&M after one year, to go to Brown University for a degree in art. She got a full scholarship. I don't see her anymore, but I am still so very proud of her. Stephanie is being pursued by Blake Corrigan, a computer whiz. I have hopes she will choose someone else. Blake hasn't dealt with his pain well. He hasn't shown her yet, but he has a mean streak. Maybe he is Stephanie's next project. She did well with me.

I recall paying too much attention to things that don't matter. I don't regret that, I just am glad Bianca came into my life to get my attention off my own hurts and on to helping others. At the end of it all, I can say, "What an exciting ride!"

Made in the USA
Lexington, KY
03 June 2018